SUGAR
FREE

SUGAR FREE

ROBIN D'AMATO

atmosphere press

Published by Atmosphere Press

Cover design by Matthew Fielder

Atmospherepress.com

Many thanks to my friend Dushka Petkovich
for reading this manuscript a million times.
(Okay, maybe only 20 times.)
And for telling me not to listen to the voices
outside my head.

PART I

Chapter 1
A Thirst So Great

The faint glow of the nightlight barely illuminated her surroundings, but seven-year-old Ginny Eastman wasn't afraid of the dark these days. What was keeping her awake tonight was an unquenchable thirst that had been tormenting her for the past several days. She imagined an enormous bottle hanging over her, continuously pouring Coca-Cola down her throat. True, part of her sleeplessness could have been caused by all the caffeine she had been consuming. That, and having to get up to pee every five minutes.

When her knees buckled out from under her the next day, her parents sprang into action. If her peeing all the time wasn't embarrassing enough (her second-grade class found this terribly amusing), her parents made her pee into a bottle. Then they took her to the doctor, who told them to take her to a hospital. Ginny's hometown, North Greenwich, Rhode Island, was a small town that had no hospital of its own. It was 1967; the town barely had traffic lights. The family climbed into their Pontiac Catalina, and Ginny's father drove to Providence Hospital. Ginny wasn't worried. Whatever this was, her parents would make it go away.

While Ginny sat defenselessly on her hospital bed, a parade of nurses in white cotton dresses came in and out of her room.

They kept asking for urine. They took blood using syringes that had enormous, one-and-a-half-inch needles. Ginny was miserable, but this would end soon. Even the food in this place made her unhappy: overcooked meat, soggy boiled carrots, grayish string beans, nothing that Ginny cared to eat. Besides, she sensed that whatever was wrong with her had something to do with food, and she was determined not to have any of it.

A harried nurse came into her room, looked at her plate, and snapped, "You've got to eat."

Ginny narrowed her eyes. She pushed the tray aside and folded her arms. The nurse mumbled something under her breath and took the offending dinner away.

Breakfast wasn't any better. Ginny looked at the runny eggs, greasy bacon slices, and cold toast and again pushed it aside. The Mean Nurse, thinking she would outsmart the seven-year-old, left the plate where it was and returned with Ginny's parents.

"She's not eating," Mean Nurse said.

Her mother looked at the food on her plate.

"Of course she's not eating. She likes her eggs cooked, and she hates bacon. Can't you bring her something else?"

"Well, she can't have cereal."

Ginny took note of the phrase, "She can't have ..." What did that mean?

"Someone can't boil a couple eggs for her and bring her some fresh toast?" her mother said.

Mean Nurse frowned. "I'll see what I can do."

Ginny could tell her parents were unimpressed with Mean Nurse. Soon, things would get better.

They didn't.

"She hasn't been eating, but her blood glucose is still extremely elevated," the doctor was saying, and her parents were nodding with concern. "We'll take some X-rays to make sure this isn't something else, then we'll make a plan."

A nice nurse came in to give Ginny a shot of something. Again, the needle was huge.

"This will make you feel better," Nice Nurse said.

It took a while, but Ginny noticed a tingling sensation and started to feel more like her normal self. Mean Nurse led her down the hall to a huge picture-taking machine. Why did they want pictures of her torso? It didn't make any sense. This whole experience didn't make any sense.

There was a rare moment when no one wanted anything from her, so Ginny sat on her bed reading an issue of *Highlights for Children* her mother had brought her. She liked the picture searches. There were ten pictures to find. Ginny had found five when her parents walked in.

Her father sat on the edge of her bed and looked her in the eye.

"Listen. You can't eat any more candy."

"Until I get out of the hospital?"

His voice became sharp and loud. "No. *Never*. Understand?"

Why was he yelling at her? She burst into tears.

"They make sugar-free things," her mother said quickly. "They have colas and candies and all kinds of things. There's Tab. Tab is just like Coke."

That was fine, but her dad didn't have to yell at her. This wasn't her fault. Was it?

Cyclamates were still legal then and tasted enough like real sugar to fool Ginny and millions of other children who were eating it to prevent tooth decay. The hospital staff brought Ginny sugar-free treats like Jello or pudding, even sugar-free cola. Maybe this wouldn't be so bad. She still wasn't eating much, but things were looking up.

Other inmates at this hospital included a toddler in Ginny's room who liked to eat his own feces. It was gross, but Ginny was too embarrassed to say anything about it. Another girl in the room, somewhat older than Ginny, had something called appendicitis. And across the hall was young Heather. She had somehow doused herself with boiling water, although there was some discussion among the nurses as to what might have actually happened. Her bandages needed to be changed often, and whenever Mean Nurse was taking care of her, the poor kid would shriek in agony.

Since it was spring in the children's ward, the nursing staff put up an Easter-egg tree in the corridor. Parents brought Easter baskets full of candy, and Ginny became pouty. She looked in envy at one of the baskets. It had jelly beans.

"Ginny!" her mother said harshly. "Don't torture yourself."

Apparently, she wasn't even supposed to *look* at candy.

Ginny was almost happy when her parents left. She didn't like to be scolded for not doing anything. She went out into the hallway to find a ball to bounce. Mean Nurse was in Heather's room changing her bandages.

"Don't stand there, Ginny! She sees you and wants to play. You're making this worse!"

Ginny didn't think she could make it any worse, and besides, why didn't Mean Nurse just close the door? Ginny ducked back into her room. The baby was eating feces again. Ginny tried not to retch.

"What's going on here?" Nice Nurse had come into the room. "You see him doing this, and you don't tell anyone?"

Ginny didn't know *how* to tell anyone. Now, Nice Nurse was being mean. Everyone was so angry in this place, including her parents. Ginny hated it here. She wanted to go home.

Stuck in the children's ward, Ginny was bouncing a ball in the main hallway to amuse herself when her knees buckled. She found herself kneeling on the floor, and she couldn't get up. Was the medicine not working? Why was this happening again?

Mean Nurse hurried to her.

"Drink this."

She handed her a cup of orange juice. Ginny drank it. Her body responded in a few minutes, and she could stand again.

"Better?"

She hated to admit that anything Mean Nurse did was helpful, but she nodded yes. Yes, that was much better.

Her parents said she had to stay the rest of the week. This was giving her a lot of time to think about her situation. This condition she had was called "diabetes." A shot of insulin four times a day. Blood taken from her three times a day. Urine testing all the time. Nurses telling her to eat all the food on her plate, then watching her every move to make sure the diabetic didn't sneak candy from someone's Easter basket. It was crazy-making, and she just wanted it to stop for a few minutes. She became overwhelmed by a disturbing thought: This was the first time her parents couldn't fix what was wrong. That was their job, wasn't it?

No one was in her room, so she ducked into the darkness and started to sob. She wasn't feeling sorry for herself. That would come later. The idea that she was no longer able to count on her parents to fix everything was too much for her young brain to process. And so, she wept.

"What's the matter?"

It was Mean Nurse.

Ginny wasn't done crying. She wanted to be left alone. That's why she was in the room. Alone. Get it? Mean Nurse took hold of a cardigan Ginny's mother had brought and was now trying to put it on Ginny. Ginny didn't want a stupid sweater.

"Go on. Put your arms in the sleeves."

Ginny tried to shake her off but then did as she was told. The sweater wasn't going to cure what ailed her, but her sadness was momentarily replaced by irritation.

Ginny's parents arrived later carrying a letter from Ginny's brother, Asher. He had shipped out to Vietnam last August, about a month after he turned 18. Before he left, Asher had been teaching Ginny how to play basketball. She wasn't yet tall enough to throw a ball that could reach the hoop, but she could dribble like mad. Asher said she had great potential for someone so short. She missed Asher. He wouldn't be treating her like a science experiment like everybody else was.

Asher had included an extra envelope for Ginny in his letter to their parents. It was still sealed! They had left it for her. Ginny tore it open.

March 4, 1967
Gin—

 Things are scary here, but I think about you, Mom, and Dad all the time, and it gets less scary. People are shooting each other and setting off bombs, killing everything in sight, children and animals, too. I think if everyone knew that beforehand, no one would come.

 My friend and I just got back from a little vacation in Hawaii. They call it 'R and R.' We didn't get to see much of the island, but it was nice to feel safe for four days. People shooting at you all the time can do weird things to your head. Maybe you won't understand that. I hope you never understand that.

 I hope you're not giving Mom and Dad a hard time. I say that, but I know you won't. You're a great kid. Keep practicing basketball, and I'll come home soon so we can play. I promise.

 Love,
 Ash

"What did he say?"

"He wants to come home, and he misses us."

"That's nice."

Ginny put the letter in the drawer by her bed with her *Highlights for Children* magazines.

Ash is sad, too, she thought.

Chapter 2

Flying Blindly

Ginny wasn't happy when she returned home, even though that's where she had thought she wanted to be. Her parents were doting on her, and it was making her crazy. She couldn't say anything, of course. They were as upset as she was, maybe more so. That didn't mean they had to smother her.

Her parents were so afraid of sugar that they ordered food with no sauce at Chinese restaurants and hamburgers at McDonalds with no ketchup so they could add their own. They bought sugar-free ketchup, sugar-free salad dressing, sugar-free soups, sugar-free sauces, and whatever else they could find that was labeled "sugar free." Ginny was thankful for cyclamates. They were ubiquitous, and Ginny felt less like a weirdo since she was consuming something other kids were eating, too.

The doctor explained that her new medicine was long-acting, with peaks for breakfast and lunch. A second insulin would kick in in the late afternoon, covering dinner and overnight. That way, Ginny wouldn't have to take insulin four times a day anymore. Unfortunately, this system caused another peak in the afternoon when the insulins overlapped and then before sleep, around ten or so. She would have to eat snacks to ward off hypoglycemia.

Ginny's mom used something called Diabetic Exchanges

to plan meals. Sometimes, the meals would be too much food, causing Ginny's urine test to be positive for glucose. Sometimes, they wouldn't be enough, causing hypoglycemia. Overall, though, the system worked well enough, and Ginny was getting used to it.

"I want to go outside and practice."

"Do you think that's a good idea?" her mother said. "Why don't you stay in?"

Ginny started to tear up. "Asher said to practice."

Her mother thought for a moment. Her daughter needed this.

"Well. Okay. Be careful. If you feel that anything's wrong, come in. I'll call you when it's time for your snack."

Ginny's father had attached a basketball hoop to the side of the house for Asher several years earlier. When Ginny was six, she would sit on the sidelines and watch Asher and his friends play. One day, after his friends had left, Asher said, "Wanna play?"

Ginny turned out to be a natural dribbler, but no matter how hard she tried, she couldn't make a basket even when she was right under the hoop. The ball hardly left her hands.

"You know. It's your arms," he said. She threw again, and this time, he helped her shot get into the basket.

"My arms?"

"Yeah. They're not strong enough. That's why you can't reach the basket."

Asher tossed the ball onto the grass.

"Come here."

They settled on a flat part of the lawn.

"Pushups," he said.

He did a couple to demonstrate.

"You try."

She did one, then fell to the grass on her second attempt, giggling.

"Yeah. No arm strength. That's your problem."

11

"It's not because I'm too short?"

"Well, that too, but let's work on something we can change."

She tried again. This time, she was able to do two.

"I prefer bouncing and running."

"That's because you're good at that. When you get better at this, you'll like it, too."

Ginny was doubtful but decided to believe him.

"Come on," he said. "Let's go back to bouncing and running."

As they played, Asher would help Ginny's shots into the basket. Ginny and Asher played that way throughout the spring. A few months later, Asher was drafted and went away. Even so, Ginny kept practicing. When it became too cold to play outside, she kept up with her pushups.

"Pushups," Ginny said now. She got up to five, which pleased her. She'd have to practice harder for when Asher came home.

"Running and bouncing. Bouncing and running."

She dribbled in a circle, and every time she came near the basket, she threw the ball in the air toward the side of the house, like Asher had taught her. She still wasn't anywhere near the hoop, but she didn't care. She kept practicing, trying to throw the ball higher and higher. When she got dizzy going in one direction, she switched hands to bounce and run the other way. Dribbling with her left hand was hard; she needed to practice that.

"Ginny! Come in for your snack!"

She stopped dribbling. This interruption destroyed her concentration.

"Ginny! Now!"

One of the problems with taking insulin was that exercise could lower blood sugar. While Ginny was bouncing and running, she was potentially bringing on hypoglycemia. She hated to admit her mother was right; she felt lightheaded, and running was more difficult. She tossed the ball into the garage and went inside.

Ginny had missed three weeks of school, but her two best friends, Tilly Quain and Renée Neuville, said they would help her catch up. There was a definite pecking order in her class, and Ginny was worried that by being out, she had lost her place. She was used to being one of the smartest in the class, not as smart as Renée but definitely smarter than that kid Bobby, although he would never acknowledge it.

The playground for the lower grades was overdue for renovation. Kids who played there would trip on the crumbling pavement, the swings' chains creaked loudly with rust, and the painted lines for hopscotch and four square were fading away. There were no immediate plans to repave, de-rust, or repaint, however. Today the intense afternoon sun was making Tilly's bright red hair appear to be on fire; one could have spotted her from a satellite. Tilly had never known her father, but people around town would say her hair color had come from him, as her mother was Sicilian and a dark brunette. Renée, in comparison, was a chocolate-brown-skinned beauty from one of the maybe two Black families in town. Ginny, with her dirty-blonde-approaching-brown hair never felt as unique as her two friends, but she wouldn't have wanted the kind of attention Renée got for being Black. When people commented on her skin color, Renée would insist defensively that she was "tanned," not Black, until someone (it was Ginny, who immediately regretted it) pointed out that most people don't stay tan throughout the winter.

Ginny's parents were pleasant-looking but average. Her father, tall and poker-faced, looked like a baseball player from the '30s, not a Babe Ruth, a man Asher said resembled a frog, but more of a Lou Gehrig or a Joe DiMaggio. Her mother could have been in one of those appliance ads Ginny saw in magazines: pretty but not glamorous. Ginny saw that was her fate as well.

"What do you want to do?" Ginny said.

"Chinese jump rope."

"Tilly, you always want to play Chinese jump rope," Renée said.

"So?" Tilly said.

Renée didn't have an answer to that.

They let Tilly go first. Renée and Ginny faced each other, put the large elastic loop that was the jump rope around their ankles, and backed up until it was taut.

"What happened to you?" Tilly said to Ginny. "My mom says you're really sick and that you could die."

"Tilly, don't say that!" Renée said.

"I'm okay. I take medicine."

"My mom says you have to test your pee," Renée said with a giggle.

"Oh, no, I don't do that."

"My mom says you can go blind and ..."

"Tilly!"

"I just can't have candy and stuff."

Tilly stepped on the rope, so it was now Renée's turn.

"No candy? Wow. I'd hate to be you," Renée said.

"I'm okay."

"And people lose their toes and feet and stuff."

"Tilly!"

"Well, they do."

"Just be quiet and play the game," Renée said.

It was hard for Ginny to admit, but most of the time, she felt unwell. Sometimes, she felt irritable and sluggish. Other times, she felt lightheaded and confused. She just wanted to feel like herself again. She felt closest to normal when she was bouncing and running, but even that often ended with her getting weak and weepy. Maybe she was just thinking about it too much. Maybe she needed more distractions.

Her eighth birthday was coming up on May 20th, and because it was a Saturday, her mother planned a party. Besides Tilly and Renée, Ginny's mother invited other kids from Ginny's second-grade class. There were presents and games, and best of all, her mother guaranteed there would be a cake she could eat.

First, her mother brought out a traditional layer cake with thick chocolate butter-cream frosting and eight candles on it that read "Happy Birthday, Ginny!" That was for the guests. Then, she brought out a special cake for Ginny. It hadn't risen very well; baking with artificial sweeteners was difficult. And there was no frosting. It looked a lot like something one might get from an Easy-Bake Oven, only bigger and not as symmetrical. It wasn't fluffy. It wasn't creamy. It was kind of dry. However, it tasted alright. Ginny could live with that.

The academic year ended with Ginny's place near the top of the class secured, thanks to Tilly and especially Renée. In July, to regain a semblance of normalcy, Ginny's parents planned a trip to Cape Cod. This would be the second family vacation without Asher. Last year, he said, now that he was almost 18, he was "too old" to go with them. Ginny didn't speak to him for a week after that. Then, he was drafted.

Having breakfast out was an Eastman family favorite pastime, one of the many perks of being on vacation. Their first morning there, however, they couldn't get in the door of the motel diner. After waiting, her father went to ask how much longer it would be.

"Another hour," he reported. "Let's find a different place."

The next diner they drove to was also crowded. Ginny was starting to feel strange, like that sensation she'd have before her knees would bend by themselves.

"Let's not wait," her mother said.

They got a table at the next place. Ginny wasn't feeling so great. She didn't think she could speak anymore, and her eyes were starting to twitch. They were darting all over, making it hard to focus.

"Could you bring an English muffin right away? She's a diabetic."

Ginny didn't mind her father mentioning her condition if it stopped what was happening. In a minute, there was an English muffin in front of her. Her mother sprinkled some sugar on it. Ginny tried to take a bite but found her throat was tightening. She put her head on the table. Someone brought a large orange juice, and her father helped her drink it down.

Ginny waited for that lovely sensation of renewed energy. Instead, she vomited all over the table, and her body went into spasms.

Her father grabbed her convulsing body and hurried toward the nearest exit. Ginny vomited again as they approached the car, this time over his shoulders and onto the pavement. Her mother got in the back seat with her so her father could drive.

Ginny's survival instincts kicked in.

Whatever you do, stay awake.

A healthy amount of stubbornness was keeping her conscious. It was possible she was shaking more violently because she refused to succumb. The car stopped. They were at the hospital. Her father carried her in, and soon, she was lying on a table surrounded by people in white coats who were holding her down as she thrashed around. She felt a needle go in her arm, and she thought, *Okay. They got me*, and she let everything go black.

She woke up in a quiet room. Her left hand was aching from a large needle stuck in the back of her hand that was attached to an IV. She wanted to get off her back, but when she tried to turn onto her side, the short IV line kept her where she was.

A nurse came into the room carrying a breakfast tray. She set it up in front of Ginny.

"Good morning," she said.

Morning? What happened to yesterday?

"What time is it?"

"About seven."

The nurse gave her a shot of insulin.

"If you need anything, there's a button to your right."

Scrambled eggs, buttered toast, and orange juice. They tasted great.

Ginny was thereafter sent to school with a roll of Lifesavers candy in her book bag. The intention was that if Ginny wasn't feeling right, she could take one or two, and all would be right with the world. Sugar was poison unless it wasn't.

Urine testing was the norm in the '50s and '60s and for the several years that followed, but it meant very little as far as actual blood sugar was concerned. These tests showed what was happening hours earlier, not at the time of the test. There was a general attitude in Ginny's house that low meant she was behaving and high meant she wasn't. If the test was positive in any way, trace (green), medium (yellow), or high (orange), her parents would lecture her about everything that was going to happen to her if she didn't act right. Sometimes, they'd just *tsk*, which, in some ways, was worse. A negative result (blue) could mean normal blood sugar, around 80 to 110 mg/dL, or it could mean a dangerous low, like 40 or below. Nothing about this system was precise enough for someone to know when to have sugar or how much to have.

As a result of Ginny's experience in Massachusetts, however, she could now sense a blood sugar drop about a half hour before any danger. And if that was happening, she knew it would take more than one or two Lifesavers to stop it.

There was another development since this incident: diabetic paranoia. This was not a recognized medical condition, nor a serious one. Ginny would get anxious that her blood sugar was either dropping or rising when it actually wasn't. Nervous and distracted, she would stop what she was doing to try to feel if her suspicions were real. If only there was a way to know what was really going on.

Chapter 3
Life Goes On

Another letter from Asher arrived, and again, there was a special envelope inside for Ginny. She ran up the stairs to where her and Asher's bedrooms were, flopped onto her bed, and tore open the envelope.

August 12, 1967

Gin—

I'm on watch duty, and it's quiet, so I thought I'd write. Mom and Dad wrote to tell me about your latest hospital stay. I'm so sorry, but I know you'll be okay. They said you fought like a trooper. Stay strong, Gin! More pushups!

I lost a friend the other night, Gin. He was a good guy, this guy Phillip. Our sergeant asked him to replace this other fellow on watch who wasn't feeling well. (There's been a lot of flu going around camp.) A rocket killed all three men in the bunker, including Phil. I offered to be the one who wrote his parents because I knew him best. That wasn't easy. Don't tell Mom and Dad about this. I didn't tell them about Phil, only you.

They expect us to work hard, but the food here is terrible. Sometimes, we can't even recognize what it's supposed to be. Meat can be called chicken or beef or pork, but we suspect it's none of those things. And forget vegetables. It's always greenish or brownish unappetizing mush. This would make you crazy, Gin. I know you like your fresh vegetables. I haven't seen anything fresh since I got here.

I have almost a year to go. I miss you and Mom and Dad a lot. Maybe the year will go by fast. Maybe I'll be home before we know it. Gotta get in some bouncing and running with you.

Very soon,
Love,
Ash

Lunchtime at the grammar school saw herds of children sitting at long tables and benches. Ginny, Renée, and Tilly, now in Miss Watterson's third-grade class, sat together at the end of their table closest to the wall. Stu, who was sitting next to Renée, offered her half of his Fluffernutter sandwich for half of her tuna, which she thought was a fair trade. Tilly swapped her chocolate chip cookies for a pack of Yodels with Stu's friend Joey, and Freddie, sitting on the other side of Stu, offered Ginny some Fritos.

"She can't trade anything," Renée said. "She eats special food."

"No, I don't. I just don't eat sweets."

"You can't eat sweets?" Freddie said. "Why not? That's terrible."

Usually, this kind of conversation would annoy Ginny, but the attention from the boys was making her more open to interrogation.

"She doesn't like to talk about it," Tilly said.

"It's alright," Ginny said. "I'm a diabetic."

"Shhhhhh. Miss Watterson's coming back."

They all went silent, and then Joey whispered to Ginny, "Can you have this? It's small."

It was a Halloween-sized candy bar. The temptation was

great, especially since it was being offered by a boy, but with the Great Thirst still emblazoned in her memory, she declined.

"Thank you. But I can't."

"Virginia! No talking!"

Miss Watterson was walking towards her.

"Stand up and face the wall."

Ginny froze.

"Come on. *Now.*"

She sounded like she was talking to a dog. Ginny did as she was told.

"Stay there until it's time to leave."

Ginny was learning a lot about humiliation without yet knowing the word. Joey was talking, too, but she was singled out. This made her angry. Mad was better than embarrassed.

Soon, Miss Watterson called everyone to line up.

"Except Ginny. You will be last."

The children from other grades were being shepherded into lines as well. When everyone was in place, Miss Watterson said, "Okay, Ginny. Join the line."

She went to stand behind Joey, and as they started walking, he motioned for her to go in front of him.

"No. Ginny's last."

The words "I hate you" repeated over and over in Ginny's head since other, more precise words had not yet entered her vocabulary. After that, Ginny took any moment she could to glare at Miss Watterson. In class, Ginny refused to smile, she refused to raise her hand, and she refused to be happy.

On a note sent home to her parents, Miss Watterson wrote that "Ginny has developed a bad attitude."

Her father found that amusing. Her mother did not.

At recess, the three friends convened on the pavement on the other side from the boys playing tag and the girls on the creaky swings. Ginny and Renée stepped into the Chinese jump rope and made it taut. Tilly jumped in between the ropes and started the sequence.

"I can't believe Miss Watterson won't let us go to the bathroom." Tilly said, then imitated her teacher: "'If I can hold *my* water, you can hold *yours*.' It's so dumb."

"She hates kids," Ginny said and laughed. "Especially me."

Tilly was doing well with the jump rope steps. Renée and Ginny watched as she completed the first round, then they raised the rope to their knees.

"Okay, Ginny. Who do you like?" Tilly said.

"What do you mean?" Ginny said though she knew exactly what Tilly meant.

"She means, who do you have a crush on?"

"Uh ... no one."

"Come on. We'll tell you ours. Mine's Bobby. Renée's is Stu."

"Bobby? Really? He's so mean," Ginny said.

"He's not mean. He's just loud. Maybe that's why I like him. I'm loud, too." Tilly stepped on the rope. "Rats. Anyway ... your crush?"

"I don't know. Maybe Joey. He seems nice."

"See? I knew you had one. Except I think he's got a crush on Renée."

Tilly switched places with Renée so she could go next.

"I'll pick someone else, then."

Tilly laughed. "You can't pick someone else. Your crush is your crush."

Ginny sensed there was something wrong with Tilly's logic. As if on cue, Joey approached the friends and stood at the side to watch.

"Can I try?" he said. "What do you do?"

"You start by standing between the ropes," Renée said, and Joey stepped in. Renée recited the steps, and Joey followed the pattern.

"That's it? That's easy."

"Hey, Joey!" It was Bobby. "Why are you playing with the girls? We're playing tag."

"I'll be there in a minute."

"You have a crush on the Black girl, don't you?"

"So what?"

"Joey likes Renée," Bobby said in singsong.

Joey lunged at him, and he backed off. Renée gave him a big smile.

"So, did I win?" Joey said.

"Now we raise the rope and you do the pattern again."

Ginny and Tilly raised the rope to their knees.

Ginny was feeling something strange … jealousy? Ridiculous. She had just decided to have a crush on him. Why did she care?

Joey went through the pattern again with no difficulty.

"Next?"

"Hips."

This proved difficult for him, but he prevailed.

"Easy," Joey said. "What's next?"

"Waist!" Tilly said. Renée and Ginny glared at her.

"We never do waist," Renée said. "Waist is too hard!"

"I'll try it."

They were right. Waist was too hard.

Stu sat next to Ginny in the lunchroom a few days later. She thought this was odd, but then he said, "Tilly says you like Joey."

"What?"

"Hey. You have a crush on Joey?" Bobby said.

"I don't have a crush. I just said he was nice."

"So, you like him."

"Yes, but—"

This was causing a commotion among the third graders.

"Shhh. Miss Watterson is coming," someone said.

Everyone got quiet and concentrated on their food. Miss Watterson walked around the table, glared at certain trouble-makers, like Ginny, and then was on her way.

"Ginny likes Joey," Stu whispered in singsong.

Bobby was making kissy faces and hugging himself.

Ginny might have to kill Tilly. This went on for weeks. It was humiliating. This, for a kid she just thought was nice.

December 31, 1967
Happy New Year!
Mom, Dad, and Gin,

We're having a little party to commemorate the time passing. There are few things to celebrate here, but we're doing our best.

I got your letters. Thank you! I'm glad you are all doing well, especially you, Gin. Mail doesn't arrive here that often, or leave here that often, actually, so I hope you get this soon. People are too busy killing each other to deliver the mail, I guess.

Sorry if that was overly cynical.

There seems to be a lull in the fighting today. I don't think it's official 'cause we would have heard about that. We were supposed to have a ceasefire over Christmas, but the North Vietnamese didn't honor it, and we wound up fighting as usual. Anyway, it's nice and quiet for the moment, and that's definitely something to celebrate.

Looks like we are having a special dinner tonight. Roast chicken with stuffing (I'm sure not as good as yours, Mom), potatoes, and gravy. I saw something green go by as well, but I couldn't identify it. I'll probably skip that!

Okay, the guys are calling me. Hope the new year is good to you, and I hope I see you all soon.

Love,
Asher

"What's 'cynical'?" Ginny said.

Her mother took a moment to decide how to answer this question for her.

"A negative attitude. Especially because of someone's experiences."

"Oh. Okay." She was going to ask her mom if she thought she was cynical, but decided to save that for another time.

Ginny came home from school and went right to her room to start working on her story for English, but found she couldn't concentrate. Miss Watterson yelled at her today for needing to pee a second time. Ginny was too mortified to tell her parents. She wanted to hide for the rest of her life.

She was tired of everything. Her body wasn't something she could count on anymore. One minute, she would be happily bouncing and running, and the next, she would need to stop and eat some Lifesavers, sometimes half a roll, before the hypoglycemia would stop. She wasn't sure what to eat anymore because even though she'd eat what her mother served her, she might get a high urine test. She didn't like getting shots, she didn't like everyone's fascination with her pee, and every time she went to the doctor, they used a needle longer than the one for insulin and took blood from her. Then there was all the talk of what would eventually happen to her. She was terrified. Ginny liked her feet. She wanted to keep them.

She lay down on her bed, pushed her homework aside, and started crying.

Ginny loved math and usually would pay attention, but today, something wasn't right. She couldn't focus. Her body was hot, her head was aching, and she was queasy. She was also starting to feel weak. She ate some Lifesavers, hoping that would take care of it. All she wanted to do was lie down. Without realizing it, she put her head on her desk.

"Ginny, are you alright?"

Miss Watterson didn't sound mad, which was unusual.

"Uh ... no."

"Joey? Can you take Ginny to the nurse?"

She had a fever of 102 degrees. The nurse called her mother. Ginny was still trembling, so she had more Lifesavers. They were still dissolving when her mother arrived.

The doctor said she had the flu.

"Usually, flu will cause an elevated blood sugar, but sometimes, it can cause the opposite."

Ginny was visibly shaking, so her mother handed her more Lifesavers. Ginny had had enough Lifesavers. The thought of even one more made her gag. Instead of trying to convince her stubborn daughter to take them, her mother produced a Hershey's bar from out of her purse. Ginny's eyes opened wide. Without a word, her mother broke off a piece and handed it to her. It melted in her mouth. In a short while, the shaking started to subside. The fever, the queasiness, and the headache, however, didn't go away for five days.

Rhode Island was not an island; it was actually many islands. And it had lots and lots of beaches, 400 miles of them. Nicknamed the Ocean State, everyone learned to swim at a young age, and during the summer months, people were all either tanned or singed.

It was a Sunday, the day before Ginny's birthday, almost warm enough to go swimming. Tilly's mother bought kites at the Woolworths and then drove Tilly and her friends to Briar Point Beach. Tilly didn't like to see her heavyset mother sunbathe. It made her not exactly embarrassed but nonetheless uncomfortable. Her mother was younger than the other moms, having had Tilly at 16, and did things that younger people liked to do, like lie in the sun. Tilly almost said she wouldn't go, but the prospect of swimming and having new kites to fly was too tantalizing.

Tilly's mother put down a beach blanket and anchored it with her large tote bag and cooler. Then she set her transistor radio to the top-40 station. She was wearing a one-piece that had a colorful swirling pattern, a straw hat with a wide brim that covered most of her dyed-black hair, and oversized Jackie Kennedy-style sunglasses. Even Tilly had to admit she looked great.

The strains of pop music filled the air as the friends ran down to the water. Ginny put her toe in and shuddered; it was cold. As she and Renée worked their way in up to their knees, Tilly took a running start and leaped in, splashing her friends.

"Tilly!" Ginny yelled.

Tilly shook the water out of her eyes and said, "You gotta just jump in."

"No, I like to ease in," Renée said.

Ginny and René were in up to their waists now and were pouring water on their arms and torsos to temper the shock of the cold ocean. The waves were minimal, and when they were all in, they swam in a circle like sharks.

"The water doesn't seem that cold now," Renée said.

"But now the air does. It's early in the season to be out here, but Mom loves to sunbathe."

René had learned to dive last year, and although she was not yet that proficient, Tilly and Ginny were impressed. Tilly showed off by doing somersaults underwater. Ginny didn't have a trick. She'd have to come up with something for next time. The friends noticed that Tilly's mother had flipped over again while they were frolicking and had now returned to lying on her back.

"Hey, Ginny," Renée said. "Your lips are blue."

Ginny stopped treading water and thought about it. She wasn't feeling right.

"Stay here. I'll be right back."

Ginny didn't like the sand on her feet, so she moved quickly toward the beach blanket. She wrapped a towel around her shoulders for warmth.

"I brought a big bottle of grape juice," Tilly's mom said. "Would you like some?" Ginny nodded. Tilly's mom took it out of the cooler. "It might be a little hard to open."

Ginny tried it. The cap wouldn't budge.

"Let me do that for you."

"Thanks, Mrs. Quain."

Ginny drank right from the bottle, not even waiting for Tilly's mom to hand her a cup.

"Oh," Ginny said and laughed. "I should have used one of those."

"It's alright. There are no cooties among friends."

The juice worked fast. Maybe this was what Ginny should be carrying instead of Lifesavers.

Renée and Tilly were walking towards them.

"We decided we're hungry," Tilly said.

"And cold," Renée said. She and Tilly reached for towels.

The song "Sweet Inspiration" was playing, so Tilly turned up the radio and left it at high volume. After lunch, the friends decided they didn't want to go back in the water. The wind was picking up.

"Why don't you girls fly your kites? I'm going to stay here and bake a little while longer."

They put their shorts and sweatshirts on over their bathing suits and headed down the beach, kites in hand, to an area where there were fewer people.

They started running. The wind that was making the air so cold elevated the kites quickly. Tilly's kite was darting and diving, but it was fast becoming a speck in the sky. Ginny's kite wasn't soaring like Tilly's, but it was steady; it had a good tail on it. Renée's kite was more in front of her than up.

"How do you get yours so high?" Renée said. "Mine is hardly flying."

"Let me see your string. Hold mine a second."

Renée's kite was soon flying overhead.

"Here you go, Charlie Brown," Tilly said. "Just hang onto it."

The erratic behavior of Tilly's kite caused it to take a last dive. It plummeted to the ground quite a way down the beach, breaking free of the string that had attached it to Tilly.

"Rats. And it was really up there."

Tilly's mom was approaching, wearing a bright yellow coverup that could be seen all the way down the beach. She was carrying the cooler and her tote bag.

"Aren't you getting tired?" she yelled.

"Nah," Tilly called back.

Tilly's mom got closer and put down the cooler.

"Tilly, where's your kite?"

"Took a dive. It's gone," Tilly said.

"Oh dear. We'll have to get you another one, then. I'm going to the car to get out of the sun. My skin's hot."

"Yeah, you are really pink."

"I am?" She inspected her arms and legs. "Good thing I brought Solarcane. You girls meet me at the car when you're done."

The girls watched her walk away, and Renée said, "You know, your mom's not fat. I mean, it's not like she's round or anything. She's just not skinny."

"She's bigger than not skinny," Tilly said. "But I guess you're right. She's not fat, not really."

The arrival of the mail truck lured Ginny away from her basketball practice.

"Mom! Dad! We got a letter from Asher!"

29

She ran into the house now, sweating from bouncing and running. Her skin was a little burned, but the air-conditioned living room felt wonderful. She waved the all-important letter at her mother.

"Look! He used three stamps! Open it!"

Her mother smiled, got her letter opener, and slit open the envelope. She started reading, then stopped.

"He's coming home in two weeks. His service has ended. And there's an envelope in here for you, Ginny."

Ginny squealed, grabbed the envelope, and ran upstairs.

June 2, 1968

Gin—

Mom says you're doing well. I know you. You will fight harder than anybody to get on top of this thing. More push-ups!

I can't believe it, but I'm finally coming home. It feels like it's been two decades, not two years. The place, the war, even the people, it's all very hard to take. There are tigers here. I'm not kidding. I only saw one once, but that was enough. Sure, they're cute in a zoo, but when you are his potential dinner, the charm wears off quickly.

Only three of the guys who started with me are going home when I do. The rest either went home already because they were injured, or they just didn't make it. One grunt is staying on. He loves it here. He's a scary guy.

Can't wait to get back to the States. Hope you've been prac-ticing your bouncing and running, because I'll be there to kick your butt if you haven't.

See you soon.

Love,

Ash

Asher entered the waiting area carrying two military-issue duffle bags. He was drawn and underfed, and his skin was leathery from the Asian sun. He looked much older than his 20 years. He pushed up his sunglasses and scanned the crowd. He didn't see his family.

"There he is!"

Ginny ran towards him. He dropped everything and grabbed her. His parents slowly approached.

"Asher ..."

"Mom."

They hugged. His father extended his hand, and they shook first, but then they hugged, too, patting each other on the back so it was a more manly gesture.

"Welcome home."

"Thanks, Dad."

There was an uncomfortable silence. Ginny was getting impatient with these adults.

"Can we go now?"

Asher laughed and picked up his bags.

"Let's go."

Ginny was out playing her version of basketball while Asher was upstairs getting settled. He said he was too tired to join her, but maybe they could play tomorrow. When Ginny was finished, she climbed up onto the porch and was about to enter the back door of the house, but she stopped when she heard her parents talking.

"Asher seems somewhat detached. And he's nervous and troubled," her mother said. "I'm worried about him."

"You're always worried, Irene. Ginny, now Asher. You're making yourself crazy."

"It's my job to worry."

"Let's give him some time to get used to being home."

There was silence, so Ginny entered the house.

"What's for dinner?"

"Steak and mashed potatoes. Your brother's favorites."

"Can we have broccoli? Do we have any?"

Her mother laughed. "Yes. What nine-year-old likes broccoli?"

"Me."

"Well, go wash your hands and let Asher know dinner's almost ready."

Ginny ran up the stairs.

"Ash?" She tried the door, but it was locked.

There was the smell of something burning, not the usual cigarette smell she noticed on her father, but something more pleasant.

"Yeah?"

"Dinner's almost ready," she said through the door.

"Okay. Thanks, Gin. I'll be down in a minute."

He did seem a bit distant, now that her mother had mentioned it. Ginny thought about it a moment, then went to wash her hands before heading downstairs.

Didn't their mother realize Ginny could hear her through the wall, especially if Asher's music was off? It was even clearer when she yelled.

"Asher, I don't want you smoking that stuff in the house. How is that going to affect Ginny?"

Ginny couldn't hear Asher's answer. Their mother was raising her voice, but he wasn't.

"I don't care if you think it won't. I think it will. I'd rather you didn't smoke it at all, but if you insist, take it outside. I know you're 20, but you're still living in this house."

What was he smoking? And why couldn't he smoke it in the house? And what did it have to do with her? Ginny didn't think she was being affected by that new-smelling smoke. She didn't understand what the big deal was.

Ginny waited for her mother to leave, and then she waited

some more. When she thought enough time had passed, she got up and knocked on Asher's door.

"Ash? Can I come in?"

At first, there was no response. Then the door opened, and Ginny entered the sanctum. Asher sat on the floor, motioning for her to join him. He took two albums out from his collection. He put one on the floor. He sprinkled something that looked like potpourri on the other one and started straining out seeds and stems, letting them roll down onto the first album. Ginny didn't understand what he was doing, but she recognized the smell.

"What's that, Ash?"

"Marijuana. Want some?"

"No. No thanks.

"Do you know what it is?"

"It's a drug, right? Is that what you and Mom were arguing about? That she thought it would do something bad to me?"

He paused. "Actually, yes."

"Well, I think she's wrong."

He smiled. "What else did Mom tell you?"

"She doesn't tell me anything. I hear stuff."

"What kind of stuff? Besides the pot."

"Well, Mom thinks you're different since you've come back."

"What do you think?"

"I haven't noticed anything." This wasn't entirely true.

"The war over there is inhuman. The things I saw ... they changed the way I think. Maybe not forever, if I work at it. Not like your situation."

Ginny thought about that.

"Do I seem different?" she said.

"You were barely seven when I left." He looked at her and smiled. "You're taller, for one."

Asher swept the cleaned pot off its album into a small plastic bag and then poured the seeds and stems from the other album into his trash can. He showed her one of the covers.

"Do you know who this is?"

She shook her head.

"John Coltrane." He showed her the other album. "Do you know who this is?"

She shook her head again.

"Bob Dylan. Next time, I'll play you some songs."

"Okay."

Asher took out some rolling papers and started to roll a joint.

"Now go on. Mom catches you in here, she'll have my head."

"Are you going to smoke that now?"

"Yup. Going out to the back porch."

"Okay. Well, see you in the morning." She got up to leave.

"Hey ...," Asher said.

She stopped.

"How about some basketball tomorrow?"

"Yes!" she said, and Asher smiled.

Chapter 4

Insulin Codependent

"These," Renée said, opening the box, "are Incredible Edibles."

There was a round contraption that looked like a circus-clown face, metal molds, tubes in different colors, and other things Ginny couldn't identify.

"What are they?"

"They're like Creepy Crawlers," Tilly said, "but instead of Plastic Goop, you pour this syrupy stuff into the molds, and it makes chewy candy."

"And Ginny, they're made with cyclamates, so you can eat them, too," Renée said.

Ginny liked the Creepy-Crawlers Thingmaker Tilly had at her house. The fact that she, too, could eat the Incredible Edibles did seem intriguing, although one of the flavors was root beer. Yuck.

"I think I'm going to have a sleepover," Renée said. She was carefully pouring colors into different parts of her butter-fly mold. She was planning a masterpiece.

"When?" Tilly tried to put her mold into the oven, but it tipped, and the blue, sticky Gobble-De-Goop poured onto the newspaper-covered kitchen table. She grabbed some paper towels and mopped it up before it dripped onto the floor.

"Drat. Sorry."

"Anyway, I'm thinking in two weeks, just after my birthday and before school starts. You two have to come."

"My mom won't let me," Ginny said. "I get my insulin in the morning. I've never slept over anywhere without my parents."

"Well, that's gotta change," Tilly said.

"You don't know my mother."

"Ask her. She might let you," Renée said.

Ginny doubted it, but it did start her thinking.

It took Ginny a few days to get up the nerve to ask. She got the answer she expected.

"No. Of course you can't go."

"Why not?"

"Because you have to take your insulin in the morning. You can't sleep over at Renée's."

Ginny stamped her foot.

"Please?"

Her mother thought a moment.

"Well, I suppose we could have Renée's mother give you your insulin, since she's a nurse."

"She's a *doctor*. But no way."

"Well then, what do you propose?"

"I can take it myself! It's not a big deal. Please?"

Her mother grew silent and concentrated on folding the laundry.

"Please?"

"No."

Ginny stormed out of the room, pushing past Asher, who had appeared just in time to hear the tail end of this conversation. He and his mother could hear the front door open and slam shut.

"What's going on?" he said.

"Just a little disagreement."

"Maybe I should go after her."

Their mother looked up from the laundry.

"Yes. Could you?"

The sun was hot, but there was a breeze, and the smell of rose bushes was wafting over from the neighbor's yard. Ginny pounded the basketball on the driveway and then threw it at the house with all her strength. It came back at her with so much force she had to duck. Asher retrieved it for her.

"Hi," he said and threw her the ball.

"Hi." Still mad but calming down.

"You've gotta give Mom some credit," he said. "She's always going to smother you. The fact that she lets you out of the house at all is remarkable."

Despite her anger, Ginny almost smiled.

"What Mom doesn't get is she makes me feel even more like a weirdo than I already do. Chasing me down to give me a snack. Telling everyone's moms to watch what I'm eating. I'm not a dog. I'm not going to eat whatever is put in front of me."

"I do," Asher said, and Ginny laughed. She bounced the ball in place a few times before she spoke again.

"Is she going to be following me around until I'm married?"

"Yes. Maybe even after that."

She tossed the ball to Asher, and he slowly bounced it, switching from hand to hand. Without warning, he dashed past her, dove at the basket, and forced the ball through the hoop.

"Hey!"

"That was my friend Phil's signature move. He showed it to me when we were on R 'n R in Hawaii. I was so jealous I practiced until I got it. Kept my mind off other stuff for a while."

"Was Phil your friend who died?"

"Yeah."

Asher threw the ball back to Ginny.

"What I didn't tell you before is that it was my turn on watch that night," he said. "Phil was subbing for me when he got killed."

Ginny stopped bouncing and looked at him.

"Yup. And I wasn't even sick. I just couldn't leave my cot. Everything seemed so heavy, so overwhelming, so hopeless. I told my sergeant I thought I had the flu. Everyone was getting it. It was a quiet night, so being on guard duty shouldn't have been a big deal. I mean, I could have hauled my butt to the post and been overwhelmed there as well as in my cot."

"But then they would have gotten *you*."

"Yes. That's right."

"That wasn't your fault."

She bounce-passed the ball to him.

"Sure feels like it was."

"It was the enemy's fault."

Asher smiled. "You're a smart kid."

Ginny thought about this for a moment. "Asher ... do you still get like that?"

"Yeah. Sometimes, I just detach from the world. I'm aware of what's going on around me, maybe even will react, but it's like I'm watching while everyone else participates."

"I kinda get like that sometimes."

Asher stifled the urge to look alarmed. He spoke carefully.

"You're still dealing with your physical situation, Gin. It's only been like a year or so. Don't let sadness consume you."

Ginny didn't respond.

"Okay?" Asher said.

"Yeah. Okay."

"You know," he said, "maybe in five years, they'll have a cure or something."

Ginny smiled. "I'll be 14. That wouldn't be so bad. But do I have to wait that long to keep Mom from following me around everywhere?"

"Yes," he said and lobbed the ball toward the hoop. When

it hit the rim instead of going in, Ginny caught the rebound.

"The thing is, it's gross," she said. "Testing pee, sweating and shaking when my stupid blood sugar goes down, peeing every minute when my stupid blood sugar goes up. I feel cruddy most of the time. Even the name is gross. Diabetes. It sounds like cooties."

"That, of course, is all in your head. No one but you thinks it's gross."

Ginny didn't look convinced. She dribbled toward the basket, stopped, and took a shot at the hoop.

"You're getting closer. Soon, I won't have to help you."

He got the rebound and shot the ball into the basket from where he stood.

"Ha. Do better than that."

Ginny obviously couldn't do better than that, but she couldn't resist the challenge. She dribbled around the driveway, headed to the basket again, jumped up, and clumsily threw the ball towards the hoop with as much force as she could muster. Not only did the ball reach the hoop this time, it went in.

She laughed and grinned at Asher.

"Hey! Look at that! How'd you learn to jump like that?"

"Chinese jump rope."

They were both laughing when their mother came onto the porch.

"Ginny!" her mother called. "Come in and get a snack!"

Ginny rolled her eyes.

"Go on," he said. "I'll be here."

In September, the friends were assigned to Mr. Hutchings' fourth-grade class. He was warm. He was reasonable. He didn't care who talked in the lunchroom or who had to pee.

"We're on the side of the school with the 'upperclassmen' now," Renée said. "The only thing better about being on this side is there's more sports stuff at recess."

"Are there basketball hoops?"

"Yeah, there's a court. Didn't you see it? Towards the line of trees, near the baseball diamond. I thought you would notice it."

"I saw a bunch of boys there."

"Sixth-graders. They take over everything."

At recess, Ginny left Tilly and Renée to go over to the court. It was calling to her like a coven of sirens. Renée was right. The boys there were sixth-graders. They were tall.

One of them, a boy named Mike, addressed Ginny.

"Wanna play?"

His friends snickered.

"No, thank you. I just heard that there was a court."

"Do you play?"

More snickering.

"My brother is teaching me."

"Here. Take a shot."

By now, Tilly and Renée had come over to see what was going on. Mike's friends were loudly complaining, but Mike handed the ball to Ginny.

"Stand on the free-throw line."

There was laughing and guffawing as the 68-pound, four-foot-one-inch tall Ginny stood on the line.

"I can only make a basket one way," she said.

"Okay. Show us."

She kept her eyes on the target, then bounced and ran her way to the basket, jumped up like a wild animal, and somehow made it in. It wasn't smooth or graceful, but she did it.

There was applause and hooting.

"Wanna join my team?" Mike said.

"Give me a couple years," she said. She was satisfied. She didn't need any more interaction with these boys. She turned and ran to her friends.

"That was great!" Renée said.

"I was so nervous. I've only made a basket a couple of times before."

"But you did it!" Tilly said. "My mom would call that 'far out.'"

"Far out? Is that good?"

"Very good."

Ginny couldn't wait to tell Asher.

Asher left the house in an elated mood that night. He was carrying their mother's car keys. Ginny was suspicious.

"Where's he going?"

"He has a date."

"Oh. With who?"

"With *whom*. Trisha. You remember her. They used to date in high school. She's back in town."

"Is she the dumb one?"

"Ginny ..." There was that tone her mother loved to use. "Yes, she's the one you didn't like." She paused. "You were an astute five-year-old."

"She used to pat me on the head."

Her mother laughed. "Yes, you hated that."

"I liked Grace. She was nice."

"I liked her, too. Ginny, your brother hasn't been socializing much since he's been home. This is good for him."

Ginny thought about it. "Okay."

"Just be nice if he brings her in to say 'hi.'"

"I'm always nice."

It was no surprise that Asher didn't return home until the next morning. Ginny was happy he came home alone. She didn't need to see Trisha ever again. Ginny hoped she would have a massive growth spurt so she could pat Trisha on the head the next time she saw her.

Asher was letting Ginny stay in his room until dinner so he could play some music for her. He said it was an important part of her education.

"The Beatles? I like the Brothers Four."

"Our parents have been depriving you of some great music. I can see you not hearing about John Coltrane, but Bob Dylan? And you shunning the Beatles the way you do has to stop."

Ginny sat on the floor cross-legged and waited for Asher to put on the album.

"This came out this week," he said. "They were playing it in the record store when I was there."

The sound of a jet airplane faded in, and then there was the fast rhythm of "Back in the U.S.S.R."

Asher saw her delighted grin and pulled out some photos from the album cover.

"This is John," he said and placed an 8" x 10" glossy in front of her. He placed the second photo and said, "Paul, who's singing this song. George. Ringo." He put down the other two photos.

"I've heard of Ringo." Ginny looked over the pictures. "They have really long hair."

"They've never been in the military," Asher said. "Do you like this music?"

"Yes."

He reached over to the album and skipped ahead. A slower song started.

"This one is written by George. That's him singing."

Ginny listened for a minute.

"This song makes me sad."

"It's supposed to."

Asher chose a few songs he thought she might like and then pulled some different albums off the shelves and played selections from them.

Someone knocked on his door.

"Should I hide?" Ginny said.

"No. Mom and I have come to an understanding." He raised his voice. "Come in. It's open."

Their mother came in, looked askance at the Beatles albums scattered on the floor, and sighed.

"Dinner's almost ready," she said.

"Thanks, Mom," Ginny said.

"The Beatles. Really, Asher."

She walked out, and Ginny said, "What's wrong with the Beatles?"

"I think she thinks they're too old for you."

"I'm not going to marry them."

Asher laughed.

"Okay," Ginny said. "John has the glasses. Ringo has the nose. Um ... George is the cute one with the mustache, and Paul is the other one."

"That's right."

"I like them."

"Good."

"I think they're far out."

Asher burst out laughing.

"Did I say that wrong?"

He was still chuckling. "No. They *are* far out. But I think you're supposed to say 'fab' for them."

It wasn't clear if Asher had invited Trisha or if she had invited herself, but their mother said it was okay if she came over for Thanksgiving; there was plenty of food. Ginny prepared for this event by hiding in her room. Unlike Asher's room, hers didn't have a lock on its door, so Ginny had to be doing something in case someone walked in. She couldn't lie there and pout, which is what she wanted to do. She was pretending to read. She chose *Alice in Wonderland*, a book she had read before. It was a hardcover, it had pictures, and it made a perfect prop.

Someone knocked. If it had been her parents, they would have walked right in, but the hesitation told her it was Asher.

"Yeah?"

"Gin. It's me."

Ginny closed the book on her thumb, as if to hold her place.

"Come in, Ash."

"Whatcha reading?"

"*Alice in Wonderland*. We're reading it in school. I read it before, but I don't remember a lot of it."

"Listen. You okay with Trisha coming over?"

"Why wouldn't I be?"

"Because you don't like her."

"I liked Grace. But it's okay."

"You sure?"

"As long as she doesn't pat me on the head again."

"I'll see to it she doesn't."

The doorbell rang.

"I'll be down in a minute," Ginny said. "Just want to finish this chapter."

As Asher went down the stairs, Ginny read a page or two to stall. She had forgotten how good this book was. Maybe she would reread it for real sometime.

"Ginny?" her father called. "Aren't you coming down?"

She closed the book and headed down the stairs.

"Don't you want to put on some shoes?" he said. "Maybe some socks?"

"Why?"

Her father shook his head. "Suit yourself."

"Ginny! Wow! You've gotten so big!" Trisha said.

Ginny scowled. "No, I haven't. I'm only four foot one."

Asher leaned over to Trisha and whispered, "Height is a sore subject in this house."

44

A small dog began lapping at Ginny's feet. It looked like a rope mop, just not as cute. Ginny tried to move her feet away from it, but the thing was persistent.

"Oh. Sorry! She has a fascination with people's toes." Trisha pulled the dog off Ginny. It didn't look like a she. It needed bows or a jeweled collar or *something* to make it less, well, ugly.

Their mother came into the room and stopped short. Ginny read the look on her face: *There is a dog in my nice living room.*

"Mrs. Eastman. Asher was raving about your stuffing, so of course I had to come."

"Trisha. How nice to see you again."

Their mother was staring at the dog, so Trisha said, "I'm sorry. I had to bring Penelope. She gets crazy if I leave her alone."

Their mother glared at her a moment more, then said, "Well, everything's ready. Why don't you all ..." She paused as if choking on her words. "... come into the dining room."

Trisha had Penelope sit under her chair. This pleased Ginny; the dog was making their mother so mad. Unfortunately, she would take it out on Asher later, but it was fun for the moment.

Before Ginny had to choose where to sit, their mother called her into the kitchen.

"Could you bring the broccoli into the dining room for me? Your father is carving the turkey. Watch it; it's hot."

Their mother had made a broccoli casserole full of cheese and Ritz crackers and mushroom soup and other good stuff. As Ginny reached for the oven mitts, Asher came into the room.

"I'm sorry, Mom. I didn't know she was going to bring her dog. I swear."

"We'll discuss this later."

"I swear." He was suddenly 16 again.

Their mother looked at him. "Okay. But if anything happens to my furniture, you're responsible."

Ginny took this as her cue. She picked up the casserole and went out to the dining room. She placed the dish in the middle of the table, then chose a seat on the other end from Trisha.

"Is everyone ready? I'm bringing the bird to the table," their father said. He and their mother came in, followed by Asher, who was saying in a hushed tone, "Nothing is going to happen to your furniture," but when he saw the look on their mother's face, he said, "Never mind."

Their mother placed the potatoes and stuffing on the table, then said with horror, "Are you feeding the broccoli casserole to the dog? On my hardwood floor?"

Trisha smiled. "She loves broccoli and cheese."

No one knew what to say.

Trisha was not invited back for Christmas.

Asher made some time to take the girls to see the movie *A Hard Day's Night*, which was playing in a revival theater in Providence. They arrived early so they could order popcorn and sodas and find the best seats.

The audience cheered after every scene and sang along to every song, even the background instrumentals. Tilly, Renée, and Ginny got into the spirit, singing when they knew the lyrics. When the movie ended, it got a standing ovation.

Leaving the theater, Asher said, "What did you think?"

"I loved it," Renée said, "but they were so mean to Ringo."

"I loved it, too," Ginny said. "George is so cute. Actually, they all are. But why wasn't John wearing glasses? It took me a second to recognize him."

"He didn't start wearing them publicly until later," Asher said. "Maybe that's why he was squinting all the time."

"I like Paul. He's got those chipmunk cheeks," Tilly said.

They got into the car, Ginny in the front and her friends in the back.

"I'm taking you two to Renée's?" Asher said.

"Yeah, I'm sleeping over," Tilly said. "Mom has a date."

Ginny bristled. Another sleepover! It was so unfair. Maybe they wouldn't even invite her by the time her mother let her go, or she'd be in college or something. Maybe her mother wouldn't let her go to college!

"Hey," Asher said, seeing her frown. "Are you okay?"

"No," she said but didn't offer an explanation.

"Wake up, Ginny. Time for your shot."

Ginny groaned but made herself sit up when she heard her father's voice. Mornings always came too soon for Ginny. She suffered from sleep inertia. Once she was awake, she wanted to stay awake. Once she was asleep, she wanted to keep sleeping. She watched him preparing the insulin, carefully rolling each vial, turning it upside down and back to make sure the zinc suspension was completely mixed. Then, he put 15 units of Lente and five units of Ultra Lente in the syringe.

"Dad, let me do it."

He scowled.

"I'm almost 10. I have to do it sometime. And Renée and Tilly keep having sleepovers, and I keep missing them. If I can do this, can I go to one? Please?"

"Your mother said no, didn't she?"

"Because of the insulin. That's all."

"Well ..."

He handed her the alcohol-soaked cotton ball and the loaded syringe. She held the needle over her arm but hesitated. Somehow, it looked longer than usual. Scrunching up her face with anticipation, she sunk it into her arm. It didn't hurt any more than when her father did it. She pushed the plunger and pulled the needle out of her arm, triumphant.

This was a step towards insulin independence.

Her mother wasn't happy about it, but a few weeks later, Ginny was invited to a sleepover at Tilly's. Ginny's father told her she could go. Tilly said they had extra sleeping bags for Ginny and Renée and that her mother would be cooking something special for dinner.

Tilly's mother served salad with the most amazing bread, something she called sourdough, which tasted great with butter. Then she served a casserole called chicken parmigiana, with pasta as a side dish. Ginny shouldn't have eaten the pasta after having two slices of bread. She thought she was going to just taste it, but she ate the whole dish because the sauce was delicious. Her parents made sauce with ketchup; it didn't compare to the real thing. Then, for dessert, Tilly's mom served pie but also fresh berries because she wanted to serve something Ginny could eat. Ginny didn't just feel full; she could feel her blood sugar spiking. It wasn't her imagination.

Since it was Ginny's first sleepover, she, Tilly, and Renée were up talking until well after midnight. They were having a good time, even with Ginny getting up so often to pee. After Tilly and Renée fell asleep, Ginny stared at the ceiling for a while, then got up to pee again. She wasn't especially thirsty, but her high blood sugar did make her cranky and distressed. As she lay awake in the sleeping bag on the floor, what she felt mostly was failure.

Sometimes, in the spring, the gym teacher would organize a class into a kickball game. It was supposed to be a treat, although it was met with great trepidation by some.

The team leaders were Carson Reynolds and Michael Hoyt. Of the boys in Ginny's class, Freddie Grisham was picked last. He was unmuscular and somewhat uncoordinated, and athletics frightened him.

"Ugh, we have Fem Boy on our team," Bobby said.

Ginny whispered to Renée, "Fem Boy?"

"Freddie."

"Why do they call him that?"

"'Throws like a girl,'" she answered.

"That's just dumb. That's mean to both Freddie and to us girls."

Carson picked Ginny first from the girls because everyone knew she played basketball and, therefore, was cool. At his next turn picking, he said, "The dark one."

"Don't call her that," Joey said. "Her name is Renée."

"Oooooh. Her name is Renée. Ooooh. Okay, Renée. You're on my team."

Kickball was not basketball. There was a coordination to someone rolling a ball at you and you having to kick it. Ginny was having trouble, but she did kick it hard enough on her third try to get on base.

"I dunno," Renée said to Tilly. "If Ginny can't do this, I doubt I can."

She was up next, and she hesitated.

"What's the matter, Dark One?" Bobby called from his position at third base.

"Oh, shut up, Bobby," Tilly said.

"Oooh ... You're so tough."

"Kick it right through his teeth, Renée," Tilly said.

Renée missed the first pitch, but on the second, she aimed at Bobby and kicked it so hard he couldn't catch it. Renée stood there, shocked.

"Run!" Tilly said.

Renée got to second. Ginny made it home.

"That ought to shut them up," Ginny said.

"Oh, they'll never shut up," Tilly said.

Tilly was always right.

Chapter 5
(I Want to Be)
Forever Young

The record store was in the middle of town, right by the center green. It was a small but busy place. A person could listen to a record in the listening booth, ask for recommendations, find rarities or bootlegs, or pick from a selection of books and magazines on the current music scene.

Asher went there often to keep up on new releases. On a previous visit, he had inquired about getting his old job back. Mr. Santini, the owner, had told him one of his workers was going to college, so he'd have a spot for Asher in about a month, and would he like to be a manager? "Yes" was the answer. "Yes, and thank you."

Ginny and Asher, meanwhile, were playing basketball almost every day, making the most of the last days of her summer vacation before she started fifth grade. Two men about Asher's age came into the yard one afternoon while they were playing. Ginny recognized them. They used to come by to practice with Asher when Ginny was younger.

"Steve! John! How the hell are you?"

Asher had said "hell." Their mother wouldn't like that.

"Can we join you?"

The men were even taller than Asher. Ginny didn't think she made it up to their waists.

"It's up to her. Gin?"

She had been getting much better at making baskets. Plus, she was getting taller. Not Asher tall, of course, but she was now almost four foot three and a half.

"Sure."

"How about you and Gin against Steve and me?"

"It's 'Ginny,'" Ginny said. "Only Asher calls me 'Gin.'"

"Oh. Sorry." John was amused, but when he saw Ginny's frown, he stopped smiling.

"Sure. You two against us two," Asher said.

Ginny was the better dribbler, and Asher had the better aim, but Steve and John were always ahead. They hardly needed to look at the basket to make goals.

Steve scored again, and Ginny said, "Time out!"

"You can't call 'time out,'" John said.

"She just did," Asher said.

Ginny went to the sidelines and took a couple of gulps of her emergency juice. It was Ginny's idea to bring juice and a package of crackers outside with her. It was weird that none of the adults had thought of that.

When she started to feel normal again, she said, "Okay. Let's get 'em."

They only lost 21 to 18. They were sure to win next time.

This year, the three friends were adding new moves to their jump-rope games, such as diamonds (crossing the ropes with their feet), jumping, or hopping. They were eager to add more, but today would not be the day. Tilly left her Chinese jump rope at home. They sat on the grass at recess, a little bored but happy to be outside in the late September weather.

"You know those Sharon Tate murders in California?" Tilly

said. "They think they're close to figuring out who did it."

This led the conversation into a dark place.

"There's also this man who keeps killing young people," Renée said.

"Oh?"

"He leaves, like, notes and stuff, but they can't figure them out. They call him the Zodiac Killer because some of the notes have astrological symbols in them. They haven't caught him yet, either."

"Ooh," Tilly said. "Kind of like one of those ghost stories we tell at camp."

Ginny had never been to camp, and it was doubtful she would be going anytime soon. The story still upset her.

"Are they close to finding him?" she said.

"My dad says no," Renée said. "My mom says he shouldn't have told me that."

Like any good ghost story, this information got under the girls' skins. They changed their positions to sit with their backs to each other to keep an eye out for danger. When Ginny mentioned this to Asher, he explained that Zodiac was in California, and the young people he was killing were young adults, mostly couples.

"Still," Ginny said.

"Worry about this when you're with your boyfriend some day and Zodiac has moved to Rhode Island. But I'm sure they'll catch him long before then. In the meantime, avoid California."

Ginny and her friends went back to Chinese jump rope a few days later and forgot about the California killers. They had a lot of new steps to learn.

Some days, the friends followed Ginny's lead and tried basketball. They had to get to the court before the boys and start playing immediately, or the sixth graders would try to bully them off the court. Ginny's bounce-and-run skills were usually enough to persuade the boys to find other things to do.

"Where's Tilly?" Renée said.

"She'll be here."

Ginny took a shot from the foul line. It didn't go in. Renée grabbed the rebound before the boys could get to it.

In a few minutes, a visibly upset Tilly ran up to them.

"Tilly, what's wrong?"

"Paul McCartney is dead!"

Renée dropped the ball, and it bounced away onto the grass.

"No, he's not," Ginny said.

"Yes, he is! Stu's older brother told him. He died in a car crash in 1966, and the band replaced him with a double!"

Paul was Tilly's favorite. Ginny understood; she would have felt terrible if it was George.

"That's really far-fetched." Renée had just learned that term and was excited to use it.

"No, it's not! There are all kinds of clues on the albums!"

"Why would they bother leaving clues? Why wouldn't they just announce it?" Ginny said.

"Because the fans would go crazy!"

"Then why wouldn't they keep it a total secret and not have clues?"

"Ginny, you never believe anything!"

"It sounds phony," Renée said. "I bet you this is a lie."

"Well, I hope so," Tilly said, not convinced.

They all agreed, though, that if this was true, it would be awful.

Now it was Ginny's turn to be upset.

"They're *banning* it?"

Her mother didn't seem to understand why this was so important.

"They discovered it causes cancer."

"If cyclamates cause cancer, why don't I have it? I eat a lot of that stuff. They should test me!"

Ginny's mother gave her a long-suffering look.

"Ginny, I can't change the law. We'll stock up on it. It's not off the shelves until February."

"February? That's too soon!"

It was almost November. Ginny's mother shook her head.

"I'm sorry. I don't know what to tell you."

"What am I supposed to do?"

"You'll use saccharin."

"But it's horrible. It tastes like chemicals."

"I use it."

Ginny was about to say, "But you don't have to," but realized this was not an argument she could win. Cyclamates would be gone in a few months. Time to stock up.

As it turned out, Ginny's father wouldn't let her stock up.

"It's poison," he said. "Stop using it."

After the announcement, stores began to dispose of boxes and boxes of cyclamates. They gave away anything that contained it: sugar-free Jello, sodas, candy, gum, pudding mixes. The kids in Ginny's neighborhood carried boxes of the sweetener and flung the flakey powder at each other. Ginny wished she was old enough to drive so she could get a few boxes. More than a few boxes. A dozen boxes. She would store them in her room. She'd learn to bake with it. Her mother wouldn't tell on her. Her father would never have to know.

Except he'd find out, and anyway, eventually, she'd run out. Ginny had to admit defeat.

Asher came home from the record store with a magazine for Ginny and her friends.

"*Life* magazine," Ginny said when she met up with them the next day. She displayed the cover. "A whole interview with Paul. See? He's there with his wife and kids."

"That could just be his double."

"For a whole interview? Tilly, if the double talks like, and sings like, and *writes songs* so much like Paul, wouldn't he want his own career?" Ginny had borrowed this logic from Asher.

Tilly took a moment to contemplate this.

"Well, they're paying him a lot of money."

Ginny bopped Tilly over the head with the magazine and handed it to her.

"Paul is alive. Stop being so upset," Ginny said.

"You think?"

"We think," Renée said.

Tilly smiled with relief.

Tilly's mother bought Tilly a portable record player for Christmas. She also gave her the collection of 45s she had acquired while working as the local record store's bookkeeper. The friends pounced on the boxes and flipped through the singles. A lot of the names didn't mean anything to Ginny and Renée (The Marvelettes? Sam Cooke? The Archies? Jackie Wilson?), so Tilly picked out some singles and stacked them on the record player to play.

The first single dropped down onto the platter, and the tone arm moved over to start playing. When the song was finished, the tone arm moved back to its starting position, and the next record dropped. Ginny and Renée had never seen anything like it.

"Stop staring at the record player. You're wasting the music."

Tilly started to dance, and soon Renée joined her. They moved like the dancers Ginny would see on *American Bandstand*.

Ginny's mother always changed the channel when there was dancing like that, but Ginny saw it often enough to know she liked it.

Tilly called out to Ginny, "Come join us!"

Ginny tried to mimic what her friends were doing. This led her to find her own groove. She moved along to the music, feeling free and happy. And she had a very clear thought:

I want to be 10 forever.

The new year brought Tab and Fresca back on the market, and Ginny's father bought a large bottle of each. New labeling announced, "Now with saccharin!" as if that was a good thing. It wasn't. The soda tasted terrible. In fact, every new sugar-free product had a weird aftertaste: ice cream, cookies, even gum. Ginny drank the soda, ate the ice cream, and chewed the gum, but she missed her cyclamates.

It was a rainy, dreary Sunday in North Greenwich. Since she couldn't play basketball, Ginny wandered into the living room to see what was on television. Asher and her father were watching something, an unusual activity for an afternoon. The adults usually saved television until after dinner.

"What are you watching?"

"NBA basketball."

"Really?"

"Come. Sit."

Ginny tried not to ask questions, but what were those strange things the announcers kept talking about? What was a hook shot? A layup? A lane violation? A shot clock?

Asher leaned over and said, "Watch this guy, Dave Debusschere. He's on the Knicks, number 22. See that? That was something called a jump shot. Dave doesn't average a lot of points per game, but he does make the long shots, and he's great with defense. The guy used to play professional baseball, too."

As the game continued, Asher would lean over and tell her about other Knicks players, like Walt Frazier and Willis Reed. He would add some game pointers and strategies, too. Ginny had never played basketball with real rules. A forward? A center? A guard? In gym class, they just got rebounds and tried to make baskets without poking each other's eyes out.

When the game was over, Ginny called Tilly and then Renée. This was information that had to be shared.

Ginny made sure to watch Sunday afternoon basketball from then on, sometimes with Asher and her father, sometimes with Tilly and Renée. Spring saw the girls with renewed enthusiasm on the court during recess. They had no idea what they were doing, but they tried fancier shots, like their versions of layups and hook shots. They rarely scored like that, but they were having fun.

Today, the boys had taken over the court first, so Ginny and Renée stood on the sidelines watching them play. They were waiting for Tilly to join them; maybe she brought her jump rope.

"Here I am," Tilly said. She was out of breath from running. "You'll never guess ..."

"What?"

"The Beatles broke up."

Renée and Ginny rolled their eyes.

"No, they didn't," Ginny said.

"Is this like that 'Paul is dead' stuff you swore was true?" Renée said.

Tilly sighed and showed them the newspaper she was carrying.

"See?"

"Oh my God," Ginny said. "The Beatles broke up!"

"Yes."

Renée skimmed the article. "It says Paul is releasing a solo album. That makes it official, doesn't it?"

"Maybe this is only temporary. Maybe Paul just needs to

sell his solo album, and then he'll go back."

Tilly and Renée looked sideways at Ginny.

"Okay, maybe not."

The three friends stood in silence for a few moments of reflection.

"Well," Tilly said. "This is a total bummer."

Ginny did a lot of practicing alone these days. Asher was working four days a week, and he was still seeing that stupid Trisha. When he was home, he stayed in his room. He'd have Ginny come in to listen to music, but he wouldn't venture out except to smoke.

Ginny was determined to become a better shooter. She'd start close to the basket until she made the shot, then back up a couple of steps, make another shot, and continue like that until she was too far back to reach the basket except with an underhand throw, which Asher said was uncool. Her father called her "a girl obsessed." That sounded negative.

"Hi."

"Ash!"

"Sorry I haven't been around. I haven't been feeling great."

"Flu?"

"No. Depressed. I've been trying to sort out some stuff in my head."

"Oh."

"Later, I have something to play for you."

"A new record? What did you get?"

"Paul's album."

She frowned.

"They've been playing it at the store," he said. "It's really good. Although with at least one song, maybe two, I think he should have had John write a middle eight for him."

"I think Paul's a traitor."

Asher laughed.

"I'm sure there was a lot going on with those guys that we're not privy to."

"Well ..."

"You'll give it a listen. If you hate it, we'll listen to something else."

"I like George. Think he'll put out an album, too?"

"I'm sure they all will."

"Well ... Okay."

"C'mon. Show me what you've got."

She was happy now. Asher was here.

While Ginny's mother was cleaning the dinner dishes, Asher and their father were engrossed with the TV. There were sounds of people yelling and cheering.

"What are you watching?" Ginny said.

"Basketball," Asher said. "Have a seat."

"On a Wednesday night?"

"They're airing the finals. This is game three."

Ginny sat between the two men, one who smelled like cigarettes and the other who smelled like pot.

"Who's playing?"

"The Knicks and the Lakers."

"We want the Knicks, right?" Ginny said.

"I'm a Lakers fan, myself," their father said and laughed when Ginny and Asher each made a face.

The score swung back and forth, sometimes Knicks leading, sometimes Lakers. They moved fast and made it seem so effortless. The score was soon close to 100 each.

"These guys are tall," Ginny said.

"Six feet and change, most of 'em," her father said.

"Wilt Chamberlain is seven-one," Asher said.

"He's on the Knicks?"

Her father grinned at her and said, "Lakers."

With seconds left and the score tied 100–100, the Knicks' Dave DeBusschere landed a jump shot to put his team ahead 102–100. Not to be outdone, the Lakers' Jerry West threw the ball from the back court in what football announcers would have called a "hail-Mary pass" and somehow made the basket as the buzzer sounded.

"That shot should've been worth like 10 points," Ginny said.

"In the ABA, it would've been three," Asher said.

"The NBA should do that. Still, that's not enough."

The score now tied, the game went into overtime. Ginny, Asher, and their father all sat forward on the couch and watched as the Knicks beat the Lakers 111–108.

"Well, watching that exhausted me," their father said. "Turn off the lights before you turn in. I'm going to bed."

"Hey," Ginny said. "They just said they're playing again Friday."

"Game four. Best of seven games."

"We're going to watch, right?"

"Of course."

The Knicks won the finals (their first NBA title), and it made Asher happy, but that didn't last long. Ginny figured he must be overwhelmed again.

Asher didn't come out of his room all weekend, even to smoke. Ginny's mom told her to leave him alone, but Ginny was worried. When she went upstairs to her room, she stopped at Asher's door.

She knocked. "Ash?"

She could hear music from behind the door. She waited a few moments and knocked again, this time a little louder.

"Yeah?"

"It's me, Ash."

There was a long pause, then Asher turned down the music and opened the door.

"Hi, Gin."

He didn't let her in, just looked down at her.

"Mom says you're sad and I shouldn't bother you. But I thought maybe I could cheer you up."

His expression didn't change. She continued.

"I can leave you alone if that's what you want."

He opened the door wider, and she entered his room.

"Is this a new album?" she said. They were yelling something she couldn't make out.

"Yep. It's Woodstock. The band about to play is Country Joe and the Fish."

She was going to ask what Woodstock was, but she didn't want to be any trouble. She'd ask Tilly or Tilly's mom later.

"Turn it up."

He nodded. "This song is called the 'I-Feel-Like-I'm-Fixin'-to-Die Rag.'"

He waited until the "Fish Cheer" was over, then turned up the music part.

Ginny listened to the song for a minute. The singer mentioned Vietnam.

"Was he in Vietnam, too?" Ginny said over the music.

Asher turned the volume back down.

"I'm not sure. Certainly, he has friends who were. Everyone has friends who were."

Ginny had to think about this. She got very quiet.

"Hey. I can play something else. Wanna hear the new Beatles album?"

"I thought they broke up."

"They did. But there's an album."

"I kinda like this song."

He smiled. "I do, too."

"But play the Beatles when this ends."

"Okay."

He turned the song back up.

"Asher ... what's a 'fucker'?" Ginny said, this time loud enough to be heard over the music. "He just called the audience 'fuckers.'"

Asher smirked. "Mom's going to kill me."

"Why?"

"Because it's a bad word. Ten-year-olds shouldn't go around saying it."

"I'm eleven."

"Still."

"Okay."

The song ended. Asher stood up to change albums.

"Is everyone against the war?"

"Not everyone, no."

"What about Mom and Dad?"

"Yes."

"How about you?"

"Yeah. Me too."

"But you went there."

"I had no choice. They drafted me. I should've gone to college like Mom and Dad wanted."

Asher put the Woodstock album back where it belonged and took out the Beatles' latest.

"You said you saw bad things over there. What kind of things?"

She thought his silence meant she had made him mad, but then he responded, "I shouldn't have mentioned that to you."

"Is that why people are against the war?"

"I think that's why some people are against war in general."

"Are those things one of the reasons you're sad?"

He put the album on the turntable and turned to look at her. "Yeah. I keep ... reliving things ... I mean, it comes on like a nightmare, only I'm wide awake."

He paused.

"Let's talk about this another time, okay? I promise we'll talk about this."

"Okay."

"Let me play the new Beatles for you. I think you'll dig it."

He brought the tonearm down on *Let it Be*. Ginny loved what she heard. She couldn't wait to tell Tilly and Renée.

Chapter 6

I Talk About Boys

The summer had been brutally hot, and although Ginny still practiced, she was close to getting heat stroke more often than not. The fall finally arrived with cooler temperatures, perfect for basketball. Ginny and Asher had plans to play Saturday morning. Ginny got up early, and since Asher's bedroom door was still closed, she went into the bathroom to pee before he got in there.

There was blood.

Nooooooo! Not yet! I'm still a kid!

She had been warned about this.

She went into the bathroom's linen closet and got out one of the sanitary pads her mother bought for her.

Her body was changing in other ways as well. She had peach fuzz all over her legs, arms, and other places it shouldn't be growing. But, more importantly, lately she felt she was losing the ability to feel when lows were coming on. These days she only had a 10- maybe 15-minute warning. Could this be related? Maybe things would go back to normal in a few days after this thing was over. She had the feeling, though, that nothing was going to be "normal" again. She should have stayed 10 forever like she had wanted to.

Ginny returned to her room and sat on her bed, holding

her knees. She felt crampy and grimy. She never wanted to move again.

Asher came out of his room and stood in her doorway.

"What's wrong?" he said.

"I don't know."

"I see. Wanna play some basketball?"

She didn't like to say no to Asher, but it wasn't like she could tell him the problem. That was beyond the realm of their brother-sister relationship. She hesitated.

"Sure, you do. Let me get dressed, and we'll play," he said.

She thought about it. What would she do if she was a professional athlete? Skip a week of playing every month? Ridiculous.

Bouncing and running felt good. The more she moved around, the better she felt. Asher stole the ball from her, but he missed his shot, and when Ginny got the rebound, she scored.

"Nice," Asher said.

Yes, she was feeling better. Bloated and, to use the proper medical terminology, icky, but better.

"Try a layup. You'll take your last two steps as wide as you can to get momentum to jump. Have those steps bring you as close to the basket as possible, and use the backboard to get the ball in."

Up until now, Ginny would stop, throw the ball toward the hoop, and hope for the best. Sometimes that worked.

"Use the backboard?"

She tossed him the ball.

"Keep your eyes on the basket as you approach. I aim at the backboard, just above the hoop, and the ball goes right in. Otherwise, it's easy to overshoot it or undershoot it."

Asher demonstrated a layup. Then Ginny tried. The ball skimmed the backboard and rolled over the rim to the other side.

"That's right. A little more backboard and that would have gone in. Keep practicing. You'll get it."

"Think I'll ever be as tall as you?"

"Not likely, but I'm sure you'll grow taller than you are now."

"Okay."

"You're a girl. You're not supposed to be as tall as me."

"Mom's pretty tall."

"Think about this. If you get too tall, you could lose your signature bouncing-and-running skills."

"I could?"

"It's easier to dart around when you're shorter."

"Far out," she said.

Mattel had stopped selling Incredible Edibles. Could've been because they contained cyclamates. Could've been because they tasted terrible. Maybe the Creepy Crawlers were just more popular. Renée and Ginny went to Tilly's house over the weekend to try the new molds she got for her Creepy-Crawler Thingmaker. The girls could now create various monster parts that could be stuck onto pencils to make standing creatures.

Tilly filled one of the molds while Renée and Ginny's creations were cooking. They were discussing Ginny's latest news.

"I use tampons," Tilly said.

"What's that?"

"It's like cotton shaped like a lipstick."

"And?"

Renée giggled. "You stick it in there."

Ginny made a face. "Really?"

"Oh yeah," Tilly said. "Far better than those pads. Far less disgusting, too."

"I'll never do that," Renée said.

"Yes, you will," Tilly said. "Once you get yours, you'll want to use them. Pads are horrible."

Ginny shook her head. "My mother will *never* go for that."

"I'll give you a box. My mom buys them all the time."

As she left the room, Renée said, "Tilly has a hip mom."

Tilly's "hip" mom drove Ginny home in the late afternoon. Asher was sitting on the back porch. Ginny was sure he was smoking pot, but she walked over anyway and sat beside him.

"Hi."

Asher smiled. "Don't let Mom see you out here."

"I don't think she knows I'm home yet."

"Think you better sit on the other side of me so you're not downwind."

Ginny changed sides. The backyard of the Eastman property was delineated by trees. It used to scare Ginny when she was younger. She thought monsters hid in the leaves, a belief propagated by her older brother. They sat together now, having unrelated thoughts. Ginny wondered what swimming would be like with this new development. Maybe tampons were the answer to that, except … eww. Asher was recovering from a morning of flashbacks, which seemed more benign now that the pot was taking effect.

"What are you doing for Halloween?" he asked.

"We'll probably go trick-or-treating, maybe in Tilly's neighborhood."

"You don't sound excited about it."

"I like to make costumes. But the trick-or-treating part is really a drag for me."

Asher was amused by her use of the word "drag." They sat a while longer, and then he said, "I've had a bad morning."

Ginny waited for him to continue.

"I've been reliving things since I woke up."

"What kind of things?"

He shook his head. "You're just a kid. I'll tell you when you're older. Maybe when you're, like, 60."

Ginny was going to say she was no longer a kid but decided against it.

"Tell me."

He hesitated. "Things like centipedes the size of my head crawling up my legs and arms. Which are more visually challenging, unless they bite you. Then you're in a world of hurt. Buddies dying in front of me from grenade explosions or mortar attacks, while I'm somehow spared. Sometimes, the blasts are so close I check to see if I got hit, too. Then there are our soldiers, stacking the bodies of the enemies, happily counting the corpses. Some of our guys enjoyed killing them, like they got excited thinking about it. Those guys scared me more than the commies. Anyway, it's so real that it's like I'm still there. Then everything disappears in a flash, and I'm back here."

Ginny was listening intently. Asher continued.

"Once something started over there, it felt like it would never end. It could be the heat. The downpours. The mosquitoes. The mortar attacks. The maiming. The dying."

He turned and saw Ginny's horrified face.

"I'm sorry. I should have stopped at the centipedes."

"No, I'm okay. I don't know how you stayed there so long."

"I didn't have a choice." Then Asher motioned toward the kitchen window, where their mother was preparing dinner. "I think you should go inside before Mom comes looking for you."

"Good idea."

When Ginny entered the house, her mother said, "Did you have a nice talk with Asher?"

Busted.

"Yeah. I did."

"Good."

The friends tried not to let their new upperclassman status go to their heads. Other sixth-graders bullied or bossed around the younger kids, but these three friends had other things to do with their time. Ginny's main concern was growing taller.

Mother Nature was playing a cruel trick on her. Her parents and her brother were tall. Couldn't she get some height, too?

At recess, the basketball court was occupied, so Ginny and Tilly were left to find another amusement: Clackers, two heavy acrylic balls on a string that made a loud noise when you swung them up and down. Tilly had a blue pair. Ginny's was clear with sparkles.

"I heard these are supposed to be dangerous," Ginny said, raising her voice to be heard over the noise.

"Nah. Just rumors. Supposedly, they can shatter."

"I would think they'd be more dangerous as a weapon. Like if someone threw them at you."

This made them laugh.

"Where's Renée?"

"I don't know," Tilly said. "I passed her at the exit. She was talking to Stu."

Renée came running up to them. All clacking stopped for a moment.

"Stu asked me out."

"He did? What'd he say?" Tilly seemed more excited than Renée was.

"Just asked me if I wanted to go to a movie on Saturday."

"Did you say 'yes'?" Ginny said.

"Of course. It's Stu!"

This made Ginny nervous. Boys? Already? It was one thing to have crushes, but to actually do something about them? How would she go on a date, anyway? She'd have to insist on eating on time. She'd have to explain herself, and people didn't always understand, so what was the point? Besides, being a diabetic was not romantic. Repellent, even. Like having her period, but every day, forever.

"Maybe I'll ask out Bobby," Tilly said.

"Isn't the boy supposed to ask?" Renée said.

"Why?"

Neither Ginny nor Renée had an answer to that.

Back inside the school, Joey approached Ginny in the hallway.

"Hey, Ginny. Do you still have a crush on me?"

The old embarrassment and humiliation took over her judgment.

"No! Of course not!" She turned her back to him and stuck her face in the drinking fountain. She was starting to breathe fast. She tried to calm down.

"Oh. Okay. Good. Just making sure," he said.

She sighed with relief. She couldn't go through *that* again. Boys. What else was going to change?

Ginny was sitting on the floor in Asher's room. She was in a sulky mood. Asher was going through his records, trying to decide on the perfect music for this occasion.

"You know, there's nothing wrong with liking someone," Asher said.

"I know, but everyone is suddenly dating. I mean, yesterday, we were kids. Today, the kids have dates on Saturday nights."

"Do you feel left out?"

"Not exactly. Kind of. Maybe. Yes. But it's because I don't want to do this right now."

Asher chose the latest, and last, Simon and Garfunkel album, *Bridge Over Troubled Water*, and then sat on the floor with Ginny. 1970 was a year of break-ups, the Beatles, Simon and Garfunkel, and the Supremes, to name a few, and deaths, most notably Janis Joplin and Jimi Hendrix. Asher bought all their last albums.

"It's okay. You don't have to. Do you feel pressured?"

"No. Not really. Left out, yes. Pressured, no."

"Then do what makes you comfortable. It's not a race."

"It's just that now my friends won't be available anymore."

"Ahhh. But they will be. How about you and I do something this Saturday? Want to go to the record store? We can pick out whatever you want."

Ginny's mood brightened. "Really? Yes!"

"Okay. It's a date."

Tilly and Renée weren't busy every Saturday night, especially after the novelty wore off. As usual, Asher was right. By the end of the fall, things were almost back to normal. Date night was only happening sporadically.

Ginny was currently trying to digest Thanksgiving. There was a lot of food, and she happily had servings of everything. Nothing she had eaten was outside of her prescribed diet, but she felt she had had too much of it. She would no doubt pay for this later with a positive urine test.

Tilly called from her grandmother's house a while later. The main phone in the Eastman house wasn't available because Ginny's parents were watching television in the living room, so Ginny picked up the call on the extension she and Asher shared. She dragged it into her room so she could have some privacy. Asher was amused that an 11-year-old needed privacy, but he understood.

"What did you have for Thanksgiving?" Tilly said.

"The usual. Turkey, stuffing, mashed potatoes, vegetables. My mom's stuffing is amazing."

"We had ham, applesauce, and sweet potatoes with marshmallows. You ever have those?"

"No. Mom never made them, and then I couldn't, anyway."

"Ugh, I ate too much."

"So did I."

"Grandma had two kinds of pie, and I had a piece of each. I'm really bored here."

"Two slices of pie!" Ginny had never heard of that.

"That was after all the other food. I made myself get sick afterward."

"What? Why?"

"So I don't get fat, like my mother."

"But how ..."

"Stuck my finger down my throat."

"But ... yuck."

"I know. It's gross, but I'd rather be able to eat than worry about it."

"I kinda wish I could do that. I'm stuffed."

"Yeah. But you're skinny. And your mom's skinny."

"You're skinny."

"And now you know why. By the way, don't tell Renée. I'd just get a lecture, and she might even tell my mom."

"No, of course not."

"Far out. You've always been cool, Ginny."

"I try."

Shopping the day after Thanksgiving and that entire weekend was too crazy for Tilly's mom. She was not a fan of crowds. The following weekend was safer. People were less frenzied. Tilly, Renée, and Ginny accompanied her to the mall, eager to spend the money their parents had given them for some new clothes.

"Where should we start?" Tilly's mother said.

They decided to walk over to the big department store. They took the escalator to the second floor.

"I'll be right over here in Women's Clothes," Tilly's mom said. "Meet me at the cashier in an hour."

"An hour. That's not enough time," Tilly said. "But wow! Look at this!"

"Cute shirt!"

"Okay. I'm definitely trying this on."

"I like this one," Ginny said. "Except, why is everything brown? Pink and brown, orange and brown, blue and brown. What happened to colors?"

"It's what's in now," Tilly said. "Bright colors are out."

The girls weren't paying attention to their surroundings, focused as they were on shopping. If they had been, they would have noticed the security guard. He wasn't standing that far away. In fact, he was inching closer.

"Hey. Look behind us," Ginny whispered.

"What? Because we're kids, that means we're gonna steal?" Tilly said, loud enough for him to hear. He didn't flinch.

"Tilly ..." Renée said but laughed.

"Maybe we should split up," Ginny said quietly.

"Good idea. I'm going to go try this on," Tilly said.

"I'm going to keep looking," Ginny said.

Tilly headed for the changing rooms. The guard held his position.

"I'm going to go look at socks," Renée said.

"Okay. Meet me back here."

Renée wasn't sure where socks were located, so she wandered around until she found them. There were racks and racks, all different colors and patterns. She picked out a few pairs.

"Ahem."

Renée turned to see the security guard glaring at her. This unnerved her, which was his intention. Trying to maintain her composure, she turned to head back to Ginny, then thought better of it and put the socks back first.

"I thought you were going to get socks," Ginny said. "Didn't see anything you liked?"

"They had so many cute ones! And that's where the colors are, Ginny! My favorites were the red ones with white hearts."

"Why don't you get them?" Tilly was holding the blouse she had tried on; she was going to buy it. "By the way, that security guy is gone."

Renée lowered her voice. "No, he's not. He's been follow-ing me."

Tilly and Ginny took a moment to grasp what she was saying. Why would security follow Renée?

Ohhhhhh.

When they turned, there he was again.

"Renée. Go get your socks. We'll wait," Ginny said.

Reluctantly, she headed to the socks. She picked out the red ones, then chose some blue with clouds and yellow flower-power ones.

The security guard was watching her. He waited, waited … then as soon as Renée turned to go, he approached her.

"Okay, Miss, come with me."

The security guard grabbed her arm.

"Let go of me!"

"Shoplifting is illegal, in case your parents never told you."

"I'm not shoplifting. I'm going to buy these."

"Come with me."

"No!"

Tilly and Ginny heard Renée's voice and hurried over.

"Let me go!"

"What are you doing?" Tilly wasn't afraid of anyone. Ginny liked that about her.

"Your friend was shoplifting. I suggest you call her mother. She's in trouble here."

"No, she wasn't! Get your hands off her!"

But the guard pulled her by the arm and dragged her off. Tilly's mother heard the commotion and came over, but not until Renée and the guard had disappeared into the back of the store.

"My daughter was *not* shoplifting," Renée's mother was say-ing to the manager. Tilly, Renée, and Mrs. Quain helplessly looked on. Ginny thought the security guard looked smug.

"I know it's a shock, Mrs. Neuville."

"That's *Doctor* Neuville. And my husband is a lawyer. We'll sue this place until none of you have jobs."

"That won't be necessary," the manager said with a smile and a lot of condescension. "This is only her first offense. We're prepared to let her go with a warning."

"She didn't do anything wrong. She was *shopping*," Tilly said. "You picked on her because she's Black!"

"Tilly ..." her mother said.

Tilly's mom was holding a lot of clothes she was going to buy, some for herself and some for Tilly. Other shoppers were looking over but didn't dare approach.

"Where is she?" Dr. Neuville said.

"In detention." The manager turned to the guard. "You can go get her now."

"You have her sitting in a room by *herself*? She's 11 years old!" Her voice had the proper amount of agitation and anger in it.

The guard returned with a sheepish, crying, and frightened Renée. Tilly's mom stepped forward.

"I think I'll just put all of this stuff back. In fact, *you* can do that." She pushed the clothes into the manager's arms.

"We're never shopping here again!" Tilly said, which she knew didn't matter to the people in charge, but she felt good saying it, and it almost had Renée smiling.

Asher was excited about Christmas this year. He had nice presents for everyone and was particularly proud of the gift he had for Ginny. She kept inspecting it as it sat under the tree, asking if she could open it early, but he wouldn't let her.

"You'll ruin the surprise."

"Okay. It's sort of the shape of a record album, but it's really thick, so maybe a book? But books aren't usually square..."

Asher smiled. "You'll just have to wait."

Christmas morning, Ginny was beside herself.

"Can I open it now? Can I open it now?"

"Ginny, we're going to have breakfast first. You can wait a little while longer," her mother said.

"Argh. No, I can't!"

"Let's sit down," her father said. "I made pancakes."

Ginny had sugar-free syrup, which had a funny after-taste because of the saccharin, but who eats pancakes without syrup? They were delicious, anyway, and Ginny almost forgot about Asher's present.

Almost.

"Now? Can I open it now?"

Asher laughed. "Yes."

She darted to the tree and grabbed her present. The paper was too pretty to rip, so she carefully undid the tape.

It was George Harrison's new solo album, *All Things Must Pass*.

"Far out!! But why is it so thick?"

"It's three LPs and a poster."

"Oh my God! Thank you! Thank you! I can't wait to tell Tilly and Renée! They'll be so jealous! We all love 'My Sweet Lord.' Tilly's mom bought her the single."

"The store has been playing the album nonstop. It's great."

"Better than Paul's?"

"Better than Paul's."

Her parents were smiling at her.

"What?"

"Open our present."

They pointed to a large box. Ginny crawled on her elbows and knees to get to it, then dragged it out from under the tree.

"What on earth?"

A turntable. Not the cheap portable record player that Tilly had that scratched up the records, but a *bona fide* turntable with a clear cover, a lot like Asher's, only his was stereo and hers had a single internal speaker.

"Thank you! Thank you! Thank you!"

"I'll set it up for you," Asher said.

"You'll still play me stuff, right?"

"Absolutely. I also bought John's album. We can listen to that today, too, if you want."

"After George."

"Of course."

She tore open the plastic covering on the album and retrieved the poster.

"Be right back."

"Ginny ..." her mother said.

Ginny ran up the stairs. Asher and his parents exchanged looks and laughed.

"Ash! I can't put this up! I'm not tall enough!"

Asher chuckled and went upstairs to help.

Ginny woke up a few days later feeling feverish. And queasy. And she had a burning sensation in her throat like she had swallowed chemicals. She wasn't weak like she often was when she got sick, and she was extremely thirsty, which worried her. She made her way downstairs and announced, "I think I'm sick."

Her mother sighed. "I thought maybe we'd skip the flu this season." She felt Ginny's forehead. "You're hot. Let's check your temperature."

It was 102.4 degrees.

"I don't feel so good."

Ginny lay on the couch and stared into space. She wasn't well enough to sleep. Her mother called the doctor. He said not to give her her insulin.

"Wait until the queasiness subsides."

This didn't sound right. Ginny always took her shot. She fell asleep for about an hour and woke up feeling sicker. Pain had developed in her back, which caused her to have trouble breathing.

"Mom?"

Her mother called the doctor, who told her to call an ambulance.

She arrived at the hospital with ketoacidosis, brought on by extreme hyperglycemia. The underlying cause was a bout of walking pneumonia. Insulin and fluids got her stabilized, but she stayed a while longer for the pneumonia. Her doctor later told her mother that he thought Ginny just had the flu, thus the directive to avoid insulin. Ginny knew this time was different. She should have said something instead of blindly following instructions. Adults, even doctors, didn't know everything. They weren't inside her body.

Chapter 7

You're Not a Kid Anymore

Students from all three of the town's elementary schools graduated to the North Greenwich Middle School. There, they were organized by brain power, with the different levels numbered. It didn't take an astrophysicist to crack the code: 7-1 meant you were smart. 7-7 meant you weren't. The school split the top level into two sections. Ginny was in 7-1a and Renée was in 7-1b. Tilly was in 7-3. This meant the three girls wouldn't be sharing any classes this year.

As Ginny entered the home room, Freddie Grisham waved her over to sit next to him. They had never been close in grade school, but he had come to her house a few times for her birthday parties when they were younger. Middle school was full of strangers. Ginny was happy to see someone she knew.

"My brother says the earth science teacher is cool, but to watch out for the math teacher," Freddie said. "Apparently, he's pretty tough and kinda mean."

Freddie's brother was a sophomore in high school. He was a good source of information.

"We survived Miss Watterson in third grade. We can survive anything," Ginny said.

"She wasn't so bad. Wait a minute. Yes, she was."

Ginny and Freddie walked with each other from class

to class. They only had to separate for gym. Ginny liked the math teacher at first sight, but she didn't say so to Freddie. She wasn't afraid of a little pre-algebra, but who knew what he might be like the rest of the year?

As she and Freddie headed to their last class, Principal Morgan approached Ginny with her parents in tow. Freddie went on to class, and then the bell rang. The corridors emptied except for a handful of late students rushing to their rooms.

"Ginny, you need to go with your parents," Principal Morgan said.

"What did I do?" she said.

"Nothing, dear," her mother said.

"What's going on?"

"We'll tell you in the car, Ginny," her father said sternly. "Come with us. Now."

This sure didn't sound like she hadn't done anything wrong. Ginny followed them to the car. What could be going on that both her parents were here? Why wasn't her father at work?

"Okay. Tell me."

Her father didn't start the car.

"It's about Asher."

Ginny felt a deep pain in her gut. What did Asher do? Did he get arrested for smoking pot like their mother predicted? Was he stealing from his job? Did he get Trisha pregnant?

"What about Asher?"

Her parents exchanged looks.

"I'm sorry, sweetheart," her mother said. "He ... died."

For a moment, there were no thoughts in Ginny's head, just a dark, murky feeling she had never experienced before.

"You're wrong."

"Ginny ..."

Her mother said this in her go-to, disapproving tone. Ginny waited for someone to tell her it wasn't true.

"How?" she said finally.

"Your mother found him. He was in the bathtub."

"He *drowned*?"

There they were, exchanging looks again.

"Tell me!"

His father nervously cleared his throat. "He ... slit his wrists."

Ginny couldn't catch her breath. She forced herself to inhale and exhale.

"He couldn't have. I don't understand."

"I'm sorry, honey. You know he's been troubled since he came back from overseas." Her mother didn't like to say "Vietnam."

Ginny spoke between sobs. "I know, but ... he was doing better."

The car was moving now. They weren't heading home. Ginny noticed her overnight bag was on the floor next to her.

"Where are we going?"

"To your friend Renée's," her father said. "We thought maybe you'd want to spend a couple nights there." He paused. "You don't want to be home right now."

It took a second, but then Ginny realized what he was saying.

"I guess Mom doesn't want to be there either, right?"

"Not until the police leave. We're going to a motel."

Ginny was getting the picture. Asher was still there.

Renée's dad brought Ginny home after breakfast on Saturday. Ginny's mother was in the kitchen. Without a word, she came over and hugged her daughter.

Ginny climbed the stairs, tossed her bag into her room, and stood in front of Asher's door. She hesitated, then entered and fumbled for the light switch. The room still had the faint scent of burnt reefer. She sat on the bed.

"Ash, what did you do? I mean, could I have done something to stop you?"

Asher had left an album on the turntable, so she went over to see which one. It was John's solo album. She turned on the stereo, started the turntable, and put the tonearm on the record. Before she sat back down, she saw an envelope with her name on it leaning against the nearest box of albums. She shuddered. With great apprehension, she took out the note.

Sept. 9, 1971
Gin—

> *By now, you know that I've done something pretty horrible. I couldn't help it. Really, I couldn't. Do me a favor, Gin. Please live forever.*
>
> *Love,*
> *Ash*

She stared at the note and tried to burn it into her memory like a ranch logo they branded onto those poor cattle Ash liked to eat. She stood transfixed, barely noticing Lennon wailing in her ear about his lost parents. Someone had cleared away Ash's baggy of pot from his nightstand, but there was a partially smoked joint in the ashtray beside the turntable. She thought a moment, looked behind her to make sure she was alone, and slipped the joint into her pocket.

"Are you okay, Ginny?"

She jumped. Her mother had entered the room.

"Just listening to some of Asher's records."

Her mother attempted a smile, but instead, she pursed her lips.

"I made you some lunch."

"Okay. I'll be down."

Ginny waited for the song to end, then turned off the stereo, leaving the album where it was. Her favorite track was "Isolation," but it was the last song on the side, and her mother was waiting for her. She went into her room, put the note and the joint in the empty diary she got for Christmas a few years ago, and headed downstairs.

Ginny's mother had been complaining all week that Ginny was "sulking," but now that it was the morning of the funeral, her mother was letting her stay home to, well, sulk. Ginny just couldn't bring herself to go; it made it too real. Her mother gave her the neighbor's number, saying, "Just in case you need anything."

Ginny didn't plan on needing anything. She was curled up on her bed, staring into space, and intended on staying there. She didn't know how long she lay there, but something made her sit up and go into her diary. She took out Asher's note. She reread it a few times, then put it back and took out the joint. She went into Asher's room, found the fancy lighter their grandfather had given him, and went out to sit on the porch.

Since it was too early in the year for the foliage to change, the trees were lush and hid the yard from the neighbors. Ginny flicked the lighter and got a flame, but just for a second. She tried again, and, holding down the striker instead of letting it go, she got a steady flame to light the joint. It caught on fire but then went out.

How did people do this?

She tried holding the joint to her lips and inhaling as she lit it. She started coughing uncontrollably. The joint went out, but she was determined. She lit it again, inhaled more carefully, and only coughed for a few seconds. She exhaled a lot of smoke. She had gotten a hit.

Not sure how much to smoke, she thought maybe three hits would be enough. She just wanted to try it, but in a couple of minutes, she was stoned. It was unsettling. What time was it? Did she need to eat? What was happening?

She went back inside and was relieved she was able to read the clock. It was noon-thirty. Lunchtime.

There was some leftover home-made quiche, which was perfect since Ginny didn't think she could figure out how to make a sandwich in her condition. She cut herself a slice and started to eat without heating it. It was the best thing she'd ever tasted. She put the rest of the quiche away, then grabbed an apple. That should do it.

She put the lighter back in Asher's room and the rest of the joint in her diary, and although she kind of liked smelling like Asher, she took a shower to get rid of the pot odor. She wasn't as stoned anymore; now she felt sleepy. After setting an alarm for her snack, she dozed off.

"You've got to stop moping."

Sulking. Moping. Ginny loved her mother's vocabulary.

"I'm not moping."

"Well, what do you call it?"

"I'm sad. I can't just forget about it like you and Dad do."

Her mother winced at this accusation but kept her cool.

"It's been three weeks. You need to start getting back to doing things. You haven't seen your friends. You haven't played basketball. You haven't listened to Asher's albums. You just sit and pretend you're reading."

She knew Ginny was pretending?

"I'm surprised you're not getting behind in school."

"I have *some* pride."

"Well, good." Her mother softened. "Ginny. You will be grieving for a long time. Start living again. You'll feel better."

Ginny hated to admit it, but maybe her mother was right. Asher himself had warned her not to get consumed by sadness. Ginny had let herself get consumed.

"Okay, Mom. I'll try."

Ginny kept her promise. She started playing basketball again. She made plans with Tilly and Renée to go to a movie and then went to a sleepover at Tilly's, dancing with her friends to Tilly's singles. She was keeping busy, and she did feel better. After a few days of this, she came home from school feeling drained. Being happy was hard work.

"Did you have a good day?"

"It was okay."

"I'll make you a snack."

"Sure. I just want to go upstairs a minute."

She went into the bathroom. When she was done peeing and was washing her hands, she started uncontrollably weeping.

The tissue box on the counter was empty, so she went into the linen closet for a new one. Wait. Razorblades. Was that what Asher used? She took one out and unwrapped it.

Why would he do such a thing?

She touched the blade to her wrist, and it cut her skin. Fascinated, she made another cut. She moved the blade to her forearm, created a thin line of blood, then several more. When the cuts began to ooze, she put her arm under the cold-water faucet, dried her arm with some tissue, and disposed of the blade in a small container Asher had labeled "used blades." Then she pulled down her sleeve and went downstairs to get her snack.

Steve and John came around a few days later to make sure Ginny was doing okay.

"How are you holding up, kid?"

"Sometimes okay. Sometimes not."

"It's still fresh in your mind," Steve said.

"You'll deal with it better as time goes on," John said.

Ginny's mom came into the room.

"Do you two want something? A drink? Something to eat?"

"No, thanks, Mrs. Eastman."

"We were just going outside," Ginny said.

"We were?" John said.

Ginny led them to the backyard and Steve said, "Twenty-one?"

Ginny proposed they play one-on-one, with the odd man playing the winner. That way Ginny could still hone her dribbling and defensive skills. Twenty-one was only about rebounds and shooting.

After they left, Ginny practiced shooting. She was trying to shoot from farther away when something occurred to her. She always shot by crouching down and pushing from underneath. Anyone could block her shots.

She got closer to the basket and tried to shoot overhand. It almost went in. She wasn't strong enough to get any distance, but this would be harder to block. She would practice it.

As she headed inside to get her snack, a dark thought took hold of her. What was she going to do with basketball, anyway? She was a girl and an average-height one at that. It wasn't like she could ever be a professional player; there wasn't such a thing for women. And what would she do, keep candy hidden in her uniform?

Besides, without Asher, what was the point?

Ginny was curled up in her room, crying. It was a Saturday after a long week of trying to be cheerful. She didn't care if her mother thought she was moping. She didn't care if she wasn't seeing her friends, or playing basketball, or doing her homework. It was just two months since Asher died, and Ginny was miserable.

Someone knocked on her door.

"Ginny?" It was her mother. "Can I come in?"

Her mother never asked if she could enter her room. Ginny stopped sobbing and croaked out, "Okay."

Her mother entered. Ginny didn't move.

"Are you okay?"

"Just sad."

Her mother sat on her bed.

"I'm sad, too."

Ginny sat up.

"Listen," her mother said. "You may not feel up to it, but I was going to go shopping in a little while. Maybe you'd like to come? I thought I'd go grocery shopping in the center of town. Maybe you'd like to go to the record store while we're there."

"Okay."

"Okay?"

Ginny sniffed. "Okay."

"Good. You tell me when you're ready, and we'll go."

The center of town had the larger grocery store, situated in a small plaza with a parking lot and other, smaller stores. Ginny liked the idea of doing something normal and mundane. She picked out some Brussels sprouts for her mother to cook for dinner, and then they went to the meat counter to buy some fish. Her mother chose tuna steaks. The rest of the grocery list was ordinary: milk, eggs, paper towels, juice, dishwashing soap.

They had to walk by the record store to get to their car. Her mother stopped.

"Want to go in?"

The record store was playing Janis Joplin's *Pearl*, an album Asher had played many times for Ginny. The store felt like a second home, one where Asher was still alive. Ginny looked through the new releases while her mother waited for her outside. She picked John Lennon's *Imagine* and the Rolling Stones' *Sticky Fingers*. She counted up her money; she had just enough, including the tax.

When she got home, she started with John's album since Asher was such a fan. John Lennon confused Ginny. The Beatles' biography by Hunter Davis portrayed him as witty and outgoing, but then Asher finally let her read that *Rolling Stone* interview from the beginning of the year, and there John seemed angry, troubled, even cruel.

She put on the album.

The title song was transcendent. How could all that anger come from a person who could write such a beautiful song? Her grief melted into the music.

She loved song after song, but when "I Don't Want to Be a Solder" started playing, it blew Ginny's little 12-year-old mind. Besides the lyrics, she found the overlapping rhythms and sounds fascinating. The clincher was the first song on the second side, "Gimme Some Truth." Asher used to call John a "truth seeker." It seemed he was right.

She was beginning to understand why John was Asher's favorite. There was more to this John Lennon guy than she thought.

Next was *Sticky Fingers*, Ginny's first Rolling Stones album. Asher had played her a lot of Stones' music, so she decided she should have an album of her own. She thought the cover with the working zipper was cool.

At the first track, "Brown Sugar," Ginny was hooked. Later in her life, the lyrics would concern her, but on first playing, the song was high-energy and danceable. Every track had something interesting, melodic, rhythmic, or all three. She would have to report this to Tilly and Renée. This was something they should know about.

The tryouts for the girls' basketball team were approaching. Ginny dreaded making this decision. The closer the tryouts came, the sadder she got. By Wednesday, she was dragging herself through the school's hallways, head down, shoulders drooped. She slumped down further and further as she crept along.

"My God, Ginny. You walk like a 90-year-old man."

She hadn't noticed she had passed Principal Morgan. She stood up straight and entered her classroom.

The Good Humor truck that was parked by the school was waiting for students to exit the building. Tilly and Renée were thrilled it was still coming around this late in the year. Tilly bought a strawberry shortcake bar, and Renée bought an ice cream sandwich.

"You going to the tryouts tomorrow?"

Tilly's ice cream bar was something Ginny had never had. She wasn't sure she would like it. She favored chocolate.

"No. I don't think so."

"But you're great at basketball," Renée said.

"It's not like I can make a career out of it."

Her friends rolled their eyes.

"You could become a coach," Tilly said.

"Great. And coach girls to spend time doing something they can't do anything with."

Ginny was in one of her moods. This would pass.

"Well, you have until tomorrow after school. Maybe you'll come to your senses by then." Tilly licked the last bit of ice cream off the stick and tossed it to the ground.

"Maybe," Ginny said, but she was sure she had made the right decision.

She didn't go to the tryouts, but Tilly and Renée did, and both made the team. Ginny tried not to let this bother her. She reminded herself that she didn't care anymore. Even so, she slashed up her arms when she got home. Then, she went out to the driveway to practice.

Ginny didn't think she was cutting herself all that often, but the marks on her arms begged to differ. This would become more of an issue in warmer weather, but for now, she could wear long sleeves. To solve the problem, she began cutting her hips. This was not only a more discreet area, but even the gym suits hid the cuts there.

Meanwhile, Ginny wanted to remove the hair growing on her legs and under her arms. Despite her current fascination with razorblades, she didn't want to use a full-sized razor like Asher's. She went shopping with her mother and bought a Lady Schick razor and a bottle of Nair. This was overkill, considering how little hair she had at the moment. She tried the Nair first. The stuff smelled toxic. Was it going to do weird things to her skin? No, all it did was take off the hair from her legs. She would use the Lady Schick for now, though. Nair smelled too nasty.

The earth science teacher picked Freddie and Ginny to do a project together. They had to include drawings in the report, which Ginny volunteered to do, so Freddie offered to organize notecards and create an outline. Then, they'd share the writing.

Freddie's family had a current *Encyclopedia Britannica*, so the pair chose to work at Freddie's. Each took a volume of the *Britannica* and sat at the dining table. As Freddie took notes, Ginny drew the various plants they needed for the report. This creative endeavor made her mind wander. She sorely regretted not trying out for the girls' basketball team. Where else would she get that kind of team experience? She had let her sadness consume her again. If Asher were still around, he would have told her to try out. He'd have good reasons, too. Asher was right about everything while he was around. It was just his last decision that was a bad one.

"You okay?" Freddie said.

"Yeah. Why?"

"You're staring off into space."

"I am?" She laughed. "Sorry."

"I guess you weren't thinking about plants."

"No. Asher. Basketball. Asher and basketball."

"Wanna talk about it?"

"Not really. Just some memories. I'll go back to my plants."

"Okay. Give a shout if you change your mind."

Chapter 8

I Really Thought I'd See You Again

Freddie was in her level again, 8-1a. He was smart and made her laugh. It was nice to have a new friend.

If Ginny was being honest, she would have to admit that the reason she didn't try out for basketball the previous year, besides being consumed with grief, was she wasn't sure how she would navigate her highs and lows. Gym class worked okay because it wasn't that demanding, and it was only 40 minutes. But this year, she tried out and made the team. What would that entail?

"Just tell Coach Fox you'll need juice on hand," Tilly said. "She's cool. She won't mind."

"She won't think I'm damaged?"

"You *are* damaged, but you're not unreliable. Just warn her."

The coach was a tall woman, close to six feet. Ginny again wondered if her own height would ever increase. It would help her game.

"Coach Fox?"

"What is it, Ginny?"

"I'm supposed to tell you ... I'm diabetic. I'll need to bring some emergency juice to practice. I won't need it all the time."

The coach smiled.

"Me, too. Twenty years now."

"Really?"

"Can you see?"

What? "Of course."

"I stopped taking my insulin regularly for a while in college. I thought I was gaining too much weight. It was a crazy thing to do. Finally came to my senses when I could no longer see out of my left eye."

Coach Fox said this with great enthusiasm. How did she function without insulin? Apparently, Ginny wasn't the only self-destructive diabetic.

"God. How long do I have?"

Coach Fox smiled at her.

"You'll be fine."

Ginny wasn't so sure.

The first practice had Ginny on the opposite team from Renée and Tilly. Ginny was the only new girl who wasn't a seventh-grader. She would have to prove herself, which would be hard; she still didn't have great aim.

Her team had possession of the ball, and this girl Colleen, who was the team's center, threw it to Ginny. She froze, but then put on her game face.

Here she goes, bouncing and running down the court. People are catching up with her. Now she's blocked. She can't shoot! She does a sneaky side pass back to Colleen, who shoots and scores!

Her confidence came back. She would still have to practice shooting, but she did make a basket when she was close to the hoop.

"Wow," Colleen said to her after practice. "You're really good."

"Thank you."

"You weren't on the team last year. Didn't you try out?"

"No. I ... I don't know why I didn't."

"Well ... welcome."

Ginny was starting to feel weak, so after Colleen was out of sight, she quickly drank some juice.

"Ginny. You got a minute?"

"Sure, Coach."

"Let's go to my office. I got you something."

It was a paperback book called *Feast on a Diabetic Diet* by Euell and Joe Gibbons. Ginny flipped through the introduction. Joe Gibbons was a juvenile diabetic, like Ginny. This was about how he managed it.

"Uh ..."

The coach saw the look on her face and smiled.

"Read it, don't read it. I found it interesting."

"Thank you," Ginny said, figuring it would be just another book about food exchanges. She didn't think she'd be reading it anytime soon.

"Ginny! Tilly's on the phone!"

Ginny quickly disposed of the razorblade she was using on her right hip, reassembled her clothing, and exited the bathroom. Then she picked up the phone she and Asher had shared, which was now in her room.

"Got it!" she yelled to her mother, and when she heard her mother hang up, she said, "Hi."

"Guess what? My mom is going away for the weekend. She said I could have a sleepover."

Ginny made a mental note not to mention Mrs. Quain's absence to her parents.

"Sounds great."

"My cousin is coming over. You'll like her. She's in high school."

Ginny's parents were thrilled that Ginny was going to Tilly's for the weekend. They felt she was getting back to her old self. Renée was already there when Ginny's mother dropped her off.

"This is Wendy," Tilly said.

"Hi, Ginny! We're going to have fun this weekend." Wendy caught Tilly's eye, and they laughed.

"What?" Ginny said.

"You'll see," Wendy said.

They had pizza for dinner. They played music and danced around. They made prank phone calls. Except for the calls, which Ginny and Renée thought were silly, they were having a good time.

"Shall we do it now?" Wendy asked.

"Yes. But we'll have to go outside."

"What are we talking about?" Renée said.

Wendy produced a large joint from her pocketbook.

Renée frowned. "What's that? A cigarette? My mother doesn't want me to smoke. She said it's addictive and bad for you."

"It's pot," Ginny said. "Ash used to smoke it."

This was the first time Ginny had mentioned her brother around them since his death. Tilly and Renée tried not to stare at her.

"Well, let's go outside then," Wendy said.

"Okay, we need to be quiet," Tilly said. "Neighbors are close by."

The girls went out to the backyard. It was chilly and wet. Ginny wished she had brought a jacket like her mother had suggested. They settled onto the damp grass, and Wendy took out a book of matches and tried to light the joint. Just as Ginny was going to offer some assistance, Wendy got it lit. She inhaled deeply and started coughing so hard that her eyes were tearing up.

Tilly laughed. "Okay. Who's next?"

Ginny reached for the joint. She carefully inhaled and passed it to Tilly.

"Take more than that," Wendy said.

Again, people telling her what to do.

"I will. When it comes around again."

The joint went around the circle a few times. Ginny sensed her friends were a lot higher than she was. They were rolling around on the grass, giggling.

"See? You didn't smoke enough," Wendy said to Ginny, much too loudly.

"Shhh," Tilly said but then burst out laughing.

"Ooooh. I've got the munchies!"

Tilly stood up. "That means it's time to eat something."

Ginny calculated. Dinner was maybe three and a half, four hours ago. She could have a snack in a little while. She followed them inside.

"We have Oreos. And peanut butter cookies. And ice cream."

"Anybody got dry mouth?" Wendy said. "I need soda."

There was Coke, and Tilly's mom had bought some Tab for Ginny. Renée and Wendy broke open the cookies.

"Do you have carrot sticks or something?" Ginny said.

Wendy thought this was hilarious. Tilly brought a box of Ritz crackers to the table and placed them in front of Ginny.

"Thank you."

"You're welcome. Cheese?"

"Yes, please."

They smoked all weekend until Sunday evening when Tilly's mom got back and drove everyone home. Ginny hoped she didn't smell too much like pot. Surely, her parents would recognize the scent, but they didn't say anything about it. Ginny hurried upstairs and changed out of her clothes. Being high all weekend made her dopey. She'd wait for the dumb to wear off before she tried doing her homework.

She was beginning to see why Asher smoked so much. She wasn't as sad after she smoked. She usually thought about Asher all the time, at least several times a day. She realized she hadn't thought about him more than a couple of times all weekend. Was she going to forget about him entirely?

This year, the three friends went out for Halloween in Renée's neighborhood. Each created her own costume, although with some parental assistance. Tilly decided to be something easy, so she chose a gypsy imitation. She wore her mother's imitation jewelry, a bandana, a white blouse, and a tiered skirt.

"You sure you don't want a black wig? Gypsies usually have dark hair," her mother said.

"I like my red hair. People will still get the costume."

Renée's grandmother had made her a blue-sequined, mermaid-hem skirt from a Simplicity pattern. Renée wore a green leotard with a seashell bra over it that was taken from an old hula costume. She topped it off with a sky-blue, long-hair wig her mother had picked up for her from Woolworth's.

Ginny was "Lucy in the Sky with Diamonds." She wore her mother's rhinestone necklace (swearing on her life she would return it) and a mask her father helped her make that used kaleidoscope-patterned contact paper around the eye holes. Her dress was blue with cloud-shaped, fluffy cotton attached.

They got high as they walked from house to house, and Renée and Tilly soon dove into their bag of candy. Besides making the costume and smoking the joint, this part wasn't fun for Ginny. Maybe next year, she could convince her friends just to get high and forget the collecting candy part. They were getting too old for trick-or-treating, anyway, weren't they?

"I ate too much candy," Tilly said when they got back to Renée's house.

"Me too. I'm not high anymore," Renée said.

"Wanna smoke the rest of the joint?"

Renée shook her head.

"Don't look at me," Ginny said. "I'm still really high."

"I'll get my mom. She'll drop you two off."

When Renée was out of the room, Tilly whispered, "I need to get rid of this candy," and she didn't mean what was left in her bag.

"Did you have a good time, dear?"

"Yes, Mom."

"Did people like your costume?"

"Yes! I had to explain it to a couple of people, but most of them got it."

"Okay. I'm going to turn in. Don't forget to eat a snack."

"I won't."

Ginny went into the kitchen. She was higher than she had planned. Needing to come down, she quickly ate an apple and some cheese. Then she went into her bag of candy and ate a small Milky Way bar. Then another. Then, a bite-sized Hershey's bar. Then she lost track. When she finally came to her senses, she put the wrappers back into her Halloween bag and, panicking, brought the whole thing upstairs. She could already feel the sugar rushing into her system. She thought about Tilly, went into the bathroom, and stuck her finger down her throat.

The next morning, her urine test was green. Not terrible. This could be very useful if she was ever in that situation again.

Ginny decided she'd skip seeing her friends that coming weekend. They'd be getting high, and she didn't want to mess up again. It was times like these when she really missed Asher. He would have made her feel better about Halloween. It was over a year since he died. Her mother was right; she would grieve for a long time.

She woke up unusually early Saturday morning and went into her diary to reread Asher's note. The diary smelled like pot! She had forgotten she had left the rest of his joint in there. She didn't want her brother's note smelling like that.

She went into the bathroom and flushed the joint. Then she started crying.

"Ash, what the heck?" she said aloud. She took out a razor-blade and started slashing her left hip. She stopped mid-attack.

"C'mon, Gin. Stop it."

After she disposed of the blade, she quietly entered Asher's room. It took her a second to find the light switch, and then she looked through his Beatles albums. She chose *Yesterday and Today.* The album cover was creepy with all those mutilated dolls on it, but she loved this record. She turned on the stereo, kept the sound down so she wouldn't wake her parents, and sat on the floor. The first song was "Drive My Car." She listened for a while, then started talking.

"I really screwed up, Ash. I didn't understand exactly what the munchies were. You could have warned me, you know. Had to resort to drastic measures."

She loved the harmonies in this song. John and Paul's voices sounded so happy.

"I dodged a bullet here, as you would say," she continued. "But it scares me that I was so out of control."

She waited as if Asher was responding and then said, "Right. I'm only human."

Her father was calling her. She got up off the floor and opened the door.

"Yeah, Dad?"

"Come down and have some breakfast with us."

"Okay. Be right down."

She sang along to the "beep-beep" in the refrain before she turned off the album, leaving it on the platter so she could listen to it later. Then she went downstairs to take her insulin and eat.

Ginny had to have a physical every year, especially if she wanted to play sports. She felt vulnerable sitting there on the table in a paper gown. It was also cold in the office. Didn't they know people would be unclothed?

"I didn't know your family owned a cat."

The doctor was referring to the slashes that were peering out from under Ginny's gown.

"Uh, we don't. I was at a friend's house. I almost sat on it, and it clawed me and ran off."

The doctor *tsk*ed. Ginny wasn't sure if he believed her.

"Well, everything looks good. You gained an inch, five foot one. According to the chart, you should be 100 pounds, and you're 110, but that's fine."

Her weight had never been an issue before. She was in great shape. She had to lose ten pounds? How was she going to do that?

"Look after those scratches," the doctor said. "You don't want to get an infection."

She wasn't sure how she would hide the cuts next time. In the meantime, she'd have to convince Tilly or Renée to get a cat.

"Who told you you're fat?" Tilly said. She was struggling to roll a joint. Wendy had made it seem so easy. It wasn't.

"My doctor," Ginny said. "Not fat. Overweight. He said at my height, I should be 100 pounds. I'm 110."

"Hmmm. Did he go by the chart?" Renée said.

"Yes."

"My mom says those charts are misleading. People are all different frame sizes. Also, muscle weighs more than fat. You have a ten-pound leeway."

"Then why didn't he say that? That's just ..."

"Isn't it, though?" Renée said.

Tilly lit the joint, but it fell apart.

"Damn."

"Tilly!" Renée said.

"What?"

"Don't say 'damn.'"

"What are you, my mother?"

She lit what was left of the joint and took a hit off it.

"Here we go."

She handed it to Renée.

"So, Ginny," Tilly said, "Tell us about Freddie."

"What about him? We do homework together sometimes."

"Uh huh."

Ginny felt herself blush. Blush! This was so unlike her. Renée started giggling.

"What's so funny?" Ginny said, annoyed.

"Of course, nothing's going on," Renée said. "Freddie doesn't like girls."

"Renée, that's just a rumor," Tilly said. "Boys in our class don't like him because he doesn't play sports."

"Anyway, we're friends," Ginny said. "Maybe I'll teach him to play basketball if that's such a problem."

"It is," Renée giggled.

Tilly started giggling, too, and said, "Renée, you are *so* high."

Chapter 9

Lost in High School

High school was baffling enough without the North Greenwich High School building adding to that confusion. The original building was small. Now, there were two floors, many corridors that looped around, and an annex that was added a few years ago. Its population by 1973 had grown to a whopping 646 students. Freshmen found it difficult to navigate. Ginny and her friends were no exception.

Ginny managed to find most of her classes, but it took some time to find the annex, where her last class, Art 1, was being held. Once she found the annex, she couldn't find the room. She ran into some other lost freshmen, and eventually, they discovered that room B404 was in the basement, down the scary staircase that looked like it went to the boiler room. The five of them were 10 minutes late. Ms. Osbourne didn't mind; she was used to freshmen getting lost on their first day.

They started by working with clay. They didn't have potter's wheels, but there was a kiln so they could bake and glaze their work. Ginny wasn't proficient at making pots, cups, or anything that should be symmetrical. The vase she was working on was lopsided. It probably wouldn't hold liquid, but she put the finished piece on the drying table anyway so it could be baked. Then she went into the hallway to the girl's lavatory to wash her clay-encrusted hands.

And she had a thought.

This restroom was out of the way. No one was down there unless they had class. Might be a good place to be sick if the need arose.

Tilly called to invite her to a party the next weekend. This invitation made Ginny happy; this was another year when Ginny wasn't in any of Tilly or Renée's classes. Tilly said when her mother returned from her date, she would drive people home if they didn't have rides.

The party was filled with people Ginny didn't know. She said hello to the three boys and the girl who were in the kitchen, but they just stared at her. How rude. Ginny poured herself some Tab and went to look for Tilly.

The stereo was blasting "Hi, Hi, Hi" by Wings. Ginny hated that song. Seriously, Paul? Current music could be good, though, like Gladys Knight and the Pips or the Staple Singers, but generally, music just wasn't as fun as it was in the 60s.

She found Tilly in the living room laughing and smoking a joint, surrounded by more people Ginny didn't know.

"Ginny! Everybody, this is Ginny! Ginny, everybody."

Ginny smiled and nodded. There was an uncomfortable silence while everyone stared at her, so she said, "Is Renée here?"

"No. She had something else to do," Tilly said with a hint of annoyance. "Want a hit?"

Grateful to be included and not thinking about how she might navigate this party high, she accepted the joint. A cat scurried past them and ran under the couch.

"You got a cat?"

"Yes. Oliver. He's about a year old. He'll come out when there are fewer people around. Right now, he's terrified."

Ginny had only mentioned getting a cat to Tilly once, and naturally, she didn't say why. She suppressed a laugh.

"Tilly! The pizza's here!" someone yelled.

"Right. I better go pay them."

She got up and left Ginny standing there with Everybody. Ginny accepted the joint one more time, then excused herself with a "Nice meeting you." She ran right into a boy, again someone she didn't know. He seemed to be older than a freshman, as did his friend.

"Sorry," Ginny said.

"Not a problem. And you are?"

"Ginny."

"Chris. This is Guy. Isn't this party great?"

"How do you know Tilly?"

"We don't. Someone at school said there was going to be a party, so we decided to check it out. There's no beer here, but the weed is excellent."

"Tilly's mother's hip, but she won't supply beer. Her daughter's a freshman."

Guy reached into his pocket and produced a pint bottle labeled Forester.

"Want some?"

Chris took it out of his hand, took a swig, and handed it back.

"No thanks," Ginny said.

"Do you smoke?"

"Yeah. Sure."

"I mean weed."

"I knew what you meant."

He lit a joint, took a hit, then leaned over and blew the smoke into her mouth. He waited for her to stop coughing, and then he kissed her. Even if she wasn't high, she wouldn't have known how to react to that.

"Uh, okay, excuse me," Chris said, gave Guy a knowing look, and departed.

Guy took her hand, led her into the TV room, and had Ginny sit next to him on the couch. He kissed her again, this time with tongue, and especially because she was high, Ginny liked it. He leaned over and put his arms around her, and then they were making out.

Ginny was happy with this for a while, but then she started to get bored. How did she tell him she wanted to stop? He was really into her. Was she going to be stuck there all night?

The answer was yes.

"Hey, you two."

Never was Ginny happier to hear Tilly's voice.

"C'mon. My mother is taking people home. Guy, Chris is looking for you. He said he's your ride."

Guy kissed Ginny goodbye, waved to Tilly, and went to find Chris.

"Wow. Way to hook up. Good for you."

Ginny didn't think she had "hooked up." Anyway, she was ready to go home.

In the car, Tilly waited for her mother to drop off everyone else, then said, "I gave Guy your number. He's going to call you."

"You did? I don't want to go out with him."

"You don't spend an entire night making out with a guy and then not give him at least one date."

"You don't?"

"No, you don't."

"Okay. Thanks, I guess."

This did not make her happy.

New England's woods at night are sensual, seductive even. The smell of damp leaves, moss, mushrooms, and turned-up soil creates a natural aphrodisiac. This was especially potent after someone had just smoked a joint.

After dinner and a movie (*Enter the Dragon*, which Ginny thought was predictable but entertaining), Ginny was in Guy's car, parked in the woods by the railroad tracks. She and Guy were making out in the front seat. Ginny was still trying to get used to the fact that Guy was old enough to drive. And drink. Every few minutes, he would produce a pint bottle and take a gulp or two. He told her he was 18. Did he know she was 14? Did he care?

"You sure you don't want some?"

Ginny guessed he was being polite, but she was getting tired of saying no. This was more a practical issue for Ginny; she didn't know how to navigate alcohol with her insulin, and she wasn't about to test it out in the front seat of Guy's Dodge Colt. She was counting the minutes until she could go home, when Guy pushed back from her and unzipped his fly to reveal an enormous, erect penis. Ginny had never seen a penis before, much less an erect one. It was a lot bigger than she had imagined, and it was straight up, flat against his belly. She found it disturbing. Guy reached for her hand and placed it on his erection. She figured that meant she should rub it, so she did. Guy groaned and tilted his head back. At least *he* was enjoying himself.

Ginny was supposed to be home by ten, and Guy honored that without her having to remind him. The ride home was unnerving. Guy was fuddled and unfocused from drinking. The winding streets of the town were often narrow, and a lot of the curves were small bridges that covered streams or ditches. Ginny tried not to cringe too visibly, although, in Guy's current state, he wouldn't have noticed anyway.

He walked her to the door and gave her a too-long, okay-that's-enough-now kiss. Ginny watched him leave, then lingered on the porch, trying to make sense of her evening. The door to the house opened behind her.

"Ginny! I thought I heard a car. Did you have a good time?"

"Sure, Mom. Guy's nice."

And a senior. She'd have to talk to Tilly about that.

"Good. Well, I'm turning in. Make sure you turn out the lights before you go upstairs."

"Yes, Mom."

Ginny waited for her mother to close her bedroom door, and then she went out to the kitchen to get some crackers. This had been an unsettling evening. She would have to ask Tilly when it was okay for her to stop seeing Guy.

The high school girls' basketball coach, Coach Lukor, was reading something on a clipboard when Ginny entered her office that morning. She didn't look up as Ginny spoke.

"Coach Lukor?"

"Yes?"

"I just wanted to tell you I'm diabetic. I'll need to bring emergency juice to practice."

The coach frowned and looked up at her.

"And?"

"That's all. I just wanted to let you know."

"Will this be a problem, Eastman?"

"No, ma'am."

"Okay, then."

That was somewhat humiliating. Maybe Ginny shouldn't have said anything.

Tilly was now smoking cigarettes. Ginny and Renée weren't interested. Neither of them liked the smell, and Renée's mother had been adamant that she avoid tobacco. Besides, they preferred pot.

"It'll keep my weight down," Tilly said. She lit her Kent Light and tossed the match onto the grass, away from the picnic lunch her mother had made the girls. She inhaled like it was weed and started coughing.

"Who told you that?"

"It's common knowledge."

Where did Tilly come up with these things?

"Ginny, you broke up with Guy?" Renée said.

"We had one date. I told him that was it."

"Why?"

"He makes me nervous."

"You're nervous about anything that's different," Tilly said.

"True, but he's too old for me. He's 18."

"Oh. That is too old," Renée said.

"Well, there's still Freddie. I saw you two walking down the hall together the other day."

"Freddie and I are friends."

"Sure. Friends," Tilly said.

Ginny didn't like the fact that Tilly was always right. Funny, she had never minded when Asher was.

Self-hatred was coming on in waves these days. Ginny would switch from hopeful to miserable and frustrated within a few minutes. Her hips looked like Oliver the cat was using her as a scratching post. Ginny didn't think these moods were following any kind of a pattern. Low sugar, high sugar, pre-period, post-period, stoned, not stoned. It didn't seem to matter.

She was thinking about Freddie. She liked him, but enough to actually let him touch her strange, unpredictable body? Did he like her? Maybe she was getting ahead of herself. Nothing had happened between them yet. Maybe nothing would. Maybe Renée was right. Maybe he didn't even like girls, and Ginny was waiting for something to happen that never would. Or maybe he did like girls and just didn't want her.

As Ginny lay despondent on her bed, her mother knocked

on her door and entered the room.

"What's the matter?" her mother said.

"Nothing. I was just thinking about something."

Her mother handed her a magazine.

"What's this?"

"*Diabetes Forecast*. It's a magazine just for diabetics." She said this as if this was a treat.

Ginny rolled her eyes.

"Just look at it. If you hate it, throw it out."

Ginny took it from her mother. "I'll look at it."

Her mother smiled and headed down to the kitchen.

Ginny looked at the poor soul on the cover, some heavyset fellow with a cane. He *looked* like a diabetic. His skin was puffy, as if he had too much sugar in his blood, and he couldn't open his eyes all the way. She saw that look on her own face at times. It wasn't attractive.

"Don't judge a magazine by its cover," Ginny said aloud.

There were articles about types of insulin and innovations doctors were studying. She thought they were interesting. There were also a lot of ads.

"Treat or treatment?" one ad read, with pictures of a glass of orange juice, a dish of ice cream, and a large chocolate bar. The ad was for glucose tablets. Were they saying diabetics waited around for their blood sugar to drop so they could eat sugar?

"Oh, yay! Time for a Lifesaver!"

She flipped the page away from the offending ad and found she was looking at an article with a small banner across the picture that said, "Forty Years with Diabetes." The article spotlighted someone who had been diabetic that long, which was impressive, considering what wasn't happening in medicine in 1933 when he was diagnosed. Were they going to give Ginny a banner when she reached that milestone? If she reached that milestone?

The feature at the back of the magazine was an article

submitted by a reader. Ginny read a bit of it but lost interest. Yeah; thirsty, yeah; confused, yeah; had to get used to it,
but she prevailed; yeah, yeah, yeah. Even though it chronicled
what she had experienced, it made her feel bitter and defensive. *Great, rub it in*, she thought.

Ginny didn't want people to pat her on the head and tell
her everything would be fine. She also didn't want people to
scare the crap out of her until she was rolled up in a fetal
position sobbing her eyes out. However, this didn't mean she
didn't want information.

She remembered something. She went to her bookcase to
find the book Coach Fox had given her, *Feast on a Diabetic Diet*.
Maybe it would be different. Maybe it was more than lists of
food exchanges, warnings, and pep talks.

Ginny started reading. There were no food exchanges. The
book recommended counting carbohydrates to match insulin intake, which, the book explained, was far more accurate.
Liberating, even. Ginny didn't care so much about being lib-
erated, but more accurate was intriguing. Maybe she could
purge less. If only foods were labeled with nutritional information. It was unlikely that would ever happen, though. In
any case, unlike the magazine, the book did not wind up in
the trash can.

Ginny's American history teacher, Ms. Thatcher, was orga-
nizing a weekend school trip to Washington, D.C. Ginny was
excited, but also nervous. She wouldn't let her mother know
that, however. She was more interested in going than admit-
ting to being worried.

"I'll talk to your teacher, then you can go."

"Don't talk to her. I can handle myself."

"I'm sure you can, but as the chaperon she needs to know."

"No, she doesn't. What's she going to do? Give me my
insulin?"

"Ginny..."

There was that tone again.

"Mom ..."

Mother and daughter locked eyes.

"Okay. But bring crackers with you and plenty of Lifesavers.

"Of course."

Ginny didn't carry Lifesavers anymore, but she knew what her mother meant. Not only were Lifesavers too small for her purposes, but they were also difficult to eat quickly. She preferred Ike and Mike's. She could chew them faster and they dissolved easily. The only problem was the box didn't close well and often they wound up all over the bottom of her bag.

After five minutes on the bus, the two chaperons handed out donuts. Ginny declined and felt smart. She could do this, no problem. Then Ms. Thatcher headed towards her, brandishing an apple.

"Here you go, Ginny," she said and winked.

Ginny's mother had gone behind her back. Having had breakfast a short time ago, Ginny couldn't eat the apple now, anyway. Diabetes was as much about timing as diet, maybe even more so. Ginny put the apple in her bag, hoping Ms. Thatcher didn't see she wasn't eating it.

The bus stopped at a McDonald's for lunch. Ginny had a fish sandwich, including the tartar sauce (she had stopped swapping out condiments years ago with no adverse effects), and then ate the apple. The other students were drinking milkshakes. Ginny was no longer jealous of that. She wanted to keep her weight down, and unlike Tilly, she wasn't going to start smoking cigarettes. Plus, making herself sick wasn't convenient on the road.

They left Washington on Monday, right after breakfast. Ginny sat toward the front this time since the back of the bus smelled like fumes and the chemical disinfectant from the water closet.

One o'clock came and went, and the bus wasn't stopping.

Ginny didn't want to say anything, but she was anxious. She started eating one of her packages of crackers. Ms. Thatcher was in the seat behind her and, seeing this, got up to talk to the driver.

"He said he'll stop soon. He wants to make time while there's no traffic."

Another hour passed, and Ms. Thatcher started handing Ginny candy through the space between the seats. Ginny had her own, but she accepted it and put it in her bag.

There was an accident up ahead, and soon they were sitting motionless on the highway. Ms. Thatcher got up to talk to the driver again. They raised their voices, and then Ms. Thatcher went back to her seat.

"He said he'll turn off as soon as he can get to an exit."

Don't worry, Ginny thought. *It's not like I'm a diabetic or anything.*

Ginny thought she had eaten enough crackers but ate some of candy, just in case. She couldn't tell if her blood sugar was dropping or if it was just nerves. The thought of going into convulsions in stalled traffic did not appeal to her.

It was after three o'clock when they got off the highway. Ginny couldn't eat now; the time for lunch had passed. She had had two packages of crackers and some candy. Ginny ordered a Tab. Ms. Thatcher came over to her.

"Ginny, you have to eat."

No, I don't, she thought, but she didn't want to make a scene. Well, more of a scene. Everyone was already looking at her.

"Order something," Ms. Thatcher said.

Ginny loved it when people told her what to do. She ordered a grilled cheese and ate half of it. This satisfied Ms. Thatcher.

When Ginny got home, her urine tested orange. She didn't tell her parents what happened. As it turned out, it hardly mattered what they told Ms. Thatcher. Maybe they should have discussed this with the bus driver instead.

Ginny and Freddie started the afternoon in Ginny's backyard. The plan was to teach Freddie some basketball.

"You think you can make me more coordinated?"

"I think you can make yourself more coordinated. Here, try to make a shot."

She tossed the ball to Freddie. He ducked. The ball went bouncing off into the neighbor's yard, and he chased after it.

"It's not dodge ball. I'm not trying to hit you with it," Ginny said.

"Old habits die hard."

"Toss it to me," she said. "Nice and easy."

He tossed the ball to her.

"Okay, ready?" She tossed it back, and, with some fuss, he caught it.

"Okay. Now try to shoot."

"Uh ... how do I do that?"

"Don't they teach you anything in gym class?"

"I think they think I'm a lost cause."

Ginny motioned to Freddie, and he threw the ball back to her.

"Put your hands on either side of the ball like this, and push. Use your body if you need more power."

His shot didn't make it to the basket, but it was in the general vicinity.

"That was good for a first try. When I started, I could barely throw. Of course, I was six."

"When I was six, I was watching cartoons and eating Cocoa Puffs."

"Wasn't your brother into sports?"

"Sure. But it didn't rub off on me."

"Let's try a game. You catch the rebound after two bounces. First one to 11 wins. You start. Right where you're standing."

"I start? Okay ..."

He shot, and the ball almost hit the rim.

"See? You're already getting closer."

"I'll just stand near the basket the whole game."

Ginny took a shot from behind their designated foul line, and it went in.

"I can see it now," Freddie said. "Eleven to zero."

"It's just practice. I won't tell anyone I kicked your butt."

Ginny won 11 to 2. Freddie was proud of those two points.

"Next time, I'll teach you how to dribble," Ginny said.

They went inside the house and started their geometry homework. Ginny wondered if she would ever have a chance with Freddie. Maybe there would be an opportunity when she taught him to bounce and run.

The school's lunches seemed inedible to Ginny, except for two things: the tuna-fish hero and the pizza. Today, the lunch lady must have been in a particularly good mood, because she gave Ginny an extra slice of pizza. Ginny calculated: Two slices of pizza, so skip the apple. This made sense, but all afternoon she felt she had eaten too much. She had time before her last class, so she ducked into the girls' lavatory near her art class and made herself vomit.

Someone entered in time to hear her retching.

"Are you alright?"

It was Ms. Osbourne. Crap.

"Yeah," Ginny said from her stall. "The school's pizza didn't agree with me."

"Do you want to go to the nurse?"

God, no.

"No. I think I'm going to be fine now."

"Well, okay."

Ginny quickly got out of there before Ms. Osbourne could see her. A face to face would have been even more awkward.

There was a girls' basketball game that Saturday, the North Greenwich Pilots versus the neighboring East Greenwich Avengers. Ginny was bouncing and running down the court, followed by two or three Avengers in hot pursuit. She bounce-passed to Tilly, who passed to Colleen, who missed the shot. The rebound ricocheted back to Ginny. She pivoted and took a side-armed shot that miraculously went in.

After the game, the coach approached her.

"Eastman, can I talk to you?"

Ginny followed the coach to her office.

"You played a great game. Nice hook shot, by the way."

"Thank you." *Is that what that was? Good to know.*

"What are those cuts on your legs?"

Uh oh.

"Cuts?"

The coach lifted her uniform leg slightly to reveal the marks on her hip.

"Oh. Those."

"You've been hurting yourself?"

"Uh ... yeah."

"Want to talk about it?"

"Not really."

"Okay. If you ever do, come see me. Okay?"

Ginny didn't think she ever would, but she said, "Okay. Thanks."

She was mortified. She had to be more careful.

Chapter 10

Give Me the Beat, Boys

Ginny noticed that the top 40 in 1974 had much less rock 'n roll. Folk rock, yes. Southern rock, yes. But songs were a lot less danceable. These days, Ginny was acquiring an album collection of her own. She liked to think Asher would have approved of her choices. Tilly was still collecting singles. She said she could get a better variety of music for her money. She agreed with Ginny that finding music to dance to was getting harder. The friends would listen to the radio together, searching for good dance prospects. Tilly jotted down what everyone liked, and then they'd ride their bikes to the local record store.

The girls split up in the store as if they were playing Supermarket Sweep; they were determined to visit every inch of the place. Once they were satisfied, they reunited in the checkout line. The young man at the counter was about to ring up Ginny's selections when an older man came over. Ginny recognized him. It was Mr. Santini, the store's owner.

"You're Asher's sister, aren't you?"

Ginny nodded.

"These your friends?"

Ginny indicated Tilly and Renée and nodded again.

"Give them 20 percent off," he said to the cashier.

"Thank you, Mr. Santini!"

He winked at Ginny.

The cashier took out a calculator to figure out the girls' discounts. Ginny was impatient and almost offered to help him, but he eventually got it. Yes, people use math in their everyday lives.

The friends placed their shopping bags in the baskets on their bikes. Renée had purchased a Beatles biography by Hunter Davies, which they all agreed to share.

"I'll read this quickly," René said. "Then we can all talk about it."

"You're treating it like a school assignment," Tilly said. "Have some fun with it."

"I like school assignments," Renée said, and they started home.

Since Coach Lukor had spoken to Ginny, Ginny had been making an effort to stop cutting herself. Getting caught was just too embarrassing. Her efforts didn't always work, of course, but they were enough that she would often stop mid-attack and throw out the blade.

Sophomore year would be another where Ginny shared no classes with Renée or Tilly. Tilly was still on the basketball team, so she'd see her there, but Renée had decided not to play this year. She said she didn't have time. She was taking Latin in addition to her biology elective.

Ginny also only shared one class with Freddie, their algebra class. Just a month into the school year, their teacher, Mr. Franklin, sprang a surprise quiz on them. Most of the students groaned, but Ginny was secretly happy. She knew she was odd. She was learning to embrace it.

Mr. Franklin slowly walked around the class, entertained

by his students' grumbling and sighing, when he stopped at Ginny's desk.

"Medic Alert?"

He had noticed Ginny's bracelet. She looked up at him.

"Diabetic," she said.

"My diabetic grandfather used to count his toes every morning when he woke up."

Ginny looked at him as if he was speaking Swahili. Then she understood. His grandfather was checking to make sure his toes were all there.

Ginny was not amused.

"How do you think you did?" Freddie said.

"It seemed okay to me. What about you?" She felt she had aced it but didn't want to brag.

Freddie did not have that problem.

"I thought it was pretty easy."

"Where are you going now?" Ginny said.

"World history. I'm taking an AP class."

"Then I'll walk with you," Ginny said. "I hate history. My brother would have said it's because I'm not good at it. I think it's because thinking about things from the past makes me anxious."

"History is not for everybody."

They reached the stairs. Ginny had to climb them to reach her next class; Freddie did not.

"Well, see you."

"Yeah. Okay."

Ginny watched him enter his class before she continued up to the next floor. She wondered: Was Tilly right about him, or was Renée?

Ginny hadn't had a discussion with Asher in a while, and she was feeling guilty. When she got home from school, she gathered a few of her albums and took them into his room.

"I'm going to play you some songs, Ash," she said. "You must be wondering what I'm listening to these days."

She placed the first album on the turntable. Asher had the better audio system, and the sound was much richer compared to hers. She could even hear the separation of the tracks.

"This is Ringo's latest, *Goodnight Vienna*. The title song was written by John."

She let the song play and then said, "It's great, right? Okay, this next one came out, like, last November."

She changed the album to George Harrison's *Dark Horse*.

"His voice is so raspy. Not sure what happened, some kind of laryngitis or something. But the music is great."

She sat on the edge of Asher's bed and let the record play for a couple of songs. She looked around the room. He had a lot of books, not as many as albums, but it was an impressive library. She thought she should read some of them one day: *Catch 22*, *On the Road*, *M*A*S*H*, *Valley of the Dolls*. They seemed interesting.

"Okay. Ash. Here's Paul's *Venus and Mars*. I'm not sure how I feel about the whole album, but I love this track."

She put on the song "Magneto and Titanium Man" and turned up the volume.

"And you can dance to this one."

She danced around his room.

"I know, you were never much of a dancer, Ash. That's okay. Let me play you something off John's album. It's just him singing 'Ya Ya' with his son, Julian, who's like 11 or something, on drums. I love John's voice here."

She played the one-minute track.

"Next time, I'll play you more of this album. I know John's your favorite."

She took the record off the turntable and put it back in its sleeve.

"Okay. That's it for now. We'll talk soon."

She gathered her albums and went to her room.

Freddie and Ginny also had a study hall together two days a week. Ginny felt study halls were a waste of time. It wasn't like someone could discuss homework with fellow students. True, not many would; most would prefer to gossip. Anyway, once the bell rang, everyone had to be quiet.

"Did you start the math homework yet?" Freddie said as they entered the room. "I'm a little confused by that third one."

"Word problems," Ginny said. "Read it carefully. There's a trick."

"Okay. Thanks."

Forty-five minutes later, they were free. Ginny often wondered why, when they built the extensions to the school, they didn't build more exits. Every afternoon people shoved each other to leave the building.

"Did you get it?"

Freddie looked puzzled.

"Number three. The problem you couldn't solve."

"Oh, yeah. I got 37. Is that right?"

"That's what I got."

"Okay, good."

They made their way through the corridors to the sunlight. Busses were lined up to collect students to take them home.

"I'm meeting up with my brother," Freddie said. "His car's over there. Want a ride somewhere?"

"No thanks. I'm going to walk."

"Okay."

He hesitated, then leaned in and kissed her. He looked surprised, as if he had caught himself off guard. He lingered there, waiting for her reaction.

"Nice," she said and meant it.

"Ginny! Freddie's on the phone!"

Ginny waited for her mother to hang up before she started talking.

"Hi, Freddie."

"I think we should go on a date."

"Sure. Where should we go?"

They paused, both realizing how ridiculous it was, trying to go on a date when neither party could drive.

"My brother offered to drive us somewhere," Freddie said.

"That seems kind of awkward, no? How about lunch, somewhere we can walk?"

Ginny pictured them strolling home via the back streets, with woods surrounding them so they could be alone. There was always her bedroom, which, with Asher gone, was isolated from the rest of the house, but not for a first date. Certain rules had to be established first.

"There's the Friendly's across from the high school," Freddie said. "Maybe we meet after school."

Ginny almost rejected that idea for being too casual, but since neither of them had a job, it made sense to go somewhere affordable.

"Perfect. Let's do that."

Friendly's was known for having over 30 flavors of ice cream, which naturally made no difference to Ginny. She would only be having a snack anyway, like coffee and half a muffin. The two friends usually had a lot to say, but today, they sat nervously across from one another, sipping their coffees and occasionally looking up and smiling. Ginny wished Asher was around; she would have asked him for some first-date advice.

It was as they were walking home via the wooded roads that Ginny decided to take charge.

"Freddie."

"Yeah?"

"Stop walking for a second."

"Okay."

As Tilly once said about the ocean, "You gotta just jump in." Ginny put aside her body issues and anything else that was making her nervous and kissed him, a long, open-mouthed kiss. When they came up for air, Ginny said, "I think this has been the problem today. Too many expectations."

"I think you're right."

"Now you kiss me."

Freddie leaned in and gave her a soft, sensual kiss.

"Okay," Ginny said, somewhat flustered. She hadn't felt this way when Guy had kissed her. This was a new experience.

"Now that we've done that, let's be ourselves," she said.

Freddie took her hand, and they slowly headed home.

After reading *Feast on a Diabetic Diet*, Ginny started to think about food differently. She didn't need to make herself sick as often because she was calculating more accurately. However, weight control seemed easier when she was expelling a good portion of the food she ate. The problem was that this made her have more lows. While, at first, this system of purging was almost perfect, it was now a routine she didn't know how to stop. She figured it was this or do what Coach Fox had tried to do: take less insulin. No way. Ginny was never going off her insulin. She would try to eat less, but when she couldn't, she had other options.

Ginny had practiced hard the past several months, and by February, she could do a proper layup. She was also getting better at her overhand shot, though she hadn't tried it anywhere except in her backyard. She arrived at practice that afternoon feeling confident and a little cocky. She put her juice bottle on the floor near the bleachers so no one would trip over it, then ate some crackers for her snack. This had been working well for her. The drills today were for dribbling. Ginny was great with her right hand but slower with her left. Everyone was slower with her left; for some, it was a new skill. As Ginny was gaining momentum, she suddenly grew tired, and her limbs became heavy. Hypoglycemia had snuck up on her. She had to quit the drill. She hadn't had to do that before.

"Eastman. Why are you stopping?"

Ginny jogged toward the bleachers with as much dignity as possible and got her juice.

"Damnit," she muttered. If Tilly could say that, so could she.

The coach approached her.

"Eastman, what was that?

Somehow, saying "low blood sugar" seemed lame, embarrassing, even. That sounded like she needed to sit and fan herself. It didn't sound as if she would soon be on the floor convulsing. There was no easy way to say that.

"Sorry, Coach. It won't happen again."

"You've been making great progress. Today was very different."

"Yes, Coach. I'll work on it."

"Okay. I'm counting on you."

"Thanks, Coach."

Freddie was waiting for her after practice, and despite it being winter, they walked over to the Friendly's to get sodas.

"Crap! Darn it! Sunnova ... sea cook."

This attempt at cursing amused Freddie.

"Everything alright, Ginny?"

"No. I totally messed up at practice today."

"I'm sure it wasn't that bad."

"It was that bad. I had to stop in the middle of drills because of my stupid blood sugar."

"So?"

Ginny glared at him.

"Did the coach say anything?"

Ginny took a sip of her Tab and made her usual face of revulsion.

"She wasn't happy. Thing is, I said it won't happen again, but I can't guarantee it."

"Don't let it."

"You don't understand. I had *no warning*."

Freddie didn't know what to say, so he said something useless.

"You could eat more."

She rolled her eyes.

"If I eat more, I'll get fat. No one wants to see a fat basketball player."

"You won't get fat."

Ginny scowled at him. He could see she was not accepting any solace right now.

"What do you want me to say? You *will* get fat?"

She laughed.

"My doctor keeps trying to adjust my insulin. I'm going to talk to him again. But it seems like a losing battle. Yeah, I could eat more. But then some days, it goes high, which makes me sluggish and irritable."

Freddy took her hand. "You're smart. You'll figure this out."

Even though she didn't want to be consoled, she smiled and said, "Thanks."

Ginny and Freddy hadn't been anywhere together as a couple, not out with other people, anyway. They went to Tilly's next party together. It was their "coming out." Filled with people they didn't know, they went through the house until they found Tilly, Renée, and some other girls in Tilly's bedroom smoking a joint. After introductions, Tilly told Freddie to scram for a while.

"Nothing personal. We're just going to have some girl talk."

"Uh ... okay."

"You're okay with that?" Ginny said.

"Sure. I'll go mingle. Don't be long."

He kissed her and headed downstairs.

"Close the door," Tilly said, and Ginny did as she was told. "And lock it."

Someone offered Tilly a cigarette, but she declined.

"You're not smoking?" Ginny said.

"I quit. Decided it was too gross. Everything smelled bad: my breath, my hair, my clothes, everything."

"Okay, what were we talking about?" Renée said.

"Killing the witch!" this girl Gretchen said, and everyone laughed but Ginny.

"Who's the witch?"

"Not who. What," Tilly said. "The witch is our code for virginity. And it must be killed."

Ginny looked around the room at the giggling sophomores, who surprisingly included Renée.

"Why do we want to do that?" Ginny said.

"C'mon. We can't be children forever."

Ginny saw nothing wrong with that.

"Ginny. You have a boyfriend. You have it easy," Renée said. "Us single girls have our work cut out for us."

"I'm sure Bobby would accommodate me," Tilly said. "We broke up over the summer, ironically because he kept insisting on having sex with me. I'm sure he'd be game."

Tilly saw the look on Ginny's face and said, "The goal is to lose our virginity before we leave high school. That gives us a couple years. No one has to rush into anything."

Well, gee, what a relief, Ginny thought sarcastically. This conversation was making her extremely uncomfortable.

"Hey, Tilly!" a male voice said through the door. "You gonna come out of there sometime tonight?"

Tilly opened the door, and three guys bounded into the room and sat on Tilly's bed, pushing the girls over so they had room. One of them produced a pint bottle from his pocket and passed it around the circle.

Ginny stood up.

"I'm going to go find Freddie."

He was in the kitchen, talking with two people Ginny didn't know.

"Come on," she said. "Let's go make out."

He smiled.

"Excuse us," he said and followed Ginny.

Ginny got home around midnight. Her parents were already asleep, so she was quiet when climbing the stairs. She was no longer high, and when she got into bed, she fully expected to fall asleep.

Instead, she started weeping.

It came out of the deep, dark recesses of her subconsciousness. The thought of having sex was a constant conundrum for Ginny. The more physical she and Freddie got, the more twisted her thoughts became. Did he cringe every time he kissed her? Did he hesitate every time he touched her? Would he be revolted if he saw her naked? Or worse, would he be attracted but then repulsed after he got closer?

Her mother would say she was "overtired." Was that even something that happened to teenagers? She turned over to her other side, which didn't help, and cried herself to sleep.

Chapter 11

The Witch Is Not Even Sick

Students in the junior class were busy getting their driver's licenses, taking college entrance exams, applying to colleges, and trying to secure dates to the junior prom. Tilly, Renée, and Ginny were also still hoping to kill the witch before graduation.

The three friends were lying on Ginny's bed with the radio on after an afternoon of playing two-on-one basketball in the backyard. Ginny's skills had far surpassed those of her friends'; playing one-on-one was no longer fun for any of them. They played for a couple of hours, and now they were relaxing before dinner. Asher's room was larger, but to Ginny, that was sacred territory. She didn't want any intruders, even her best friends.

"I thought you were going to ask Bobby?" Ginny said.

"I was," Tilly said. "But he's turned into such a jerk. He's gotten worse since we broke up. I don't want to knowingly have sex with a jerk, especially my first time."

"He is completely annoying," Renée said. "What happened to him?"

"Tilly broke his heart," Ginny said, and Tilly threw a pillow at her.

"Wait. Turn that up," Renée said.

It was Paul Simon's "Loves Me Like a Rock." They sang along to the song, dancing on Ginny's bed with their arms and torsos, and when it was over, Ginny turned the radio back down to conversation level.

"I hear Stu's taking Colleen to the prom," Ginny said.

"Those two didn't have three words to say to each other, and since he asked her, they're inseparable," Renée said.

"Think they've done it?"

"Tilly!"

She laughed. "Sorry. I can't help wondering. You know who has, though: Joey and a lot of girls who have gone on dates with him. Apparently, he's very persuasive."

"How do you know this stuff?" Ginny said.

"People tell me. They don't realize I tell you two everything."

"How about you and Freddie?" Renée said. "Have you two even discussed it?"

"He's been kind of hinting around. I figure maybe something will happen prom night. That's traditional, right? I can wait until then."

"It's a long time until June," Renée said. "Ask him to take you to Homecoming."

"Freddie? Ha. He doesn't get along with jocks," Ginny said. "He certainly has no interest in going to an event that reveres them."

"You're a jock. He gets along with you," Tilly said.

"I don't make fun of him."

There was a knock on the door, and Ginny's father came in. "Aren't you girls hungry? Dinner's ready."

"Thanks, Dad."

Ginny turned off the radio, and they followed him downstairs.

No, Freddie and Ginny did not go to Homecoming. They did, however, spend New Year's Eve together at Freddie's house while his parents went out for the evening. Freddie and Ginny felt more comfortable spending time there now that Freddie's brother was at college. And tonight, they had the whole house to themselves.

Over the summer, Freddie had taken a chance and put his hands on Ginny's breasts, even touching skin. He was rubbing them now as they kissed.

"I'm getting hot," Ginny said and unbuttoned her shirt a little. Not subtle, but she was a girl on a mission.

Taking her cue, Freddie unbuttoned the rest of her shirt. Did she detect some hesitation there? When she looked at him expectantly, he reached behind her and unhooked her bra. He kissed her harder.

He moved his mouth to one of her breasts and started sucking. Ginny couldn't believe how good it felt. More of their clothes came off, first Ginny's shirt, which was practically off anyway, then Freddie's. The kissing continued until an overly excited Freddie unzipped her jeans and pulled them down, underwear and all. Ginny half expected him to be repulsed. She was relieved that he wasn't. *All in your mind, Ginny,* she thought.

Was this going to happen?

"Damnit," he said.

Ooh, probably not. "What?"

"Condoms."

"Right. Damn."

"There may be some in my brother's room."

He got up to go to the other room

"Wait ..."

Ginny didn't want to stop doing what they were doing for a condom hunt that might be fruitless.

"Next time," she said. "This is nice anyway."

Freddie started rubbing gently between her legs, which felt great. To reciprocate, she unzipped his fly and started rubbing him, too. For two people who really didn't know what they were doing, they both were satisfied.

Tilly's mom not only didn't mind her daughter and her friends getting high in her house, but lately, she was supplying the pot. What they had tonight was strong, and instead of making the girls giddy, it made them stupefied. And introspective. And hungry. Tilly's mother brought them Ritz crackers, cheese, and sodas. Ginny did a quick carbohydrate estimation in her head to decide how much to eat. She figured 10 crackers with some cheese. She hoped she wouldn't get so high she didn't remember how to count to 10.

"I've decided I want to be a veterinarian," Renée said.

"I thought you wanted to be a doctor," Tilly said.

"I want to be a doctor, but I love animals. Either way, I'd be in school a long time. Might as well do what I want."

"Where are you applying?" Ginny asked.

"My parents want me to apply to Harvard, but Cornell has a better veterinary school. I'm hoping to go there, much to my parents' dismay."

"I can't believe your parents would be disappointed if you went to Cornell," Ginny said. "I mean, it's not like you're saying you want to go to a community college."

"I want to go into advertising," Tilly said. "I want to be the person who comes up with stuff like 'Taste that beats the others cold!' So, I'm heading to New York City, hopefully to FIT."

"What about you, Ginny? Still want to be a basketball coach?"

"I don't really want to coach. I want to play. My parents won't let me apply to colleges based solely on that, though. I'm hoping to get into UCLA. They have good women's basketball, and it's a good school. Everybody's okay with it. Besides, they have scholarships."

"A scholarship? But you're so short," Tilly said.

"Not an athletic scholarship. Yes, I'm aware I'm short. I'm five-five and a half, and that's probably all I'll ever be. I called, and they have non-scholarship spots on the team, so I'm going to try out."

"That would be so great if you got on a college team," Renée said.

The girls passed the joint around until everyone refused it. Tilly put it out, and they all reached for the crackers.

"I have to say," Tilly said, "the witch is very healthy these days. I think she's eating Wheaties."

"Mine, too," Renée said.

"The witch is very sick in my corner. We came so close New Year's Eve, but we didn't have any stupid condoms."

"Ah, there but for the grace of condoms go thee. Or is it thou? Thy?" Tilly said.

"Anyway, it looks like we won't be waiting for the prom after all. It'll be, like, any day now. We just need to have the right place."

"And condoms."

"Right. And condoms."

However, it was a while before Ginny and Freddie even got close to having sex. Often, it was an inconvenient time or place that thwarted their efforts. Ginny's father walked in on them once while they were making out, and Ginny was reluctant to pursue anything further for a while after that. The closest they got to sex was one day at Freddie's house, but his mother barged into his bedroom when they were both undressed. That was a total ice bath, and neither one wanted to try again, maybe ever. The universe was trying to slow them down. Maybe Ginny would be waiting until the prom after all.

To make things even more difficult, Freddie got a job

at the library. It took up his weekends and certain evenings during the week. Between Ginny's basketball and Freddie's new work schedule, it was hard to find time to get together. Ginny was worried that, without seeing Freddie regularly, she would revert to hating her body, hating being touched, hating herself, all of it.

Not having Freddie as a distraction was also bringing some nagging, underlying fears to the forefront. How would she survive college with her various self-destructive behaviors? What would a college coach do if, like Coach Lukor, she saw that Ginny was habitually slashing her skin? Most likely, people had already noticed and just didn't say anything. Freddie only mentioned the cuts once; Ginny's reaction told him to drop it, immediately and forever.

Ginny went into her bathroom and threw out her razorblades, even the new packs. Maybe that would take away the temptation. This would still require discipline. Did she have any? She needed to talk to Asher.

She went into his room and put the Beatles' *Abbey Road* on the turntable. She waited for the intro of "Come Together" to finish, and once John was singing, she started to whisper.

"Ash, what am I gonna do? Mom almost caught me purging the other night. She knocked on the bathroom door to tell me Renée was on the phone. I never knew a person could stop mid-heave, but I did."

She waited a moment, then said, "That was your cue to laugh."

The song continued, and so did Ginny.

"Anyway, I just threw out my razorblades. That's a good start, right? And as for purging, my original reasons for making myself sick were practical ones. Stopping is the practical thing now, right?"

She looked at the ceiling.

"Right," she said.

There was a knock on the door, and her mother walked in.

"Ginny. Do you want cauliflower or broccoli with dinner?"

This all-important question momentarily blew Ginny's concentration. She tried not to look annoyed.

"I love them both. Will the cauliflower have Alfredo sauce?"

"If you like."

"Then let's have that."

Her mother paused a moment at the door. "Something" had started playing.

"That's a pretty song," she said and closed the door behind her.

"Mom is coming around to the Beatles, Ash," Ginny whispered. "It only took her a dozen years."

Ginny wanted to dress for this dinner. It was not a night for jeans and a T-shirt. She put on a blouse, satiny black slacks, and pumps. She had to walk around her room a bit to figure out how to walk in them, but they did look nice. She even put on eye shadow and lipstick.

Freddie arrived a little early, but she was ready.

"I can't believe you're taking me to a real dinner. How ... *adult* of us!"

Freddie smiled weakly. "You don't turn 17 every day."

"Are you alright?" Ginny said. "You seem bummed."

"I'm fine."

"You look like you want to throw up. Are you sure you're okay?"

"I'm okay."

He wasn't. Ginny decided not to pry.

Freddie had borrowed his dad's car for the evening. He had made a reservation, although the restaurant didn't require one. The place was all but empty when they arrived.

Ginny was too excited to look at the menu.

"I bought my gown for the prom," she said.

Freddy didn't react, so she continued.

"It's not poofy, pastel, and frilly like everyone else's. It's a dark color, midnight blue, and it's slinky and elegant."

"Ginny ..." Freddie put down his menu. "I think ... I'm gay."

Talk about a conversation killer. Since words were escaping her, she simply stared at him.

"I mean, I am gay. There, I said it."

"But ... But, I mean, we make out and stuff," she said, then lowered her voice. "We almost *did* it New Year's Eve. And that time when your mother caught us ..."

Freddie couldn't look at her.

"There was always something ... not right," he said. "Really, I am gay."

Ginny picked up the menu and stared at it.

"Stop saying that," she said.

"But it's true."

"I know. Just stop saying it."

"Okay."

She seethed a moment, then said, "Nice timing, telling me on my birthday."

"Sorry, I just figured the prom is coming up, and you'd expect—"

"Who is it?"

"Who's what?"

"Who did you fall for that made you realize?"

"Doesn't matter. He's straight, anyway."

"Well, then you know how it feels."

"Yeah. Okay. I deserved that."

Ginny pretended to study the menu.

"Could you do something for me?" Freddie said.

She glared at him.

"Just don't tell anyone yet?"

Fat chance. Ginny wanted to tell everyone. She wanted to shout it from the rooftops. She wanted to scream. She wanted to cry. What the hell was he doing with her for the past two years, anyway?

She would keep his secret, of course. *Fem boy.* Man, the other kids knew he was gay back in grade school.

It wasn't even ten o'clock when she got home.

"You're home early."

Ginny didn't know what to tell her mother. Freddie had food poisoning? He was getting up early the next day? He had another date?

"We both got tired. The dinner was great, but then all we wanted to do was sleep."

That seemed to satisfy her.

"Well, I'm glad you had a good time. Freddie is good for you."

Ginny forced a smile and nodded.

When Ginny got upstairs, she sat on her bed and reached across to pull the phone over to her. Nope, she couldn't call Tilly. She couldn't call Renée. What could she say that wouldn't out Freddie?

The junior prom was in a couple of weeks. What was she going to do with her gown? She guessed she could wear it next year. It was too late to find someone to go with her this year. Besides, everyone would assume she was going with Freddie.

Her phone rang.

But if someone called *her* ...

"I got it!" she yelled. "Hello?"

"Ginny. You're still up."

"It's only ten o'clock, Freddie. I'm not even out of my clothes yet."

"Listen, how about we go to the prom anyway?"

"Really?"

"Sure. It'll be fun."

"You know, we could pretend we're still together until the end of the school year. That's, like, a month."

"You would do that?"

"I would."

"The thing is, Gin ..."

"Ginny."

"Sorry ... *Ginny* ... is I thought about not saying anything until the summer. But I didn't want to pretend with you anymore. I mean, we're friends first."

Ginny didn't respond.

"Aren't we?"

"Yes. I guess we are."

"Good. I love you, Ginny. Just not that way."

"Thanks, Freddie. I guess I love you, too."

Ginny's parents' bedroom had floor-length mirrored closets, making it a perfect place for Ginny to model her dress. Freddie wouldn't be picking her up until seven thirty, but she needed time to get ready. She hardly ever wore makeup and never did anything special with her hair. Her mother offered to help, and Ginny was grateful for it.

"This dress is perfect on you. Except ..."

Ginny's mother was trying to adjust the top of the dress. Ginny was muscular, but her shoulders sloped.

"I have an idea."

Her mother went into one of her drawers.

"Shoulder pads?"

"They're not for your shoulders."

Ginny laughed. "Oh."

"There. Much better."

Ginny looked at herself in the mirror. Yes, the falsies made the dress fit. Her hair and makeup proved to be a much bigger project. Her mother had bought her a variety of new makeup.

Ginny had no idea what to do with it all, but her mother did. The result was quite a transformation.

Freddie arrived right on time.

"My God. You make me wish I was still straight."

Ginny burst out laughing.

"What?" Her mother hadn't heard what he said.

"Private joke," Ginny said.

Freddie didn't like to dance freestyle like everyone else. He preferred partner dancing. Ginny didn't know anything about partnering, but she followed Freddie's lead. The other kids were giving them side glances as they made their way across the floor, but Ginny and Freddie didn't care.

They stayed until the end. It was after midnight when Freddie walked Ginny to her front door.

"Can I kiss you one last time?"

"Sure."

It was a nice kiss. Ginny was going to miss this.

"A new doctor? Why?"

"You'll be 18 next year. You can't keep going to a pediatrician."

There was a lot of logic in that statement.

"Well, okay. Who is this guy?"

"It's a woman. Dr. Hummel. She's a diabetes specialist."

Ginny probably wouldn't be able to hide her lacerations from this doctor. Would she believe that these were old scars?

As it turned out, she didn't even have to undress. First, they talked. Then Dr. Hummel put a small brown bottle in front of her. It had little color swatches on the side.

"What's this? Looks like a bottle of test strips. I have test strips."

"Yes, they are test strips. For blood sugar."

Ginny's eyes went wide.

"You're kidding."

The doctor smiled. She opened a new lancing device, loaded it, and handed it to Ginny with an alcohol swab.

"Prick your finger with this. Put the blood on a strip, and we'll read the results."

Ginny did as she was told.

"Now compare the strip to the bottle.

"Looks like, maybe, 130. That's high, right?"

"When did you last eat?"

"Uh ... about an hour ago."

"It'll come down."

Ginny couldn't believe this.

"Where do I get these?"

"I'll write you a prescription."

"What if it goes high? I usually go out and shoot some hoops, but that doesn't always work."

"If it's over 200, take a unit or two of regular insulin."

"Really?" This might do away with the need for purging.

"Yes, really. Just be careful not to overreact to rebound highs."

"Rebound highs?"

"A temporary high after a low. You don't want to be chasing your blood sugar all over the place."

No, she didn't. Before now, she wouldn't have even known that she had rebound highs.

When Ginny got home, she sat on her bed and stared at her new bottle of test strips.

"Well, *this* is far out," she said aloud.

Dinner wasn't ready yet, so she picked up the phone and called Freddie.

"I just got blood glucose strips," she said.

"Uh ... what's that?"

"Strips that test blood sugar. Actual blood sugar. I can tell what's going on."

"Ohhhhhhh."

"Yes."

"That is good news. I have news, too."

"Oh?"

"I think I have a boyfriend."

"Way to take the wind out of my sails, Fred. Who is he? Where'd you meet him? Come on, I want details."

"He's in college. Ben. I met him in a bookstore in Providence. We were talking, and he asked for my number."

"Bonding over Le Carré, were you?"

"Anne Rice. Ben and I both love vampires."

"When were you going to tell me?"

"I was going to wait to see if it was going anywhere. I've only been on two dates. Sorry about your sails."

After she hung up, Ginny pricked her finger and tested her blood: it was about 90. She put the bottle of test strips and her lancing kit in her bag. This was a change she could live with.

Habits die hard, and for Ginny, constantly vomiting any time she ate her fill was almost comforting. However, now that she could test her blood, it might be easier to stop. Vomiting was disgusting. Why would she continue to do it when half the time she already felt like a dirty sponge? Maybe she could avoid some of her lows. And a lot of her highs.

This could be revolutionary.

Chapter 12

He Only Loves Me for My Mind

High school seniors received certain perks simply by staying in school for four years. A study hall, for instance, could be spent anywhere on the school property. At lunchtime, a senior could leave the school grounds on the condition that she would be back in time for her next class. Ginny and Freddie took advantage of this on the first day to go to lunch at Friendly's.

"I wonder if a manager at Friendly's is on the school board," Ginny said. "This place is full of seniors. It's not like there are a lot of places in walking distance from the school."

"I imagine this will quiet down once the novelty wears off."

Ginny took out her test strips.

"You're so cavalier about doing that in public."

"Is it weird?"

"A little."

"Good."

The food arrived: a tuna melt and a Tab for Ginny, a burger and a Coke for Freddie, and fries for both. Ginny missed being Freddie's girlfriend. She missed being *somebody's* girlfriend. The more she hung out with Freddie, the harder it would be to find someone else, but Ben had dropped Freddie over the summer, and Freddie needed a friend to lean on. Ginny was his closest friend and the only one so far who knew there had been a Ben.

When they got back to the school, Freddie entered at the door by the gym, which was his next class, and Ginny entered through the annex. She was worried that she had overeaten, so she went to her secret lavatory to get sick. She opened the door to a stall, then stopped.

"Maybe you don't have to do this," she said aloud.

She took out her test strips. 140. Not terrible, as long as it didn't go much higher. Too bad she didn't have any insulin in her bag. Wait. Why didn't she? She wouldn't want to carry a whole vial of insulin; it would go bad. She could, however, carry a syringe with three or four units for emergencies and toss it if she didn't use it.

Ginny couldn't bask too long in this revelation. Her next class was at the other end of the school. She climbed the stairs to the main level and found the corridors full of seniors rushing back from lunch. She joined them, hoping she was going in the right direction.

"Fight! Fight!"

First, there was confusion, and then students turned and moved quickly towards the shouts. Ginny tried to stand her ground, but people were jostling her from all sides. She ducked into a classroom doorway and let the rush of students sweep by her. The bell rang. No one paid attention.

Tilly was working her way through the crowd.

"There you are," she said.

"What's going on?"

"Bobby said Freddie made a pass at him, so Bobby's friends started beating on him."

"Oh my God. Is he okay?"

"Someone called an ambulance. I told Principal Seymore I'd come find you."

Ginny could hear sirens.

"But I never said anything," she said, mostly to herself. "Not to anyone, not you or Renée. Not anybody."

"People have a way of finding things out. Wait. What are we talking about?"

Ginny almost laughed. "Freddie's gay."

"He is?"

"He told me just before the junior prom. He wouldn't make a pass at someone here. He's not an idiot. Someone just wanted to start something. I don't know how they found out. I didn't say anything to anybody."

"It's not your fault," Tilly said.

"This is so awful. Damn everyone."

Ginny was quiet on the ride over to Providence Hospital except for the occasional sigh. Tilly, in the driver's seat, sensed her mood and remained silent as well. They didn't know what condition Freddie was in or what exactly had happened. Providence wasn't that far away, but the drive seemed like a cross-country trip.

Freddie was in the emergency room getting stitches in the back of his head. The bridge of his nose had a smaller gash, which could get by with a simple bandage. The doctor said he could go home after they were sure he didn't have a concussion.

"Oh my God! Freddie!"

"Ginny. Tilly. What are you two doing here?"

"Had to make sure you're okay. Are you?" Tilly said.

"More humiliated than injured, I think. It was mostly just shoving until someone hit me with a hockey stick."

"Those guys are cowards. They're only tough when they're in a pack."

"Thanks, Tilly."

Ginny leaned over and kissed Freddie's cheek.

"I'm so sorry."

"You didn't do anything."

"I'm sorry, anyway."

Freddie was back at school several days later. He hadn't been absent because of his injuries; the principal had suggested he stay home "until things calmed down." Renée shared some classes with Freddie and supplied notes and assignments, but no one was happy. It was like Freddie was punished, not the culprits.

When Freddie's parents questioned Principal Seymore, he said, in effect, "Boys will be boys."

"I can't punish every boy who starts a fight. Besides, there's no clear evidence as to who started it. Some people say it was Freddie."

Freddie didn't want his parents to know he was accused of making a pass at Bobby. He didn't want them to know he was gay, although he had a hunch they might already know. Even so, he was happier just letting it drop.

It was a warm September night, and Tilly, Ginny, and Renée were sharing a joint in Tilly's backyard. Ginny noticed that if she focused on one star, the other stars would stop moving. She didn't need the whole sky swirling around above her. It was distracting, and her friends had to keep repeating themselves. Ginny didn't have the heart to tell them the sky was more interesting than they were. She sat up, abandoning the planetarium show.

"Well, so far, the witch is *not* dead in my village," Tilly said.

"Mine neither," Ginny said.

"Well, of course not. I mean, you were with Freddie."

"Renée!"

"What? I mean, it's not like everyone doesn't know now why they broke up."

"It's fine, Till. How about you, Renée? Witch still alive in your corner?"

"Well ..."

"Really?"

"We were at a party a month or so ago. He asked; I said yes. I really regret it now."

"Who was it?"

"Joey."

Tilly and Ginny exchanged looks.

"He's always had a thing for you," Ginny said.

"How was it?" Tilly said.

Renée grimaced. "It was okay. It was over quickly."

Tilly shrieked with laughter.

"What?"

"Good sex isn't supposed to be over quickly."

"How do you know this stuff?" Ginny asked.

"My mom gave me a book: *The Joy of Sex*."

"Sheesh. My mom and I don't talk about *anything* like that," Ginny said. "She still doesn't know I use tampons."

"My mom gave me a book, too, but it was very clinical," Renée said. "I think the intent was to *remove* the joy of sex. In any case, it didn't help at all with Joey."

"Maybe Joey needs to read *The Joy of Sex*," Ginny said.

The girls were quite high, so they lay back on the grass and watched the moving stars. Soon, they'd be going in to get some snacks and drinks.

With Al Stewart's album *The Year of the Cat* on the stereo, Ginny was doing pushups. She liked having a beat while she exercised, although nothing too fast. She heard the phone ring, so she turned down the music.

"Ginny! It's Tilly!" her mother called from downstairs.

Ginny got off the floor and picked up the phone.

"Looks like there's a problem," Tilly said.

"What's up?"

"Renée thinks she might be pregnant."

"Oh, God."

"She got one of those new home-pregnancy tests. It was positive."

"Are those accurate?"

"Not as accurate as a doctor. I told her I'd drive her to get tested. Wanna come? I think she could use the support."

"Sure. When?"

"Tomorrow after school."

Ginny had basketball practice. She never missed practice. She'd talk to Coach Lukor in the morning.

"You're missing practice? You better have a good reason, Eastman."

"I do, but I can't tell you what it is."

"Oh?"

"I have to help someone in trouble. That's all I can say."

The phrase "in trouble" resonated with the coach, though Ginny didn't realize the implications when she said it.

"Oh. I see. It's not you, is it?"

"No, Coach."

"Good. Okay. See you tomorrow."

Since Renée hadn't heard positive or negative yet, Tilly suggested they go to the mall over the weekend so Renée could get her mind off things. Ginny offered to drive. Her parents didn't need the car, but her mother was never happy about her driving anywhere. It was such a small car, she hadn't been driving long, etc., etc. Her father stepped in.

"The girl needs practice, Irene. The mall isn't that far away. She'll be with her friends. Let her go."

So, Saturday morning, Ginny picked up Tilly and Renée. She was feeling confident behind the wheel. This was going to be easy. Tilly was beside her in the passenger seat, and Renée was in the back, silently contemplating her fate.

"What are we shopping for?" Tilly said.

"Baby clothes," Renée said and burst into tears.

Ginny somehow kept control of the car. "What? When did you find out?"

"This morning. My parents are going to kill me. What am I going to do?"

"What do you want to do?" Tilly said.

"I can't have a baby, can I? I'm supposed to go to Cornell."

One could almost hear the thoughts flying around inside the car.

"Well ... It's legal now," Ginny said. "Your parents don't have to know."

When Renée didn't respond, Tilly spoke up.

"We can drive you. You won't be alone."

"But won't I go to hell?"

Ginny and Tilly looked at each other, and Ginny said, "I guess that'll be part of your decision."

Renée came home from the mall and went right to her room. She didn't bother turning on a light; she didn't deserve light. What was she going to do? Would she go to hell? Why hadn't she insisted that Joey use a condom? How was she going to tell her parents? How was she going to raise a child? What was she going to do about school? What was she going to do for work? Would she have to live off her parents? Would she have to leave town? Would her parents forgive her? Would God forgive her?

She groped around in the dark for the phone and called for an appointment.

Tilly called Ginny a couple of days before the event.

"Turns out we're not going."

"Renée changed her mind?"

"She tripped and fell down the stairs."

"Oh my God! Is she alright?"

"Pretty banged up, but very lucky. But here's the thing ..."

Ginny thought about it. "She's no longer pregnant."

"Exactly."

"And do we think this was not an accident?"

"We do think that, yes."

"She could have seriously injured herself."

"I'm not sure she cared."

Ginny opened her mouth to speak, then changed her mind.

"Anyway," Tilly said. "I told her we'd still come over after school Thursday. She could use the company."

"One could argue ..."

"Yeah?"

"That throwing yourself down a flight of stairs isn't any better than having an abortion. I mean, if you're worried about going to hell, it's pretty much the same thing."

"Let's not mention that to Renée."

"No, let's not."

Renée was covered in bruises and scrapes, and her right arm, which had stopped her fall, was in a cast and a sling. Tilly brought her some peanut butter cookies her mom had baked,

Renée's favorite. Ginny was trying not to think about the cookies, but they smelled incredible.

"I guess you never told Joey," Tilly said.

"No way!"

"I wonder how many other girls have had this issue with him," Ginny said.

"The boys always get to walk away," Tilly said. "There ought to be a law."

"How would they enforce it?" Renée said.

"They could if there was a way to prove who the father was."

"Right. That'll never happen," Ginny said.

"Eastman."

"Yes, Coach?"

"Come here a minute?"

Ginny jogged over to her.

"How's your friend?"

"Oh. She's fine now, Coach."

Damn it. She shouldn't have said "she."

The coach nodded. "I hope there were no drastic measures."

Ginny looked her in the eye. The coach knew something.

"Oh. Uh, no, ma'am. Everything turned out fine."

"Good. Okay."

"Anything else, Coach?"

"No. That's all. You can return to practice."

"Yes, Coach."

Ginny and Freddie were walking home along the back roads through a watercolor painting of yellow, green, red, and orange foliage. Leaves were landing around them as they walked, and the air smelled like musk and wet grass. Ginny was watching the ground, looking for woolly bears. She thought she heard a car motor, so she looked up. Freddie must have heard it, too, because he turned around.

"Damn."

"What?"

A car was crawling behind them. Heads and arms and even feet were hanging out the windows, and the passengers were roaring with laughter. The driver beeped his horn and waved.

It was Bobby.

"Should we walk faster?" Ginny said.

"Nah. We shouldn't let them get to us."

The car pulled up alongside them. Someone shouted, "It's the fag and the fag lover!"

A barrage of rotting tomatoes pummeled them. Then the car sped off.

"Yuck. Oh my God. What the hell?" Ginny said.

Freddie was wiping the red, slimy goo off his face. Ginny had lumps of tomato gunk in her hair and all over her clothes.

"Well, we know who they are," she said.

Freddie scoffed. "Doesn't matter."

Ginny wanted to argue with him, then saw his point.

"When do we graduate?" Freddie said and laughed bitterly.

"I'm telling you. If you make a big thing out of it, it's just going to make things worse."

They were sitting in the kitchen at Ginny's house. Ginny had changed into something clean, and Freddie was wearing her father's shirt and shorts while Ginny's mother washed his clothes. Ginny was staring off into space, plotting revenge.

"I know what you're thinking. Drop it. Seriously."

"But it just makes me so mad."

"There's nothing anyone can do. Those guys'll just come after me again, and you, too, if you're with me."

"It's so unfair. Why should they get away with it?"

"Because I'm sure a lot of people would be amused by this, not horrified."

Ginny looked at him, defeated.

"C'mon. We have homework to do."

Ginny tried hard not to show anyone in school how upset she was. She never brought up the incident, except to Tilly and Renée. There were eight months left until graduation, and everyone wanted to make it out of there unscathed, or at least less scathed.

Tilly had wanted to have a Halloween party, but she was disappointed with her classmates. Tilly didn't want members of the senior class in her home right now. In the end, she invited Renée, Ginny, and Freddie over for pizza and soda.

"Are people still bothering you, Freddie?" Renée said.

"The main offenders make a point of avoiding me during gym class, as if I have some kind of disease. I feel like saying, 'None of you is my type,' but it's probably better just to leave it be. Bobby mutters 'fag' under his breath when he passes me in the hall, but that's more his problem than mine. I'm hoping soon everyone'll be more worried about getting into college than about what I may or may not do."

"It got better for me in high school," Renée said. "In grade school, people would say things like, 'You're okay. You don't act Black,' or they'd call me 'the dark one,' stuff like that. When I was dating Stu in middle school, people—adults!—would come up to me and say I was going to have 'chocolate-milk babies.' And Stu's father just hated me. Wouldn't say hello; would just glare at me and walk out of the room. It seems better now, but maybe people just hide their prejudices better, like they're trying to maintain a certain amount of civility. I'm okay with that. Hate me, love me, I don't care; just let me exist in peace."

"People had their suspicions about me early on. They'd call me names, push me out of line, mock me, stuff like that. It stopped when I started dating Ginny."

Ginny was alarmed. "Is that why you dated me?"

"Come on. No way. I was thrilled. I thought I finally liked a girl. Which I did, just not in the right way."

"And now you can catch a ball," Ginny said.

"Which I truly appreciate."

"A toast." Tilly handed everyone a can of soda. They popped the tops all at once with one big click and hiss.

"Here's to getting through our last year in one piece."

The Pilots were doing well this year, and by February, they were contenders for the playoffs. Ginny was spending every spare moment either practicing or watching basketball on TV. Meanwhile, college acceptance letters arrived. It was no surprise that Tilly chose FIT; Renée, Cornell; and Ginny, UCLA.

Practice had been intense. Coach Lukor was determined to get the girls a championship. Ginny was experiencing blood sugar lows, but nothing that was interrupting practice. She'd do a test in the locker room beforehand and then afterward and react accordingly. Usually, a little extra juice or crackers would take care of any hypoglycemia.

After a particularly brutal practice, Ginny was shaking. It took a while for her to feel like herself again. When she finally exited the school, Freddie was sitting on the stoop.

"Hey. You didn't have to wait for me."

"I was in the library working on something, so I thought I'd meet you. Are you the last one here?"

"Yeah. I was having issues, so I had to wait a bit."

"You sure you want to walk? I could get my mom to pick us up."

"I'm fine. You know I hate that. My mom's overprotective.

Don't you be like that, too. Let's just go."

When Ginny got home, she went to her room and put George Harrison's latest album, *Thirty-Three & 1/3*, on her turntable. She liked to lie on her bed upside down and close her eyes so the music would surround her. It was like George was in the room with her.

She was feeling agitated. She sat up and did a blood test: 180! This must have been the "rebound" high Dr. Hummel mentioned. She went into her bag and took a unit of regular insulin to ensure her blood glucose didn't go any higher. Then she went back to listening to George.

The Pilots blasted through the playoffs and were on the verge of becoming champions, until they played the last game. They were behind at least ten points for most of the game, until the fourth quarter, when they rallied. In the last 20 seconds, the opposing team took a shot that went in part way, then ricocheted out of the basket. Ginny grabbed the rebound. No one there could bounce and run like Ginny. She made it more than halfway down the court before her opponents double- and triple-teamed her. Continuing forward could get her a charging penalty, and she couldn't see through the tangle of arms and hands to make a pass. Turning her shoulder to her opponents, she dribbled back a couple of steps, then jumped up, and, using an overhand throw, hurled the ball towards the basket. She fell to the floor, landing on her butt.

The ball danced around the rim of the basket. No one breathed. It went in as the buzzer sounded. Her team went wild.

"What kind of shot was that?" Tilly asked.

"I don't know. I just tried something."

"You got the last basket of the Class of '77, North Greenwich Pilots girls' basketball team," Tilly said. "That is far out."

It was. Then why was Ginny so sad?

"Her name is Matilda?" Renée whispered in Ginny's ear.

"You didn't know that?"

"No. I just thought she was Tilly."

"That's the problem with graduating. They insist on reading your full name."

A sheepish Joey approached them.

"Hey. Congratulations, Renée Neuville. Valedictorian. Good for you."

"Thanks, Joey."

"Hey. Are you going to Tilly's party?"

"Uh ... Yeah."

"Maybe I'll see you there, then."

"Okay."

They watched him walk off, and Ginny said, "What was that?"

"He can be nice when he wants to be. If he couldn't, he wouldn't get so many girls fawning over him."

"Ha. That's not always true," Ginny said, and Renée laughed.

The graduation party at Tilly's had one major change: beer. Most seniors were now old enough, or approaching old enough, to drink. Tilly's mother wouldn't supply hard liquor, but a couple of kegs seemed safe enough, even though Tilly and Renée wouldn't be 18 until August.

As usual, people brought liquor, anyway.

The party was what one would expect from these young people, a lot of whom were new to drinking. They were overdoing it and vomiting all over the house. Tilly, Renée, and Ginny still preferred pot, especially after seeing what the effects of alcohol were doing to their friends.

"If one more drunk retches in front of me, I'm going to scream," Renée said.

The three friends grabbed Freddie and escaped to the backyard so they could smoke in peace. Tilly was taking a chance that her guests wouldn't destroy the house any more than they already had.

"I don't know how I'm going to clean all this up before my mom comes home tomorrow night," Tilly said. "I don't think I'll have enough time."

"We'll help you," Ginny said, and the others nodded in agreement.

"Life was simpler before people hit drinking age," Tilly said.

"Life was simpler before we hit puberty," Renée said.

"Life was simpler in kindergarten," Ginny said, and although she was serious, they all laughed.

Freddie was Ginny's ride, which was fortunate, as he hadn't smoked very much and didn't drink anything. Ginny wondered how other people were getting home. Tilly would probably let the drunker ones sleep it off at the house.

Freddie didn't see her to the door like he used to. The porch light was on, but the inside of the house was dark; her parents had gone to bed. Ginny climbed the stairs to her room and was overwhelmed with loneliness and despair. She might not see these friends much next year, maybe not ever again. Ginny was never a fan of change, and what was coming was huge.

PART II

Chapter 13

California, Here I Come

Sun. Fun. Seafood. Fruit. Palm trees. Roller-skating. Surfing. Basketball?

The weather in Rhode Island could vary greatly, even within the same day. In Los Angeles, on the other hand, the weather was far more consistent. In 1977, it was warmer and much drier than the Northeast. Since the city imported water to keep itself hydrated, and many of its signature palm trees and other vegetation were not native to the area, some of its own inhabitants accused it of being a former desert. This was an interesting urban legend, but not true.

Ginny's roommate was already in the room with her parents when Ginny arrived. Sheena was shorter and wider than Ginny was, with thick glasses and a loud voice that revealed a heavy New York, possibly Long Island, accent. The two introduced themselves. Ginny now knew one person on campus.

"Want to come get lunch with us?" Sheena said.

"Maybe another time. I'm going to unpack."

Ginny did some unpacking and then went down to the dorm lobby. If she was going to meet people, she reasoned, she shouldn't hide in her room. She brought her schedule and her orientation papers, settled in a chair, and then stopped to test her blood sugar. It was around 180.

"Damn," she said aloud.

She looked around to make sure no one was watching, took out her syringe of regular insulin, and, hiding it discreetly between the arm of the chair and her left thigh, took a unit.

"Hi."

Ginny quickly tucked the syringe away in her bag and looked up to see a fellow coed wearing a T-shirt for the women's Bruins basketball team. It was fresh out of the package; it still had crisp folds.

"I'm Lila."

"Ginny. Fellow basketball enthusiast, I see. Are you on the team?"

"I wish. I'm just a freshman."

"Me, too. Are you going to the tryouts?"

"Yeah. You?"

"Yup."

Ginny moved her paperwork off the chair next to her, and Lila sat down.

"I actually went to a basketball camp last summer," Lila said.

Ginny didn't know there *were* basketball camps.

"How was it?"

"I was the only girl. Couldn't even make it through the drills. And the guys wouldn't pass to me or anything. Man, they were ruthless. I thought high school was bad."

"It was," Ginny said, and they both laughed.

"At the camp, they had us dribbling with two basketballs. The guys were switching hands, bouncing them through their legs, all kinds of stuff. I could barely keep both balls bouncing."

"Geez. I've never done any of that. I wonder if that'll be part of the tryout." Maybe she could practice that a little before then. It was intimidating but also intriguing.

"I felt like I was being coached by the Harlem Globe Trotters," Lila said. "Anyway, what's your major? Sorry, that's a lame thing to ask, but I haven't met anyone yet besides my roommate. She's really shy, like afraid-to-talk shy."

"My roommate is the opposite: really loud. Anyway, I'm majoring in Athletics and Phys Ed. You?"

"Journalism. Although everyone is telling me if I want to be a journalist, I should pick a specialty."

"What about sports?"

"Interesting. I wonder how far a woman could go in sports journalism."

"Probably not far. I doubt they let many women journalists hang around men's locker rooms."

"They say the team loses a lot of freshmen in the first semester," Lila said.

"I know. What was I thinking? What if this makes me hate basketball?"

"Then you'll make another plan."

"Right. Sports journalism."

On the day of the tryouts, Ginny did what Dr. Hummel had told her to do and ate an extra slice of toast and an extra egg. The doctor had felt this would be easier than trying to adjust her insulin just for practice days. Her blood sugar before the tryout was about 160. She hoped it wouldn't go any higher.

They started with drills. Ginny fell into her usual rhythm and tore through them easily, even the shooting drills. She felt aggressive and in control. She loved this sport.

Next, she was part of a scrimmage. No one there could dribble or pass like Ginny. She was surprised. She guessed the better players had scholarships and were already on the team.

She was exhausted by the end, and when she finally arrived at the lockers, she sat for a moment on a bench to collect herself. She took out her test strips. She hadn't used a lancing device all summer. These days, she'd just grab a lancet and stab her finger. The result was around 50. She was running solely on inertia that last scrimmage. She drank some juice and waited to feel normal again.

"What's that? A pregnancy test?"

One of the players was indicating her bottle of test strips. The urge to say something sarcastic was great. She resisted.

"I'm diabetic," she said. *Not that it's any of your business.*

"Oh," she laughed. "I thought it was a pregnancy test."

Sure. Say it again. It wasn't stupid enough the first time.

Ginny glared at her until she went away. She was not making any friends here. She hoped no one she pissed off got on the team. That could be awkward.

She made the team.

She made the team!

Lila did not; at least, Ginny didn't see her name on the roster. She wanted to call Tilly and Renée and tell them. Also, Freddie. Were they in class? Eating? Having sex? She wrote letters instead. What were they all doing? Had they made new friends? Did they like their schools? She wrote similar letters to each of them.

With that task accomplished, Ginny looked over the practice schedule. Mornings, five days a week, for three hours. She wasn't going to have any time to socialize. She might not even have any time to study. Bouncing and running. Did she really want to make a living teaching people to do this? What had she gotten herself into?

And when was she going to find time to kill the witch?

Lila had seen a flier for a frat party just off campus, and since both she and Ginny were feeling isolated, they decided to go. Neither one of them wanted to invite their roommates, Too Loud and Too Quiet. And what does a person wear to a frat party? The only shoes Ginny had with her were sneakers. Wait, she had one pair of sandals. That would work.

They entered the frat house and almost turned around and left. The party was full of what appeared to be upper-classmen. Everyone was freakishly tall, even the women. It seemed they had stumbled onto a basketball players' frat.

"Hey, come in. Don't be shy."

He was tall and chiseled and blond. Ginny recognized him from the university newspaper: Dashiell Hollander, class of '79, basketball star.

"Hi, Dash. I'm Ginny. This is my friend Lila."

"Well, come in. The kegs are against the windows in the back room. Make yourselves at home."

As they passed him, Dash swatted Ginny on the butt. She turned and glared at him.

"Nice," he said. "You work out."

"She plays basketball," Lila said to Ginny's dismay.

"Oh? You must be a point guard."

Yes, Ginny wasn't tall. Rub it in.

"We'll have to scrimmage sometime," he said.

Don't count on it.

As they left him, Ginny hissed, "Why did you tell him that?"

"Because he was being smug and obnoxious, and I wanted to deflate his bloated ego."

"I'm afraid nothing will do that."

The women continued to push their way into the room.

"Okay. Now, where did he say the keg was?"

"Back room by the windows. But I hate beer."

Lila laughed. "So do I. Let's hope they have something else to drink."

They needn't have worried. There were all kinds of alcohol

and plenty of mixers. Ginny poured herself some vodka with seltzer and added a slice of lime. This kind of drink was kinder on her blood sugar than beer or wine.

"Ladies!"

Another towering man approached them and put an enormous hand on each of their shoulders.

"Hold on, Max," Dash said. "That little one on your right. She's mine."

Ginny scowled. "I am not yours!"

"Ooh. She's feisty."

Coming here was whose idea?

"Excuse us," Lila said and extracted herself from under Max's paw. As Ginny followed her, Dash leaned over and said in her ear, "I want to get into those pants."

"I doubt they'd fit you."

The frat party was not a total bust. Once the novelty of freshmen Lila and Ginny wore off, the frat boys spent most of their time playing drinking games. Lila and Ginny met some other coeds who, despite drinking too much, could carry on a conversation. A joint was lit and passed around, but Ginny declined. She felt she was playing better without it.

"Okay. Who is your nominee for most obnoxious frat guy?" this woman named Alice said.

"Have we met them all yet? This is only one frat." Ginny said.

"Okay. Who is your nominee for most obnoxious frat guy here?"

"Dash Hollander!" they all said in unison.

Ginny and Lila felt a lot less cloistered after going to this party. UCLA was going to be okay.

The next step, as far as Ginny was concerned, was to get birth control. If she wanted to kill the witch, which she did, she needed to be prepared, and considering Renée's experience, she was not going to put herself in that position, ever.

"You can get anything you need at the student health center," Lila said.

"I don't know. I was thinking of going to Planned Parenthood."

"You're over 18. They can't tell your parents. And there you'll have to pay for it."

"I know, but I think I want to go off-campus for this."

"Gee, Ginny, it's not like you're getting an abortion. And how are you going to get there?"

Ginny hadn't thought about that.

"Do they have bus maps at the student center?"

They did. Ginny spent over an hour on a bus to Planned Parenthood to get an IUD. She rejected the idea of birth control pills, figuring the side effects wouldn't be good for a diabetic. But her mission was accomplished.

"I still think you could have just gone to the campus health center," Lila said. They were practically whispering because they were in the lunchroom.

"I could have. I didn't."

"You don't have a boyfriend. Why do you need birth control?"

"Because I plan to have one, one of these days. I want to be prepared. A friend of mine in high school had sex just once and got pregnant. I want to avoid that."

"You could ask the guy to use a condom."

"I suppose. I just think I'd rather be sure. Getting pregnant would really suck right now."

"Well, you have to have sex first."

"Yes, there is that."

Morning practices were going well, but Ginny still had blood sugar concerns. Sometimes it would be a little low, sometimes a little high, sometimes very low, sometimes very high. She was eating the same thing every morning. What was going on? She hoped this wouldn't keep her from playing. She didn't indulge in her frustrations about this all the time, but she was often upset. Then, those familiar, disconnected, overwhelming bouts of sadness would come over her. Maybe she was over-tired, as her mom would say.

The next morning's practice, she was dribbling down the court during a scrimmage, blasting by the opposing team, when her knees buckled. She managed to stay standing, but she was in trouble.

Damnit.

She threw the ball to Denise, a fellow freshman, who made the shot. Denise always made the shot.

"Time!" the couch called. "Eastman, are you okay?"

Crap. How embarrassing.

"No. I need a minute."

She walked with difficulty to the sidelines and grabbed her juice.

"Okay, everyone, take five."

Coach Moore approached her. This was bad.

"Eastman? What is it?"

She wanted to cry, also a symptom of low blood sugar, but she held it together.

"Low blood sugar. I'm diabetic."

This information stuck in her throat; she hoped to make it at least until Christmas break without this being an issue.

"Are you going to be okay?"

"I just need a couple minutes. Then I'll be fine."

"Okay. Good."

What was she going to do? Would the coach think she was too unpredictable to play? Would she replace her with someone else? Shouldn't she replace her with someone else? Ginny was questioning everything: her abilities, her decision to do this in the first place, even her leaving Rhode Island. She wished she could have her blood sugar tattooed on her arm. She couldn't just drink juice all the time in anticipation of potential lows because then she'd have highs, which had their own issues. Her test strips helped, but it was just about impossible to test in the middle of practice, much less a game.

There would never be a perfect time to play, a perfect time to eat, more than a few days in a row of perfect numbers. This was her condition. This was never going away, and she could either deal with it or stop living. Perfection, as much as Ginny wanted it, was unattainable. This was lucky because if diabetics had to be perfect all the time, they'd all be dead. Besides, perfection was relative, wasn't it? A perfect square was not a perfect circle.

Asher told her to live forever. That's what she was going to do.

This was still nagging at her days later, so she called her new L.A. doctor, Dr. Fisher.

"You know, Jackie Robinson was diabetic."

"Really?"

"It wasn't common knowledge. A lot of people didn't even know he had it until he died."

"He *died* from it? Great."

"That was never clear. He was 53 and had serious heart problems."

"Was he still playing when he was diagnosed?"

"Diagnosed at 33, retired at 37. Look, you've been dealing with this a long time. I wouldn't question yourself so much. You know what you know."

This conversation prompted Ginny to head to the school library. She flipped through the index cards and looked up Jackie Robinson. Would any of the books about him mention he was diabetic? She chose a couple and then decided to look at the reference section.

Encyclopedia Britannica didn't even mention diabetes for Jackie Robinson. *Encyclopedia Americana* listed the cause of death as a heart attack but did mention his health was suffering from diabetes complications. However, nothing talked about how he dealt with diabetes as a player. Where would she find that?

Maybe she didn't need to find that. "Know what you know," right?

"Ginny!"

Dash was coming towards her. Ginny never thought she'd run into Dashiell Hollander in a library.

"How's it going?" he said.

"Okay ..."

"Look. I think we started off on the wrong foot. Let's say we try again. Hi, I'm Dash."

He was trying so hard to be likable. She played along.

"Ginny."

"Okay, Ginny, can I take you out for a cup of coffee?"

She looked him in the eye. Tigers do not change their stripes. He wanted sex, and she wanted to lose her virginity. That alone made him seem attractive.

Dash took Ginny back to his bedroom at the frat house. They kissed for a while, and when it was obvious to both of them what they each wanted to do, the clothes started tearing off quickly.

Damn. The guy could do centerfolds. It seemed rather disproportionate, however, him being so tall and her being, well, not. But just the act of taking off her clothes was turning her on. Him having a perfect body was a bonus.

They went back to kissing, and he stuck his finger inside of her. She flinched, although it did feel good. He looked her in the eye for a moment as if he was looking right through her. He smirked.

What? she wondered.

He put his head between her legs and started licking. At first, Ginny thought, *What the hell?* but soon, she realized how good it felt.

"Oh my God."

He took his time, but Ginny was getting impatient. Something needed to happen soon, or she would go crazy. She wasn't sure what, exactly, but pressure was building.

He stopped and started kissing her again, and the next thing she knew, he was inside of her.

It was painful. She hadn't expected that.

He put his hand between her legs and started rubbing. The sensation she was having before came back, and she no longer minded the pain. Then something did happen, and what Ginny felt next she had never experienced before: a pleasant electric current running throughout her body. She was making strange sounds and gasping. What was going on?

He did a final push, stayed inside her a moment, then slowly climbed off her.

Unfortunately, Dash would now go back to being Dash.

"My housemates will be back in a little while. Maybe you should go before they get here."

"What? Oh. Okay. Uh, where's your bathroom?"

Ginny cleaned herself up as best she could, then quickly got dressed. The witch was dead, and Ginny was happy.

Dash was dressed when she returned to the bedroom. He had a dopey smile on his face.

"We're good together, aren't we?"

"Uh ... yes. Yes. We are."

"Cool. Maybe I'll call you or something."

"Yeah. Okay."

Ginny practically ran out of the house, then walked at a more normal pace once she was closer to the dorm. She hoped no one saw her. Seriously. Dash Hollander? What was she thinking? She worried that he would call, but then she realized she had never given him her number, nor had he asked for it. She supposed he saw her as a conquest, but he was one, too.

Ginny didn't tell anyone about Dash. The only people she'd want to tell were Tilly and Renée, and she hadn't heard back from them, so what was the point? She figured Dash would tell everyone on campus, but so far, no one seemed to be whispering behind her back or laughing in her face. Could he keep quiet about this? Doubtful.

Sheena insisted on having breakfast with Ginny the next morning. Lila was in the cafeteria with her roommate, Eileen, and the four took a table together. Ginny was tired of eating the same thing every morning, so she was trying the pancakes today. She had her sugar-free syrup in her bag, and since she didn't have practice today, she felt she could experiment a little.

"You can't eat that, can you?" Sheena said.

Ginny regretted telling her anything about her condition. "Watch me."

Dash and three other giant men entered the main room of the cafeteria. Ginny thought they were going to sit at the empty table beside them, but they veered off and found a table on the other side of the room. Dash didn't even look at her. She had mixed feelings about this. Was she so bad in bed that he wanted nothing to do with her? Or was it just that, now that he'd had her, he was no longer interested? What about the part of her that wanted nothing to do with him? Why wasn't that the strongest emotion she was having?

"What's the matter, Ginny?" Lila said.

"I'm just thinking about something."

"That's why we smell smoke," Sheena said and laughed loudly. The others rolled their eyes.

The line to return trays was adjacent to the basketball players' table, and Ginny braced herself for comments. None was forthcoming. The guys were immersed in conversation.

"I don't have to worry about women," one of them was saying. "Women love me."

Ginny remembered him from the frat party, Max, she thought his name was.

"Me too." That was from a particularly funny-looking guy. Ginny wanted to laugh.

"Anyway, the ones who don't, I don't care about." That was Dash.

"And with birth control, it's gotten a lot easier."

"Yeah," Dash said. "I just assume they're all on the pill."

Ginny leaned over and whispered in his ear, "*I'm* not."

Ginny couldn't see the look on his face, but Lila could. As they were leaving, she said, "What did you say to him?"

Ginny smiled. "Oh, nothing."

The active list for the first game would be posted today. Ginny was trying not to get her hopes up. She was a freshman, and an impaired one at that. Why would Coach Moore choose her? Ginny was still embarrassed about having to take a time out from that scrimmage, even though that was more than three weeks ago.

Players were clustered in front of the roster board, and most were happy. Only two could be scratched per game. Ginny finally got to the front of the group. Shooting guard Ann Meyers, of course, was a starter. She was a senior and an intimidating player. Forward Denise Curry, at six foot-one, was a starter. She was a freshman, but boy, could she play. Ginny scanned further down the players list. No, she wasn't a starter, but that didn't surprise her, nor did it upset her. But then, she saw her name. She was on the active list! She would be in uniform! Her odds of getting off the bench were low, but it meant she had a shot. And if not this game, maybe one in the future.

Once final exams were over for the fall term, UCLA students had two weeks off for Christmas break. Ginny planned to go home and sleep.

Her flight was the three o'clock nonstop to Boston. Then, she'd take a bus to Rhode Island. She stared out the window; they were above the clouds. If she looked behind her, she saw the sun still up over L.A. If she looked forward, she saw a full moon glowing in the night sky over Boston. Pressing her face against the glass, she could almost see both the sun and the moon at the same time. She'd have to be sitting on the wing to see this fully.

She had spent the last four months too busy to think straight. She wasn't used to having time to herself. It was late when the car service dropped her off at her parents' house from the bus station. The place seemed smaller, a little drab, a little unhappy. The Christmas tree was up in the corner, trying to make the house more festive, but even that was making Ginny sad. Maybe she would feel less alienated in the morning.

She climbed the stairs to her room. The door to Asher's room was open. All his stuff was gone! Just the bed and a dresser were left. Where were his albums? His stereo? His books? His clothes? How was she going to talk to him if his room was gone?

"Mom!"

It was after eleven o'clock. She knew her mother was turning in, but this was important. She ran down the stairs to her parents' room.

"Ginny. What's wrong?"

"What happened to Asher's room?"

"We're making it into a guest room."

"Where's his stuff?"

"All of his things are in the garage."

Ginny ran to the garage. Boxes marked "Asher" were piled

up along one of the walls, but there were no labels indicating which boxes were which.

Where were the albums?

"Ginny! You can go through those things tomorrow."

Tears of frustration were forming. She couldn't believe it. Asher's room was sacred. Didn't they understand that?

She went back into the house.

"I don't know why you're getting so upset," her mother said. "Your brother has been gone seven years now. We kept all his things. We figured you could go through the boxes while you're here and take what you want."

Ginny wanted the room to be intact, just the way it was. That way, part of him was still around. Now, Asher's spirit was no longer in the house. She had lost him a second time.

"You don't get it."

"Explain it to me."

Ginny left the room without answering. Her father, having overheard the conversation, came out of the bedroom.

"In case you were wondering," her mother said. "The answer to the question, 'Will Ginny be upset if we take down Asher's room?' is 'Yes. Very.'"

Tilly invited Ginny and Renée for a sleepover "for old times' sake." Ginny reminded her she didn't smoke anymore.

"But you two can."

"You'll get a contact high," Tilly said. "Are you okay with that?"

"I guess so. It's hard being on the team. Not smoking makes a huge difference. I can't smoke, not right now."

"We'll open the window. That way, the smoke will dissipate."

When Ginny got to Tilly's house, Renée's car was already in the driveway. Tilly's mother said to go on upstairs. A cloud of smoke hovered over Tilly and Renée, and they were giggling. Ginny found a place to sit outside of the cloud.

"Why are you sitting over there?"

"She's trying to avoid the smoke," Tilly said. "You know, Ginny, smoke moves around."

"I know. I just figure I won't sit right in the middle of it."

"Looks like your team has a shot at the playoffs," Renée said. "That must be exciting."

"I'll probably be on the bench, but it'll depend on what happens during the game. Ann and Denise can carry the team all by themselves, but that wouldn't be sportsmanly."

Renée giggled. "Sportsmanly. That doesn't sound right."

"Sportsmanish?" Tilly said and laughed.

"Sportsmanlike?" Ginny said.

"I think it's sportsmanlike, but that doesn't sound right either," Renée said.

"What were you talking about again?" Tilly said.

"Oh, I don't know." They all laughed, and Ginny added, "I think I might be getting a contact high."

"Anyone heard from Freddie?" Renée said.

"No. I wrote him when I wrote you two, but he never answered."

"Probably having a fabulous time in New Haven," Tilly said.

"I thought he got into Duke," Renée said.

"He did, but he decided on Yale," Ginny said. "He thought Duke sounded too stuffy. Founded by Quakers or something. Maybe my letter never got to him. I should try to call him while I'm here. He might be home for Christmas."

"Call from here, and we can all talk to him," Renée said.

No one answered the phone at the Grisham house. Ginny remembered that his family liked to go away over the holidays. She'd have to write him another letter when she got back to California.

When Ginny returned to the dorm, she could hear music in the hallway. She hadn't heard anything like it before. It was some kind of rock, but faster and with a steadier, stronger beat. She immediately thought of Tilly and Renée because it was great dance music. She stopped in her room to drop off her suitcase, then walked down the hall to find which room it was coming from.

She found it, the corner room at the end. She put her head against the door and thought of Ash, of how many times she had listened against his door. She knocked.

A pale, bony guy with Buddy Holly-like glasses that were too big for his face answered the door.

"Hi. I'm Ginny. I was just wondering about the music you're playing."

"Oh. Yeah. The Talking Heads. Uh ... Wanna come in for a minute?"

He handed her the album cover. It was bright red and said "Talking Heads '77" across the top.

"Which song is this?"

"'Don't Worry About the Government.'"

"This is great."

He motioned to her to sit in the only chair in the room, and he sat on the bed. He had a corner room, which was bigger than the one she shared with Sheena, and its window faced the courtyard. The next song was great, too, but then they got to "Psycho Killer," and the owner of the album leaped up and started dancing, or rather, hopping and jerking to the beat.

The door opened, and someone said, "Oh. Sorry, Ken. Didn't know you had a girl here."

Ken turned down the stereo.

"It's not like that. She heard the music, and I told her to come in."

"That's one way to do it. Hi, I'm Gavin."

"Ginny. Actually, I should probably go."

She turned to Ken. "Nice meeting you. I'm in 6E."

When the door closed behind her, she heard Gavin say, "Sorry, man."

Sheena was out with some friends, giving Ginny an opportunity to do some schoolwork. She had calculus to do, and then maybe she'd work on an English assignment due Monday.

Except someone knocked on her door.

"Ken. Hi. What's up?"

"I was wondering if you'd like to check out a punk show at the Masque tonight."

"Uh ... the what?"

Ken dropped his head and started mumbling. "It's a club. X is playing. I thought maybe you'd—"

"I'd love to. I don't have practice tomorrow. What time?"

Ken lifted his head to look at her, confidence restored. "I'll knock on your door around ten."

Ten? That was usually when she headed home.

"OK. Sure. Uh ... what do I wear?"

"Black. T-shirt and jeans. Sneakers so you can dance."

Ginny was excited about this, but who the heck was X?

Ken's older sister dropped Ginny and Ken off, then sped off to start her own night.

They were in a dark alley.

"There's a club here? This reminds me of a horror movie."

Was he going to kill her and keep a collection of her fingers in his dorm room's minifridge? Perhaps she should have asked him about that before they were in the alley. Other people were heading in the same direction, though, and Ginny could hear the faint sound of music.

"You'll love X," Ken said. "They'll go on around eleven. We're early enough that we can stand at the front of the stage."

Ginny looked around to see what other women were wearing. Ken was right: black jeans and T-shirts. But their makeup! Black lipstick, heavy eyeliner, and blue eyeshadow surrounding their eyes, not just on the lids. If Ginny tried to look like that, she'd feel like an imposter; it just wasn't her. There were normal-looking women in the crowd, too, which made her feel a little better. Neurotic was not cool, so she had to stop it.

The club was just a basement. The paint was peeling off the walls, and everything was covered with graffiti. It was as if the place had been abandoned but was pried open just so this band X could play there tonight.

"Wanna drink?"

"Oh. Uh, not yet."

Ken looked disappointed.

"Do you mind if I have one?"

"Not at all."

X's songs were varied, mostly fast and aggressive, and the crowd was jumping up and down and going wild. What struck Ginny about the band was their odd harmonies. The female vocalist had a pleading sound, like a cat left out in the rain. She had overdyed black hair, cut like a rag mop. That's where a lot of women in the audience had taken their hair inspiration.

The show ended after one o'clock, and as the audience trickled out of the club, Ken used the pay phone and called his sister's beeper.

"I'm going to the restroom," Ginny said. "Wait right here."

Ginny peed, then washed her hands and checked her blood. Around 120. She had weathered this night nicely.

They went outside to the alley, where people were drinking, smoking cigarettes and weed, and making out. Ken maneuvered her past them and towards the end of the alley, where he had told his sister to meet them.

"Nice night," Ken said. Ginny smiled. He was going to kiss her.

"Did you like the band?" he said.

"Yes. Their harmonies were getting to me after a while, but I think that's just me not being used to them. It started to sound the same, you know? Like all minor, no major, no mixing it up."

"I get it. Their harmonies get to me, too, sometimes."

"Anyway, they were great. Their lyrics especially."

"Exene is a poet."

"Is that the lead singer with the sour harmonies?"

He laughed. "Yes."

"Do they have an album?"

"Not yet. I don't think they have been playing that long."

He looked into her eyes. Ginny was prepared for him to kiss her, when a car pulled up and honked its horn.

"Damn. I mean, there's my sister."

She smiled. "Okay. Next time."

Sunday afternoon, Ginny was feeling isolated and gloomy. She had had a great time with Ken last night. What was her problem?

She went downstairs to the TV room in the lobby. She turned on the set, flipped through the channels, and found a basketball game. She didn't follow either team, but this would still be entertaining. She missed Asher. She missed Tilly and Renée. She missed Freddie. She missed her home with her mom's home cooking and her albums and Asher's albums and Asher's room. She wasn't sure any of those things would cure her current state of mind, however.

Lila came into the room and sat beside her.

"I thought I heard basketball."

"You did. 34–27, 76ers."

"I went back to the frat house last night. I was going to take myself to a movie, but that seemed lonely and pathetic. At least the frat was loud."

It seemed Lila was also experiencing the lazy-Sunday-afternoon blues.

"Were Dash and that huge guy, Max, there? He's got to be over seven feet."

"Yeah, they were there. They live there."

Lila started to say something, then stopped.

"What?"

"Nothing. Not important. How was your date with Ken?"

"It was fun. Ken's a nice guy. Business major, but a music freak, so he's not boring."

"Cool. Will you see him again?"

"Definitely."

"Oooh," Lila said at the TV. "Julius Erving, nice shot!"

"He keeps doing that."

"You heard the Knicks traded Walt Frazier?"

"And they're paying for it. They've been losing."

Eventually, the game restored their enthusiasm for life. The 76ers won 87–73, and the two friends felt a little happier.

Jan. 22, 1978

Ginny—

I'm so sorry I haven't written. I just got your second letter, and you're right; it's shaming me into writing. Things are a little intense here in New Haven. School is okay, but my love life is on fire.

Sorry, you don't need to hear that it's on fire. Let's just say I think I'm in love. His name is Matthew Haku, he's a junior, and he's from Hawaii. His father owns a hotel (or two!) there. And did I mention he's gorgeous?

I finally came out to my parents. Turns out they didn't have a clue, or at least said they didn't. (Yes, my grade-school 'bud-dies' knew, but my parents didn't.) It was a big scene, and my dad is still not talking to me. (Mom is.) The fact I told them over Christmas maybe had something to do with it. Mom thinks he'll come around. That probably means she'll be talking to him. We'll see.

I'm so happy to hear you got on the Lady Bruins, although that doesn't surprise me in the least. You're meant for great things, Ginny. They should create a pro league soon just so you can play on it. I can't believe you have time to take college-level calculus with all you're doing.

Two things that New Haven has are fabulous pizza and fabulous Italian pastries. They always talk about gaining the 'freshman 15,' but I think I'm surpassing that. Matthew says I need to put on some weight, but I don't think he meant like that. Sheesh!

I'll definitely write sooner next time. Right now, I have a class (Ancient History) to get to, and then I'm meeting Matthew.

Best,

Freddie

With Ken's roommate home for the weekend, Ken and Ginny had Ken's albums spread across the floor of his dorm room: Johnny Thunders, Patti Smith, Elvis Costello (whom Ken was imitating with those glasses, not Buddy Holly), the Dead Boys, the Stranglers, among others.

Somewhere in the middle of Patti Smith's *Radio Ethiopia*, Ken made his move. They made out for a while, and then Ginny unhooked her bra under her T-shirt. That was all the invitation Ken needed.

Clothes came off slowly in a mutual strip tease. Ginny found this lack of urgency refreshing. The only man she had to compare Ken to was Dash, and she preferred Ken. Ken was making love to her. Dash had used his vast experience with other females to impress her. She had learned a lot, but she felt she could have been anybody. Dash might have been a good candidate to kill the witch, but Ken was better as a potential relationship. And he wasn't an asshole.

UCLA's women's basketball team was indeed going to the playoffs, and Ginny contributed to the win that got them there. She made four points consisting of one field goal and two free throws. She did better with rebounds (five) and assists (four). She was thrilled to have been a part of it. They had to use her in the playoffs. They just had to.

"You did good out there."

Ginny turned to see Ann smiling at her, but before Ginny could say "Thank you," she had moved on.

Chapter 14
Know What You Know

Ginny started her summer in Rhode Island with the lingering rush of having been on an AIWA championship team. She couldn't believe they let her play, though she suspected Coach Moore only sent her in because the lead was wide enough. They beat Maryland 90 to 74, so there was plenty of room for error. Still, she didn't screw up; she did what she had to do, and there were no casualties on the court. She wondered how the team would do this coming year now that Ann had graduated. Ginny's four or five measly points per game weren't going to lead anyone into another championship.

Unlike Asher's room, Ginny's room was just how she left it. She was back there now, surrounded by possessions she didn't want to bring to L.A. nor throw out. What if her parents decided to take apart her room as well? Would all of her things be in a box in the garage next to Asher's? With that in mind, she went into her bookshelf and grabbed her old diary, first checking that Asher's note was still there. It was. She placed the journal safely in her bag.

While she was waiting for Tilly and Renée to arrive, she looked around her room. She wanted to keep her albums and the turntable, but she couldn't take them to L.A. now. She and Lila were talking about maybe getting an apartment together in the next year; she'd take them then. Books, old notebooks, old clothes, maybe she didn't need any of this stuff. The treasure was in Asher's boxes.

The three friends settled in the Eastman's garage. Ginny's father took down the boxes from the top of the stack so they could go through them.

"This box is all clothes," Tilly said.

"So's this one," Ginny said. "But I must have this shirt."

It was a well-worn, olive-drab, button-down fatigue shirt with four front pockets. The sleeves were practically as tall as Ginny.

"How are you going to wear that?" Tilly said.

Ginny rolled up the sleeves. The shirt was hanging down to her ankles.

"I guess I'm not."

"Hey," Renée said. "I've got books."

"Good. I want some of those," Ginny said.

"He's got lots of this guy Hunter Thompson," Tilly said. "My mother loves him."

"Do you want to take them? Just leave me one."

Tilly handed her *Hell's Angels*.

"Thanks. If you see *M*A*S*H* or *On the Road*, I want those, too."

Renée handed them over and said, "You know you can just buy these in any bookstore."

"I want Asher's copies."

The girls took what they thought sounded interesting (Salinger for Renée, '60s or '70s themes for Tilly and Ginny) and put the remaining books back in the box.

"What do you think will happen to the rest of his stuff?"

"My parents will probably donate everything somewhere. But not until I tell them they can."

They heard Ginny's father calling.

"Girls! Come have some lunch."

"Are we still girls?" Ginny said.

"What do you want him to call us?" Tilly said. "'Women! Oh, women! Come have lunch.'"

This got the three friends laughing, and they headed back into the main part of the house.

One of Ginny's college instructors recommended that if a person wanted to coach, one should start now. Volunteering at a school or basketball camp would be good experience. Ginny started with a camp not too far from North Greenwich, a five-day boys' day camp. No girls, but basketball was basketball, right?

The kids were in their early teens, about ten of them.

"Hi, I'm Coach Eastman," Ginny started, and she heard one of the kids groan, "We got a *lady* coach. She probably doesn't even *play*."

"I am a lady coach. And you are?"

"Not a lady player," the kid said, which got a laugh. He was tall and blond, a Dash-in-training.

"Okay, Not-a-Lady-Player. Now that we've had that introduction, how about the rest of you introduce yourselves?"

They said their names, and one of his friends pointed to Not-a-Lady-Player and said, "And that's Trevor."

"Let's start with some dribbling to warm up."

Trevor went to the end of the line. Ginny had the kids dribble up the court right-handed and down the court left-handed. Most of them were having trouble on the way back. Trevor ran awkwardly, the way a kid does when he has a growth spurt and his body hasn't caught up with it, but he was a decent dribbler with either hand.

Ginny told the kids to form a circle to do a ball-handling drill. They switched the ball hand to hand, then around their waists, then between their legs. The basketballs were flying out of their hands.

"Don't get frustrated. Losing the ball is not the end of the world. Just keep trying."

Trevor was proficient at this drill. Ginny approached him.

"Okay, you got this. See if you can pick up the pace, especially on those between-the-legs switches. And go ahead and take the ball over your head, then down to your toes as well."

At the end of the day, Ginny stayed on the court to take a couple of minutes of practice herself. She started by dribbling up and back, then again, alternating hands. Then she circled around and did some right and left layups. Her left-hand layups still needed work, but she had nailed them during games, so with practice, they'd be back. She bounced and ran past the three-point line, then turned and tried her overhand jump shot. It bounced around the rim, but it went in.

She heard clapping behind her.

"Nice, Lady Coach."

She grabbed the rebound before she turned around.

"Trevor ... Thanks."

"Where do you play?"

"UCLA."

He nodded. "Sorry I said you didn't play."

"Not every coach does. It's okay."

A car horn honked.

"Well, my dad's here. See you tomorrow?"

"Yes, you will."

It felt like it was no time at all before Ginny was back to her other reality in California. Class registration was in full swing. While Ginny had loved her previous term's calculus class, there was a sad reality. She found she was too distracted to pay it the proper attention. Between practice, the game schedule, clubs, and sex, finding time to concentrate like she needed to was hard. She had gotten an A-minus in the class last term, but that was a gift. There was a reason why classes for athletes were rumored to be dumbed down. She should have taken Variable Topics in Mathematics instead of Integral and Differential Calculus. She would have been bored, though. This term, as much as it pained her, no more calculus.

The team's road schedule worked well for Ginny. A lot of the games were in the evenings, and her insulin wasn't as much of a problem right after dinner. The team played a particularly good game in Tulsa, and Ginny was pumped. She had only scored twice herself but had handled the ball with ease and was crucial in facilitating the coach's plays. She played for 15 minutes. Whatever doubts the coach (and Ginny) might have had, she quashed them. She felt heroic.

A young man wearing a Blondie T-shirt approached her.

"Great game. You gals clobbered us."

"Well, Denise is a force to be reckoned with."

"You're being too modest. I saw you in action out there."

"Thank you. You're a student here?"

"Yeah. Sophomore. Go Golden Hurricane! Yay! But really, I think you're great." He slipped his arm around her shoulders. "How about coming back to my dorm? I have beer and weed, and my roommate is out for the night."

She maneuvered out from under his arm and said, "Thank you, but I'm seeing someone."

"So?"

"So, I don't fool around."

"Everybody fools around. Hey, I have condoms."

"Really, no thanks."

"Oh, I get it. You're not into guys. Who's the lucky girl? Someone on the team?"

"I'm not into girls. I just don't want to be with *you*."

"Dyke," he muttered.

"Excuse me?"

"Dyke!" he barked and stormed off.

Teammate Anita was in earshot and, seeing the look on

Ginny's face, came over.

"Listen," she said, "that won't be the last time you hear that. Women athletes always get that shit. Don't let it get to you. It's more a reflection on them than us. It's not who you sleep with. It's how you play."

"Thank you. My first groupie. That guy was a real jerk."

Anita laughed. "Yes, he was."

Speaking of jerks, Ginny noticed that Dash wasn't on the Bruins' roster this year. He was a senior. Did he already make it into the NBA? Why hadn't she heard anything?

In the meantime, there were tryouts coming up for the women's national team, predicated on a recommendation from the coach. Would Coach Moore even think about recommending Ginny? There was already Denise, who was also a sophomore, plus Jennifer and Anita, who were juniors. What chance did Ginny have?

A good chance, it turned out. Coach Moore recommended her. It was now up to Ginny whether she would grab this opportunity. This required some soul-searching. Could a juvenile diabetic make it as a national player?

"I think you'd be the best one to answer that question," Lila said. "You alone know how it affects you. I wouldn't bother with anyone else's opinion."

While Ginny considered this, Lila added, "I mean, you know what you know. You've been playing so far. If it gets too much, you can decide then, but I think you should give it a go. Just—"

"Just?"

"Just don't make it common knowledge."

This was excellent advice.

There was word that something called the Women's Professional Basketball League (WPBL) was starting its first season. This got Ginny thinking. Should she continue studying to be a coach? Would she be ready to give up playing by the time she graduated in 1981? She never thought she'd have an opportunity to be professional.

Bounce and run. Could this be a career?

Ginny didn't make the national team, and she was somewhat relieved. Trying out was good experience, though. She suspected part of the problem was her lack of height. At just under five foot six, she wasn't the shortest player ever, but she was the shortest at the tryouts. She had to become spectacular in the next year or so, or she'd never make it to the WPBL.

With Ginny spending more time on basketball, Ken was exhibiting signs of petulance.

"You're never around."

"I know. I'm sorry. Basketball has been taking a lot of my time lately."

"I suppose that gets priority."

"Right now, it does. Next year, I might try to go professional."

"Right. You're going to play for the NBA?"

She didn't like his dismissive tone.

"WPBL."

He laughed. "What's that?"

"It's the Women's Professional Basketball League. Or it will be soon."

Ken thought about this for a moment, then said, "How soon? Can we have sex tonight?"

Ginny laughed. "We'd better!"

"One …"

Ginny was doing pushups.

"Two ... Three ... Four ..."

"How about I sit on you to add weight?" Sheena said.

Ginny ignored her. "Seven ... eight ... nine ..."

Sheena walked by, and Ginny thought for one horrible second that she *was* going to sit on her.

"Ten ... eleven ..."

Sheena walked over her, which made her flinch and lose count.

"Uh ... eleven ... twelve ... Ow!"

Sheena stepped on her hand as she was coming back over her. She laughed.

"Sorry. Just one more thing, and I'll be out of your way."

"Thirteen ... fourteen ..."

Sheena walked over her again.

"Bye!"

And she was gone.

Ginny couldn't wait until she and Lila found an apartment together.

"Sixteen ... seventeen ..."

Someone knocked on the door.

"It's Ken!"

Ginny gave up on her pushups. As she let him in, he said, "I got into my honors economics seminar."

"You did? That's fantastic."

"Let's go celebrate. Where would you like to go?"

"Uh ... I got an exam tomorrow."

"Okay. Maybe we can go out tomorrow night. Or Thursday."

"Thursday's Thanksgiving. Aren't we going to your parents' house?"

"Oh yeah. Okay, Friday?"

"Great."

"Maybe I can find some music for us to go to."

"Music would be great."

Ken kissed her. "Good. It's a date."

"Two dates, if you count Thanksgiving."

"That's not a date. That's family."

Ken's sister lent him her car. Ginny and Ken could go anywhere in L.A. Ken decided anywhere would be Madame Wong's in Chinatown.

"Who are we seeing?"

"The Alley Cats."

"And they are?"

"Punk."

"Okay. And we're going to see them at a Chinese restaurant?"

"It's not a restaurant anymore."

They struggled to get in the door. Ginny didn't like being sardined into this club, although it was a little better once they were inside. It still looked like a Chinese restaurant, just without the tables.

The Alley Cats picked up their instruments and started playing something fast and melodic. The lead singer had marbles in his mouth or else a lot of loose teeth; Ginny couldn't make out one word. People were dancing, and soon that included Ginny and Ken. One of the songs was the Rolling Stones' "Under My Thumb," played at the speed of light. The whole set was like that, and, except for one more cover, Elvis' "Jailhouse Rock," they played mostly original songs. The show lasted about an hour. Ginny and Ken were jumping around the whole time. It felt great to be dancing in such a frenzy.

Ginny was wobbly as she exited the club and quickly ate some Ike and Mike's.

"Everything okay?"

"Yup. I'm great."

Saturday, Ken went out drinking with his friends, so Lila and Ginny headed to a movie. Lila suggested *The Deer Hunter*. Word was it was a must-see event.

The women hadn't known what to expect, and they were silent as they left the movie theater. They were silent as they walked several blocks past the nearest bus stop. They were still silent when they came upon the next stop and sat on the bench to wait.

It was Ginny who spoke first. "Do you think all that Russian roulette stuff was true?"

"I don't know."

"Asher never talked about it, but then, he was never captured."

"If what he saw was half as intense as this movie, he was a strong man."

"He was," she said.

"Did he ever talk about Vietnam?"

"He tried to avoid it, but I kept asking him. I'm sure he toned it down for me 'cause I was pretty young, but he gave me a good idea."

"Wow. Maybe I shouldn't have chosen this movie."

"It's okay. I feel a little closer to him now."

Ginny didn't have Asher's room anymore, but when she was alone in her dorm room, she'd turn the radio on and have a conversation with him. She'd have some time tomorrow.

The WPBL was showing a lot of promise. The league made it through the 1978–79 season without any noticeable hiccups. Ginny was now determined to try out for the league. She had time. She wouldn't need to try out until next year for the 1981–82 season. She would continue to volunteer as a coach over her summers. Considering women's leagues' track records, she would still need something to fall back on.

Just before Christmas '79, the Soviet Union invaded Afghanistan. This wouldn't have meant much to Ginny, and in fact, she didn't pay enough attention to the news to know about it. She heard about it from Ken, a highly political, left-leaning animal, who felt it was his duty to keep her informed. The United States announced it would be boycotting the 1980 Summer Olympics in Moscow, part of several other actions it took in response to the invasion. Many people, including Ken, felt the Olympics should never have been politicized. Moreover, it was devastating to U.S. athletes who had been training for this, some of whom had put off going pro to participate in the event.

Ann Meyers, who was currently playing for the WPBL's New Jersey Gems, made NBA history when she signed a contract with the NBA's Indiana Pacers, the first by any woman. While she participated in the tryouts, she wasn't chosen for the final squad. Nevertheless, this caused a stir among the current Lady Bruins. The NBA was interested in a female player? Had to be rumors. Just rumors.

Lila and Ginny found an apartment together just after Christmas. Ginny asked her mother to send her albums and her turntable. She couldn't ask her for Asher's collection; it would be too heavy to ship. Ken wanted Ginny to move in with him and his two roommates in a house they would be renting in Silver Lake, but Ginny didn't want to live with three men. Besides, it was a trek out to Silver Lake without a car. The apartment Ginny and Lila found was closer to the school and right on the bus line. Ginny was looking forward to spending her junior year with a new roommate in an off-campus pad. All that was needed now was for her to get into the WPBL.

Chapter 15

A Victim of the Insane

Ginny had to give up one of her camp jobs that summer to go to the WPBL tryouts. There were rumors that league pay was minimal, and checks were often late or even non-existent. Ginny went to the tryouts anyway. If the league recovered from its rocky start, this would be a great opportunity.

"How do you think you did?" Tilly said under her towel. The three friends had been in the ocean so long their skin was puckering.

"Pretty well, I think. I expected there to be more people there, but I think a lot of women are drafted without having to try out."

The August sun was brutal, even as late as four in the afternoon. The friends bought sodas from the food stand before heading to the car. Since Ginny was driving, Tilly and Renée could get high on the beach. They finished the joint in the parking lot, and then the giggling passengers climbed into Ginny's parents' car. Suzi Quatro was on the radio, and the three friends sang along. Ginny was going back to California in a few days, and as usual, she was torn. She missed hanging out with Tilly and Renée, but at the moment, everyone's other lives were more pressing.

Ginny took it easy scholastically during her senior year. She only needed three classes each term to have all the credits she needed to graduate. She could spend all the time she wanted bouncing and running, and she had time to volunteer at a local high school, coaching the girls' varsity team. She was a celebrity in their eyes. She could get used to that.

The Daily Bruin
October 10, 1980
    UCLA Bruins Guard Virginia Eastman Signs to San Francisco Pioneers
    Senior Virginia Eastman of the UCLA Bruins will join the San Francisco Pioneers for its 1981–82 WPBL season. The Pioneers made the playoffs in 1979 with an 18-18 record. That year, they defeated the defending champions, the Houston Angels, in the quarterfinal round before losing to the New York Stars in the semis.

Ken often spared Ginny his opinions and theories, knowing that politics made her anxious. She liked people to get along, and in her mind, politics only tore people apart. She agreed with a lot of what he told her, but she could only listen to so much before she started to hyperventilate.

At Ken's insistence, Ginny voted on November 4, 1980, her first presidential election. She voted for Jimmy Carter. While she was upset that he lost, Ken was acting like it was the end of the world as they knew it. She wanted to be supportive, but she found it fascinating to watch the country have this one-day revolution, a peaceful transition of power, even though it meant the country was moving several steps to the right.

One thing that improved Ken's mood was the release of John Lennon's album, *Double Fantasy*, his first album after a five-year hiatus. Ginny and Ken played the album over and over, although they started skipping some of the Yoko songs. They felt a bit guilty doing this, but not enough to play the album through. Ginny thought she'd buy the album herself, but Ken dissuaded her.

"Then, when we're eventually living together, we'll have two copies. You're here all the time, anyway."

There was enough logic in that statement to keep Ginny from buying a copy. Part of her wanted to buy it for Asher, but for now, she didn't really need to.

Since Lila liked to do schoolwork in silence, it was dead quiet in Lila and Ginny's apartment that Monday night. Ginny would have preferred music, but she was okay without it. Both women were deep in concentration when the phone rang. They jumped about a foot. Ginny went to answer the phone.

"Ken. You sound upset. Is everything okay?"

"No. Can I come over?"

"Sure. What's going on?"

"John Lennon is dead."

"What?! How?"

Lila came out of her room when she heard Ginny raise her voice.

"Shot outside his apartment building by a crazed fan."

"I thought they had gun control in New York City."

"The guy was from Hawaii. Traveled to New York to hunt him down."

"Oh my God. Oh my God. Oh my God."

"I know."

"Sure, come over. Uh ... Bring *Double Fantasy*?"

She put down the phone.

"What's going on?" Lila said. The phone rang again.

"John Lennon was murdered in New York. Hold on a second. Hello?"

"Ginny?"

"Tilly? You must have heard."

"Yeah. I'm freaking out."

"Me, too. Ken is on his way over. This is horrible."

"I'm thinking of going up to the Dakota."

"Alone? What time is it there? Go with someone."

"Yeah, okay. I'm sure I can find somebody."

"Are you okay?"

"No. But I'll manage."

"Call me tomorrow."

"Okay. Yeah. Tomorrow."

When Ginny hung up, Lila said, "What's the big deal?"

Ginny looked at Lila as if snakes were growing out of her head. She suddenly didn't feel as close to her.

"I mean, it's sad and all," Lila said, "but I don't get the hysteria."

"He meant something to people," Ginny said when she could find her words.

Lila shrugged. "Okay. Well, I'm going back to my room."

Ginny wondered how Asher would've reacted to this news. He wasn't around to speak for himself, and despite the number of times she talked to him, she knew he wasn't really there. Right now, she felt kind of silly for ever pretending he had been.

She couldn't wait for Ken to get there. She needed a hug.

Dec. 9, 1980
Hi Ginny—

I'm writing this The Day After. My brain still can't wrap around what happened last night. It was so sad at the Dakota. Some people were carrying Beatles signs, but most people just had pictures of John, or quotes from him, stuff like that. One sign read, 'Dear God—Please take Bruce Springsteen and give us back John.' I think there are better people to trade in than Bruce, but I suppose one needs to offer someone of comparable value. I mean, offering Donny Osmond wouldn't cut it.

That being said, let me change the subject to something positive. There are some great clubs here. CBGB's is where everyone goes, but it's a pit and claustrophobic and smells and, well, you can imagine. Anyway, there are other places, like Hurrah's, the Mudd Club, or Club 57, where I've seen some bands new to me, like the Bush Tetras, the Contortions, and the Sick F*cks (What a name. I kid you not). There are also free concerts in Central Park during the summer, where we saw the Talking Heads, B52s, the Pretenders, Blondie, etc. etc. ... It's been great.

I just broke up with this guy Ned. I should have known from his name he'd be a loser! He was kind of bossy and no fun. He never wanted to go out, not even to dinner. He practically begged me to give him a chance, so I went out with him for a while, and then he cheated on me. She can have him. Too much work for so little return.

Ken sounds great. Fun. Likes music. Dances. Thinks you're awesome. Except for the whole business-major thing, but you don't want them to be perfect, right?

I'm so glad you got into the WPBL! I've never heard of the team you mentioned, but fingers and toes crossed that this lasts a while.

One more thing. This morning, I saw a piece of graffiti that read, 'John Lennon lives.' First, it was Paul is dead. Now it's Lennon lives. Typical Beatles fans, not dealing with reality.

Well, writing made me feel better, for now. We'll talk soon, probably before you get this.

Love,

Tilly

Chapter 16

La La, How That Life Goes On

Signed to the Pioneers, Ginny prepared to leave Los Angeles. She finished her senior year (cum laude, thank you very much), then started looking for apartments in San Francisco. Lila had potential roommates lined up. Everything was ready.

"Of course, I get on a professional team, and the league folds before I have one day of practice."

"There's no hope?" Lila said.

"Teams have been dropping out left and right, including the Pioneers. I think it'll take a miracle to save it. The New Jersey Gems are still hanging on, but I don't know who's left for them to play."

"But you got in," Lila said. "That's fantastic. It's not your fault the league vanished."

"Maybe there won't ever be a women's league. It's so frustrating."

"I bet something's going to come up."

"Hopefully before I get too old."

"Right."

"Ken will be happy. I've been kind of ignoring him."

"He has to get used to being a second fiddle. Athletes'

wives need to understand the sacrifices."

Ginny laughed. "He understands. He just doesn't like it."

Dr. Fisher presented Ginny with something that looked like an enormous calculator. It was about the size and weight of a brick.

"What is that?" Ginny said.

"A blood glucose meter," Dr. Fisher said.

"Why can't I just use my test strips?"

"You can, but the meter will read them for you. Much easier and much more accurate. And this screen lights up. What do you do now if you're in the dark?"

"I wait until there's enough light."

Ginny stuck the test strip into the meter, lanced her finger to get some blood, and in one minute, it beeped loudly and displayed the result: 117.

"That's really precise. Amazing. But does it have to beep like that?"

"I'm sure you can turn the sound off."

Ginny lifted it off the counter.

"It's enormous. And heavy."

"Well, it's up to you if you want one or not. The technology is there."

"Of course I want one. I wish I had one of these years ago."

Ginny wasn't going to carry that thing around with her everywhere. Why did it have to weigh 4,000 pounds? It was also expensive, close to $450. Her father said he would help her. The first thing she would do would be to figure out how to turn off the irritating beeping.

Because of the failure of the WPBL, Ginny was back to her original life plan: coaching. She didn't have to stay in California, but she preferred a job in a major city near one of the coasts. Los Angeles, New York, Boston, they would all do. What she was finding were openings in schools in Des Moines, Milwaukee, and Pittsburgh. She hoped she wouldn't have to resort to that.

She thought her graduating *cum laude* would help with the job market. It wasn't as good as clearing five foot ten, but it wasn't bad. Also, her almost playing for the San Francisco Pioneers should certainly add some weight to her resume.

The phone rang.

"Hi. What are you doing?" Ken said.

"Looking for a job."

"Cool. Might you move with me to Minnesota?"

She laughed. "Minnesota!? Uh, no."

"You sure? I was just offered a job in Minneapolis."

Ken was being serious? He had an office job in L.A. He was a manager of ... something. Ginny didn't understand what it was he did, exactly, but he could manage his boring stuff anywhere, couldn't he?

"I love you, Ken, but not enough to move to Minnesota."

"You'll be missing out. There are a lot of lakes and waterfalls there."

Ginny laughed. "As intriguing as that sounds ..."

"How about we get married?"

"Ken, we can't even agree on what state we want to live in."

"A minor issue. I guess that's a no, then?"

"It's a 'not right now.' Let's figure out where we're going to be. Minnesota. Sheesh."

"Can I come over this weekend?"

"Sure."

"You sound less than enthusiastic. Is everything alright?"

"Yeah. It's not you. I've been feeling down since I've stopped playing so intensely. I need to go to the gym and do more bouncing and running."

"You're not getting that rush of endorphins you're used

to. And you haven't been having as much sex, either. Er ... have you?"

"Of course not. I'd tell you if I suddenly fell under someone else."

"Well, that's the least you could do."

It was with great anticipation that Ginny bought her first soda made with aspartame. It had to be better than saccharin, or why would they bother? These days, they were saying saccharin also caused cancer and that maybe it was the combination with the saccharin all along, not the cyclamates themselves.

She popped the can, took a sip ... and it tasted a lot better. However, it wasn't thirst-quenching. It had this strange, thick quality that kept it from feeling like liquid. Did they expect people to drink this stuff? Saccharin-based soda had that awful aftertaste, but at least it was hydrating.

"How's the aspartame?" Ken had gotten out of the shower in time to see the soda unveiling.

"Kind of weird, actually. Tastes good, but it has a slimy texture."

"I didn't think soda was supposed to have texture."

"It isn't."

Ginny took one more sip from her soda, then got up and poured it down the sink. Then, she took out her meter to check her numbers.

"Wow. You weren't kidding when you said the meter was 'a little large.'"

"Not very practical, but a lot more accurate. See? 97. I would have estimated 120."

"I'll get dressed, and we'll go to lunch."

"Afterwards, I'm going to the gym. I need to cheer up. I haven't heard from any of my job applications."

"You will." He kissed her. "I have some paperwork I can do while you're out. You do what you need to do."

Ginny started to feel better. She wasn't playing as much as when she was on the team, but what she was doing was great for her mental state. And she finally got some answers to her applications. She went to pick up the phone to call Ken, but it rang first.

"Ken. I was just going to call you."

"We need to talk."

Ginny almost laughed, hearing that from Ken. It was so clichéd.

"We do?"

There was an ominous pause on the phoneline. She carried the phone to the couch so she could sit and wait for him to speak.

"Here's the thing. I took the job in Minnesota."

Now, it was Ginny's turn to pause.

"Ginny?"

"And I've just been offered an assistant coaching job for the women's team at Queens College. In New York."

Ginny played with the curly phone cord, wrapping it around her fingers, and waited for Ken to respond.

"Come to Minneapolis, Ginny. They offered me a great salary. And I can put you on my insurance."

Ginny slid off the couch to the floor.

"C'mon, Ken. What would I do in Minnesota? You can't tell me you can't find the same kind of offer in New York. I'm lucky to have landed this. Anywhere."

This conversation had more pauses than a Pinter play.

"Ken?"

"I guess we have a problem here."

"Guess so." Another pause. "When do you leave?"

"Couple weeks."

Ginny grabbed her heart melodramatically and fell over. From the floor, she said, "You're blowing my mind here. First, why didn't you tell me you wanted to take the job? And second, what the hell, Ken?"

"I know. I know. Look, it's not like our relationship is going anywhere. I get the feeling you'd be okay keeping it like it is forever."

Astute of him.

"Anything else I should know about?" Ginny wanted this conversation to end. Now.

"No, I think that's it."

"Okay."

"We'll talk before I leave."

Ginny hung up and stayed on the floor to recover. She hadn't realized how much she needed Ken until now. She thought he was the one thing that wouldn't change, that he'd always be around in some way. But Minnesota? That would be a long commute.

"Are you okay?" Lila had entered the room. "Why are you on the floor?"

"Ken just broke up with me."

"I thought he wanted to marry you."

"He wants us to move to Minnesota."

"Minneapolis is nice. Is it Minneapolis?"

"It doesn't matter. I don't want to live there. I just got a job offer in New York City."

"Really? That's great. Punk Boy doesn't want to move to New York?"

"Apparently not."

"Uh ... do you want me to help you up?"

"No, I'm comfortable here. I'll get up in a while."

"Okay. Well, I'm heading to work. I'll see you later?"

"I'll be here."

It took several hours for this reality to sink in, but then Ginny started to panic. What was she going to do without Ken? She needed to call Tilly. It was almost eleven p.m. in New York, but this was Tilly, right? Wouldn't she be up?

"Hello?" Tilly sounded alert.

"It's Ginny. Did I wake you up?"

"Nah. I'm watching TV, some idiotic crime show. What's going on?"

"Ken and I broke up."

"No!"

"Our geographic issues couldn't be resolved. Neither of us would budge."

"Where did he want you to move to again? Minnesota? What is he thinking?"

"And I just got a job offer in New York. Queens College."

"That's great!"

"Yes, except the idea of him moving there with me fell like the proverbial lead balloon."

"You're not changing your mind, are you?"

"And follow him to Minnesota? Noooooooooo. Queens wanted a female coach as part of their roster, someone with playing experience. I'm not going to find anything so perfect. In fact, I doubt I'd find anything else right now. Ken's been asking me to marry him for the last couple years or so. He really wanted me to settle down with him. But now, only in Minneapolis."

"How are you feeling about this?"

"Weird. I don't want to follow him, but I don't want to lose him, either. Ha. He's supposed to be on call for me whenever I want to see him. I want to have my cake and eat it, too. Excuse the expression."

Tilly laughed. Ginny continued.

"But here's the thing. I've only ever had sex with Dash and Ken."

"So?"

"And I haven't met anybody of potential relationship material for a long time."

"So?"

"So, what if I never have sex again?"

"So?"

Ginny burst out laughing. "You have a way of putting things in the proper perspective, Till."

Chapter 17

Basketball Jones

A new league, the Women's American Basketball Association, was recruiting for their 1984-85 season. Ginny had been an assistant coach in Queens for the past couple of years, but while she tried to keep in shape, she had reservations about playing full-time again.

"You're not going to try out?" Tilly had always been very encouraging about Ginny's career. Sometimes, like now, it was annoying.

"I'm good where I am. I like Queens. I can come into Manhattan to see you whenever I want. Of course, you *could* come to Queens once in a while."

Tilly and Ginny were sitting in Tilly's main room, having coffee. The apartment was in a Manhattan neighborhood called Chelsea, not far from Tilly's alma mater. After graduating, she had landed a job as a Marketing Assistant at an uptown advertising firm. She had been crawling up the ranks ever since. The apartment was a nice size, especially, according to Tilly, by Manhattan standards. On her first day there, she had called Ginny from the empty space.

"I'm so excited. My first New York apartment!"

"You sound like you're in a wind tunnel."

"I know. The furniture is on its way. There's nothing here,

no furniture, no rugs—"

Then she shrieked.

"Aaaaah! There's a huge water bug sauntering across my kitchen floor!"

"Oh, yuck!"

"You can't believe how big this thing is. It's like a Kafka roach. It's human size. I may have to move out."

"Oh, God."

"Wait a minute. I have an idea."

Ginny heard a loud thud.

"There."

"What did you do?"

"Stunned him with the Manhattan phonebook. Now I'm standing on it. He's done for."

"How big is this phonebook?"

"Like a Sears catalog."

There hadn't been any Kafka sightings since, and Tilly didn't have to move out. These days, she had framed posters on the walls and sleek, modern furniture. The place looked like she had hired a decorator. (Ginny asked; she hadn't.)

"I haven't heard from Renée in a while. How is she? Last I heard, she was at Cornell getting her veterinary degree."

"Oh, she's still there," Tilly said. "She graduates this year, but now she's thinking of specializing."

"That woman loves school."

"She really does. Want more coffee?"

"Uh, no, but I should eat soon."

"Oh, right. Want me to call for a pizza?"

"Perfect."

"I'm going to get mine without cheese. How about you?"

"Why on God's blue-and-green earth would you get a pizza without cheese?"

"I'm on a low-fat diet," Tilly said. "It's supposed to help you lose weight."

"Geez, Tilly. You look great. Why are you going on these weird fad diets?"

"It's not a weird fad diet. A lot of people are doing it."

Ginny was going to point out that "a lot of people are doing it" was kind of the definition of a fad, but decided to drop it.

"If you can stand pizza with no cheese, who am I to argue? But cheese on mine, please."

While Tilly picked up the phone to order, Ginny took out her meter. Meters had shrunk some since the first one she had. They were now about twice the size of a pack of cigarettes. The reading was 78, but if the pizza came soon, she'd be fine.

Ginny always felt a tug at her heartstrings whenever she prepped her students for games. Even though she told herself she felt otherwise, it was hard not to miss playing.

Ginny signed up to use one of the school's courts to keep in shape. It reminded her of Rhode Island, playing in the driveway, either practicing alone or with Asher. Asher would be proud of her. She had gone further than either one of them could have expected; she had made it onto a professional team. The fact she never got to play as a pro was secondary. When she was growing up, there were no pro teams to aspire to. She had exceeded her dreams. Then why did she often feel so lost and defeated?

She always started by bouncing and running, running and bouncing, all around the court. She did a layup, then circled the court again. She tried a jump shot, but the ball hit the rim and bounced over her head to the other end of the court.

"Ooh, bad break," a man said.

One of the men's coaches, Frank Duffy, was chasing her rebound.

"Frank. What are you doing here?"

He started singing, in falsetto, "'*Basketball jones, I've got a basketball jones ...*'"

She laughed. "What the heck is that?"

"You've never heard 'Basketball Jones' by Cheech and Chong?"

She laughed. "No, I have not."

"I drive my wife crazy singing that around the house."

"I'm sure she appreciates that."

He threw her the ball and said, "You can really play."

"Yes. When I'm alone, I get almost every rebound."

"C'mon. Half-court. First one to get to 21 pays for coffee," he said.

Ginny could feel the adrenaline kicking in. She was back in Rhode Island, playing with Asher, only now she needed no assistance getting the ball through the hoop.

Students gathered and stood by the entrance to watch. Some were rooting for Frank, but most were rooting for Ginny. Who knew? Ginny was still the master of bounce and run.

Except for height, they were evenly matched. Frank would score, and then Ginny would score. But it was the interplay between shots that was downright balletic. Soon, it was 20 to 19. Frank shot over Ginny's head to make the last goal but missed. Ginny got the rebound and did a layup to score. The small crowd of onlookers went wild.

Ginny hadn't smiled like that in a long time. She and Frank shared a high five, and Ginny said, "Thanks. I needed that."

April 26, 1984

Ginny—

Sorry I haven't been in touch much, but now it's official: I'm a veterinarian! I passed my NAVLE (North American Veterinary Licensing Examination) in March, and I've landed a residency in Philly. I'll be close to you and Tilly. We've GOT to get together soon.

In other news, I'm seeing someone. His name is Barry, and he works in the same clinic I do. I think you'll like him. He's smart and funny, and not at all arrogant, I don't think, but I may be biased. You and Tilly will have to meet him and tell me what you think!

I'll call Tilly, and we'll find a day to get together. New York City is only a train ride away.

See you soon. Can't wait.

Renée

The three friends met at Tilly's centrally located apartment. Neither Ginny nor Renée had smoked pot in a long time, but Tilly was intent on at least one of them joining her.

"You have no more exams. You don't have to run around like Ginny does. And you already have a job. Do they do random drug testing at the clinic?"

"No. It's not in the employee handbook, anyway."

Ginny laughed. "You actually read your employee handbook?"

"What? Aren't I supposed to?"

"Don't mind Ginny," Tilly said. "She just feels left out because she doesn't want to smoke with us. Have just one, maybe two hits."

This turned into five or six, and Tilly and Renée became quite stoned.

"Funny. I remember giggling a lot on pot. I'm feeling decidedly ungiggly," Renée said.

"I know. This pot is a stoned high. I couldn't get the giggly kind."

"I like it, though," Renée said. She started staring at her hand. "Ever been to a palm reader?"

"No. There's one in my building," Ginny said.

"There's one down the street. We should go."

"Nah, I don't feel like moving."

The friends agreed that going down the street would be too much effort.

"Tell us about Barry," Tilly said.

A dopey smile appeared on Renée's face.

"He's from Philly. He's Jewish, which is freaking out my parents. I'm not sure if that's because he's white or because he's not Christian, or both. He's smart and cute, like teddy-bear cute. Not too tall, but taller than me."

Tilly laughed and said, "She's in love, L-U-V!"

Renée was flustered, but then she laughed. "I do sound like that Shangri-Las song, don't I?"

It wasn't giggly pot, but the women were laughing.

Four of Ginny's players called the next morning to say they wouldn't be at practice. This always happened during final exams. Ginny reworked what she had planned for the day, then she took a shower and started to get dressed.

"Crap. My insulin."

Although needles had greatly shrunk in the past several years, Ginny took her shot right through her thick, long-sleeve shirt. Then she gulped down some breakfast. She quickly grabbed her jacket and her bag, then stopped.

She felt her blood sugar dropping. Fast. Her eyes couldn't focus. She was in trouble. She took a handful of Ike and Mike's, sat down, and fumbled around in her bag to get her meter. The reading just before she took insulin was 115. Now it was 43. She took her emergency juice from her bag and drank it down. She waited. She still felt low. She took another reading. 47. Good, it was going up. She stood up to go, but she was still shaking, so she tested again. Meter reading: 29. It was like she had taken 18 units of regular insulin instead of Lente, but she knew she hadn't done that. The regular insulin was on the bottom shelf in the refrigerator, not with the other insulin.

She got another bottle of juice, then sat in front of the meter and kept testing. It went up to 39. Then down to 23. More juice. 47. Then 32. This continued for a while until the numbers finally started to rise and stayed there.

She called the school to tell them she was running late, then went to her refrigerator and took out the vials of Lente and Ultra Lente. The Lente insulin looked like it wasn't mixed. She did mix it, didn't she? She turned it upside down and back a couple of times and saw that the zinc particulate was still collected at the bottom of the vial. Why was it so hard to mix? And why hadn't she noticed?

This was a dangerous rookie error. She had reacted quickly, but now it would screw her up all day since her entire day's dosage of Lente had just hit her all at once. She'd have to carry a vial of regular insulin (her four-unit syringe of emergency insulin wouldn't cut it) and a few syringes. She called her doctor, who told her how much to take and when. Having a meter would be crucial today.

It took a couple of days for Ginny to get back on track, and then she felt sad and lonely. She forced herself to go to the gym. As she was practicing hook shots and her overhand throws, the court was invaded by Frank and two of his friends: Joe, whom she knew from the department, and Orin, whom she'd seen around but hadn't yet met.

"Can we join you?" Frank said.

If it was just Frank, she'd have said yes, but the other two … just not today. Frank read her face.

"Okay. Maybe another time," he said.

"No, it's okay."

"Okay. Joe and I will team up, and we'll play you and Orin."

Orin was under six foot. Pairing him with Ginny was ridiculous.

"Only if you tall people throw beyond the three-point line," Ginny said.

"What, are you scared of a little height?" Frank said.

"In basketball, yes."

"C'mon, Ginny. We can still beat them," Orin said.

Soon, Frank and Joe were winning, 12 to 4. After a while, Ginny realized Orin wasn't passing her the ball. What kind of team playing was that? Joe missed his shot, and again, Orin got the rebound and kept the ball, even though Ginny was alone right near the basket. He missed his shot, and the ball went foul.

Ginny's sadness had turned into anger. It was energizing.

"Time!" Ginny yelled. "Orin ..."

"What?"

"Pass me the goddamn ball."

"What?"

"We're supposed to be a team here. You're taking all the rebounds. Pass me the ball."

He didn't answer. Ginny was getting the feeling their handicap wasn't just their lack of height. By giving Ginny Orin as a teammate, these guys were bullying her out of her court time. Did they know Orin was an ass? Why had they brought him?

Frank's team had the ball. Joe missed an easy shot, and Orin got the rebound. Frank and Joe double-teamed him.

"Pass it to me!"

Orin started dribbling right to Frank, who immediately stole the ball. His resulting layup was beautiful.

"Fine," Ginny said under her breath.

Ginny retrieved the ball. This was where short could be an advantage, since she could run faster and dart around her opponents. Frank cornered her anyway, but Ginny passed by bouncing it between Frank's legs, and Orin shot and scored.

"Nice move," Frank said.

The next rebound went to Orin, and he was again blocked by Frank and Joe. Ginny went around behind him and stole the ball.

"Hey!"

She dribbled it up to the basket before her opponents realized what happened and did a layup.

"Hey, Orin," Frank said.

"Yeah?"

"I think you should pass her the goddamn ball."

After the game, which Ginny and Orin lost, 21–14, Ginny sat on the sidelines and guzzled some water. Playing was nice, but she would never get on a team with Orin again. Anger was killing her endorphins.

"Ginny."

She looked up.

"Orin."

"Wanna grab some dinner tonight?"

He was asking her out? He'd probably make her pay for dinner, selfish creep.

"I don't think so."

"What? Why?"

"Because you infuriate me."

His empty-headed smile irritated Ginny, but he wasn't smart enough to remove it from his face.

"Oh, c'mon. It was just a game. C'mon, come out to dinner with me."

As attractive as his whining was, Ginny got up from the bench.

"Okay, guys," Ginny said. "I still have fifteen minutes here. I want the rest of the time for myself."

Joe and Orin grumbled something that sounded like "bitch," but Frank said, "She's right. We've taken enough of her time. Let's go."

"What's she practicing for, anyway?" Orin said as they were heading for the door. This was a question Ginny asked herself all the time. But then, what were *they* practicing for?

Her decision to skip tryouts for the WABA turned out to be a good one. The WABA's first and only season lasted two months. They were gone by December. Ginny was relieved she passed on that opportunity.

Ginny talked to a few of her ex-teammates at UCLA. It seemed a lot of them were playing in Europe. The pay was decent, even good, and there was a demand for players. Ginny didn't want to play in Europe. Going overseas meant she'd have to change the timing of her insulin and figure out meal issues all over again, and then change back when she returned to the States. Besides, playing in Europe seemed like surrendering. Asher would have never wanted her to surrender.

The Queens College Knights had been playing well so far this year. True, it was only January. Although they had never won a championship, over the years a few alumni had made it onto the national team and into the WPBL. Queens wasn't UCLA or Tennessee, but at least it wasn't, say, Minnesota. Ginny wondered how stupid Ken was for a moment, then moved on.

Ginny was having one of her weepy-for-no-reason days, a mood that, back in the day, would have her slashing herself. She decided to go to the gym and try to bounce and run until it subsided. She got 20 minutes of dribbling and shooting in before Frank, Joe, and Orin invaded the court. Orin still annoyed her. Today she insisted on being teamed with Frank, and they won 21–18.

A sweaty Orin approached her after the game.

"So. Wanna have lunch?"

"Orin ... No. Still no. Always no."

"Ouch."

As she headed out the door, Frank caught up with her.

"How about me?"

"How about you what?"

"How about you have lunch with me? Without Orin."

She laughed. "Sure. Without Orin."

They went to a diner near the school, one of those curios with the metal paneling on the outside and the fabulous fifties décor inside. The booths even had mini jukeboxes hanging at the end of the tables. Ginny ordered a Greek salad, and Frank ordered a burger. This reminded Ginny of Asher. He used to love his beef.

"I was wondering ..." Frank said. "Would you maybe want to go to dinner with me this weekend?"

"Like, a date?"

"Exactly like a date."

"I thought you were married."

"Separated, almost eight months."

"Oh. You never mentioned ..."

"It was supposed to be temporary, but somehow things have gotten more permanent."

"Only if you warn me if you're going to reconcile."

"Reconciling is not likely, but I promise."

"Too much 'Basketball Jones'?"

"Oh, I'm sure I found a lot of other ways to annoy her."

Maybe Ginny would be having sex again in her lifetime.

Frank's apartment was smaller than Ginny's, but it was closer to the restaurant. It was now morning, and Ginny and Frank were huddled under the comforter, trying to keep warm; Frank's apartment suffered from inconsistent heating.

"Mmmm. I don't want to move," Ginny said.

"There's no reason you have to, is there?"

"Not at the moment. Soon, I'll need to take my insulin and eat something, but I'm okay for now."

"Your insulin? Really?"

"Yes. Really."

"I didn't know."

"Well, I don't have 'Diabetic' tattooed on my forehead."

The radiator started clanking and steaming. It seemed an outside temperature of 32 degrees was the magic number for this landlord.

"Ha! Heat!"

"It's a sign," Ginny said.

"Yes. A good one."

Chapter 18

Hear Me Roar

There was yet another attempt at a women's pro league in 1986, the National Women's Basketball Association (NWBA). They held a draft, franchises held tryouts, and although they lasted five whole months, somehow, no games were ever played. Ginny hadn't even heard about them until after they disbanded.

Frank arrived at the lady coaches' offices, and when he saw that Ginny was alone, he closed the door.

"Frank. What's going on?"

"There are openings for coaches at SUNY Flushing. They're having a whole reorg of the department."

Ginny had passed by their impressive campus many times. It wasn't far from Queens College.

"Flushing is Division One, right?"

He nodded. "I just interviewed there. They asked me if I knew anyone who'd be interested in coaching the women."

Frank took a business card out of his pocket.

"I told them you'd call."

"You know, men can also coach women. And vice versa."

He held up the card. "You want to call or not?"

"Yes. Thank you."

Frank smiled. "The least I can do for introducing you to Orin."

Renée and Barry were getting married, and Frank agreed to go to the wedding with Ginny. This meant he had to buy a proper suit, as anything he already had was old and, as he put it, "tainted." Ginny was part of the wedding party and already had her dress, which was not too scary a prospect. It turned out Renée had great taste.

Frank and Ginny went to the Macy's in Queens Plaza. No point in going all the way to the Mother Ship in the City. The Queens Macy's was sprawling, built in the '60s to be convenient for cars. It took a while to find Men's Clothes and even longer to find the Big and Tall department.

"I suppose I should buy black."

"I think you could also get away with navy or dark gray. Just not lavender or something crazy."

"Lavender?" He laughed.

"Here you go ..."

It was an electric-blue jacket with wide lapels and shiny black pants.

"Good lord, no."

"Just in case you wanted to be on MTV."

The March wedding took place in Philly. Reneé looked stunning, as brides do, and her four bridesmaids (Tilly, Ginny, and two cousins) looked elegant in their sleek, pine-green dresses. Tilly put those new Fujifilm Disposable Cameras on every table so people could take candids.

Renée had chosen the music, all '60s and '80s, and there were few songs that gave people a chance to sit down. Barry was dancing with everyone: men, women, kids, the waitstaff, everyone.

"Ginny ..." Tilly approached her on the dance floor. "Come

to the ladies' room with me." She had to shout this in her ear.

"But this is 'Heart of Glass.'"

"Sorry. Come. Now."

When they entered the ladies' room, Tilly checked under the stalls to make sure they were alone.

"What's going on?"

"Barry's a pig."

"What?!"

"He made a pass at me."

"Oh, c'mon. He's just having fun."

Tilly shook her head.

"No?"

"He grabbed my butt, pulled me close to him and said, 'Are you really a redhead?' And he planted one on me."

Someone entered the ladies' room, and the two friends fell silent. They waited for the older woman to finish, waited a little longer while she fanatically washed her hands until they puckered, and then, after adjusting her dress and hair, she left.

"Okay," Ginny said. "How drunk is Barry?"

"Quite."

Ginny sighed. "Well, maybe we don't tell Renée about this. Maybe it was just a dumb mistake."

"It was dumb, alright."

"Hopefully, no one was taking pictures at the time."

"Oh, God. Hopefully not. Whose idea were those cameras, anyway?"

They went back out to the dance floor, where Barry was visibly drooling on a young woman in a low-cut dress. Every few beats, he'd dip his face into her breasts and shake his head wildly.

"Told ya. He's a pig."

Ginny scanned the crowd. Renée was on the other side of the room, collecting envelopes and hugging guests.

"Maybe he just has a problem with alcohol," Ginny said.

"He's about to have a problem with me."

"I bet he won't even remember tomorrow how he behaved tonight."

"I can't yell at him?"

"No. But don't dance with him anymore, either."

To celebrate Frank's divorce papers being signed, Ginny and Frank started looking for an apartment together. They decided to stay in Queens, close to the school. It was far more affordable than Manhattan.

"I've been making progress with the list of apartments," Frank said. "Maybe you can look it over before I start making phone calls tomorrow."

They did find an apartment a little closer to Flushing U but a little farther from the subway. Neither had a lot of possessions. Frank was coming from a studio, and Ginny from an apartment the landlord had made into a one-bedroom by putting up a wall. Having more space trumped the slightly longer walk to transportation.

"We could each have a room and still have a sitting room." Ginny was unpacking her clothes and didn't see Frank frown.

"I thought we'd share one bedroom and have a weight room in the other."

"That would be great!"

"Okay. You don't need your own room?"

"No. I was just saying. This place is huge."

"Oh. Okay. Yeah, we lucked out. I think I was the first to see it."

"And there's room for Asher's albums."

Frank raised his eyebrows. "How much room do you need?"

"Like, a lot. Don't worry. We can stack the boxes."

North Greenwich High School Class of '77's 10-year reunion was set for the second Saturday in June 1987. Tilly rented a Jeep Grand Wagoneer and brought everyone to Rhode Island for the event. The big moment for Ginny, however, was after the reunion: rescuing Asher's records. The boxes were still in the garage where they had been stacked 10 years earlier.

"Which ones are the albums?"

"Not sure," Ginny said. "They never marked them. The couple that are already open are books and clothes."

"I bet these are them," Frank said. He dragged a box over and opened it.

"Bingo."

Ginny looked at the box. "Yes. But that's not all of them."

"Oh."

"I can't believe Freddie brought his partner to the reunion," Renée said. "That was so great! People were muttering under their breaths. I loved it."

"Old Bobby was giving them the stink eye," Tilly said.

"Which one was Bobby?" Barry said.

"The round, balding guy with the skinny wife."

"Tilly!" Renée said, but she was laughing.

"How else would you describe them?"

"Ginny. Did you ask Freddie ... you know ... about his health?"

"I did, although that was probably rude of me. He said he and Matt are both negative. For now, I guess. I don't quite understand it that well, honestly. Anyway, Freddie said they're renting a house in Maui. He says we're welcome to come out whenever we'd like."

"Okay. Let's go tomorrow," Tilly said.

It took some time, but all five boxes of albums were identified. The stereo was in its own box; Ginny wanted that, too. She also took her grandfather's lighter and a few T-shirts to sleep in, but she didn't know what to do with anything else.

"Now what?"

"I'll ask my dad to help you guys get the boxes into the car."

"There's nothing heavier than vinyl, you know," Frank said.

"Why do you think I've left them here all these years?"

"Great. And we're in a three-floor walk-up."

Ginny's parents must have been paying the yearly American Diabetes Association membership fee and keeping her mailing address up-to-date, because she was still receiving the latest issues of *Diabetes Forecast*. She would dutifully flip through the magazines, but the issue for September 1987 made her do a double take.

Rocker Bret Michaels was on the cover, long-haired, shirtless, and tattooed. Bret talked about tattoos in the article (a no-no for diabetics because of infections) and cautioned against getting them. He talked about surviving on the road. He talked about surviving, period. It was a great interview.

The reader reaction to this issue was predictable. Ginny could hear the *tsk-tsk*ing all the way from Queens. How dare they put someone like that on the cover? How dare he advocate tattoos and probably drugs as well? How dare they choose a photo of him without his shirt on? How dare Bret Michaels be diabetic? Someone wrote in to say she burned the issue on her stovetop. Ginny guessed the woman thought the issue was possessed or something. At the very least, unclean.

Ginny wrote in:

November 9, 1987
To whom it may concern:
Thank you for putting Bret Michaels on your cover. That was very brave of you. I know you received a lot of backlash for it, but I thought it was great. I usually can't relate to anyone in your magazine. This time, I could.
Sincerely,
Ginny Eastman.

Chapter 19
You Don't Know Me

In 1991, there was yet another attempt to create a women's pro basketball league, the Liberty Basketball Association. Rumor had it they were going to put players in skin-tight unitards, like they were gymnasts or something, shorten the courts, reduce the size of the ball by an inch, and lower the baskets to nine foot two. They reasoned this would make women's games more exciting. Ginny was not interested in supporting these indignities. When the NBA put its male players in Speedos, maybe she'd consider working for a league like that. Probably not even then.

There was a televised exhibition game, but the league folded shortly afterward. Ginny felt that was about how long an enterprise like that should have lasted.

Frank and Ginny had delegated Asher's albums and stereo to a corner of the sitting room, away from the windows and the heater, closer to the bedrooms. Frank had bought a new cartridge for the turntable when he first set it up and put the speakers in opposite corners of the room. Ginny had been systematically playing the records in alphabetical order so she didn't miss anything. It was taking her years to get through the collection. She was currently on Steppenwolf's *The Second.*

Frank came home during "Magic Carpet Ride" and stood a moment to listen.

"Nice tune," he said. "I have news."

She turned down the music.

"Flushing hired a new head coach for the men's team."

"Was it you?" Ginny said. "It should be you."

"Not me. They hired some guy who was coaching for Tampa. Think his name's Dashiell something."

"Dash Hollander?"

"Yeah. That's it. Know him?"

"He's a misogynist, hound-dog creep. At least he was in college."

"I guess that wasn't on his resume."

"He was a big deal. Then he just sort of disappeared. I'm surprised he never went pro."

"All I know is, he was head coach at Tampa. Now he's coming to Queens."

"Great."

"Problem?"

"He was just obnoxious. Maybe he's mellowed. Anyway, you should have gotten that job."

"You're only saying that because you live with me."

"No, I'd say it regardless."

Flushing's coaches mingled in the main hall of the Athletic Center. Exactly Dash's style to leave his minions waiting. After 15 minutes, the door opened, and someone Ginny didn't recognize entered. The only thing about him that resembled Dash was his height. He had put on weight, and his fabulous, silky-blond hair was darkish and graying. Moreover, this man had a pronounced limp, which thwarted his signature arrogant strut.

People were approaching him with handshakes and smiles. Ginny waited her turn. Dash was almost unrecognizable. Was she as well?

"Ginny! I heard you were coaching here, Short Stuff. It's so great to see you."

"Nice to see you, too, Dash." She wanted to ask about the limp but didn't want to be rude. Wait, this was Dash. She could be rude. "What did you do to your leg?"

"Oh, this? Broke my ankle skiing in the February of my junior year. Blew my chances for the NBA. I probably could have tried out later, but I was too bummed to go to physical therapy. Kind of felt defeated, you know? Like it was too much of a haul, and I figured I probably would never fully recover."

What was this she was feeling for Dash? Pity? Sympathy? Empathy? This would never do.

"That sucks, Dash. I was wondering why I never saw you playing pro. Anyway, welcome to Queens. I'm sure we'll be running into each other."

She turned to go, and Dash slapped her butt.

"Yeah. You still got it," he said.

And you don't, she thought, but she let her scowl be her only reaction.

On a cold, windy afternoon in the city, Tilly was making tomato soup and grilled cheese for Ginny and Renée. She brought a tray with three bowls of soup to the table and returned to the stove to finish grilling the sandwiches. Ginny and Renée stared at their too-hot-to-eat soups. Ginny stirred hers to cool it down, but the steam was unrelenting.

"I met someone," Tilly said.

"Someone, like, a relationship, or someone like a fling?"

"I think he's got relationship potential. His name's Duncan. He's a designer at the firm."

"That's great, Till. Hope this goes better than Fritz."

"God, yes. So far, Duncan's cool. Let's hope he stays that way."

Tilly brought the sandwiches to the table and sat down. "How's it going with you two? Renée, how's Barry?"

Renée tried her soup again. Still too hot.

"I think he's having an affair," she said into her soup.

This elicited stares from her friends.

"What?"

"He's been making excuses about staying out late. We've stopped talking. We've stopped having breakfast together. He isn't as eager to have sex with me. I don't know how to approach him. I mean, it could be my imagination."

"I doubt that," Tilly said.

"I don't know. I go back and forth. Some days we're fine, but more days we're not."

"I think you need to say *something*," Ginny said. "Even if it's just, 'Hey, is everything alright?'"

"I suppose. But he's always accusing me of not trusting him."

"The thing is," Ginny said, "if you don't say anything, things can only get worse."

"Worse?"

"You know ... no one talks about the proverbial elephant in the room."

Renée didn't look convinced, but she nodded. She carefully took a sip of soup.

"This is great, Tilly. Thanks."

"*Mi almuerzo es su almuerzo.* I don't know if I said that right. I think it means, 'My lunch is your lunch.'"

Ginny and Renée laughed.

"I guess I'll talk to Barry," Renée said. "It's just that he gets so touchy."

"Maybe that's because he has something to hide," Tilly said.

Renée sighed. "Maybe he does."

Ginny entered the university's Athletic Center, eager to do some bouncing and running, but she stopped. She heard a basketball bouncing in one of the other courts. She slowly opened the door. Dash was shooting baskets. Ginny closed the door a little so he wouldn't see her, but not so much that she couldn't watch. He could dribble, although not quickly, and he could still shoot some impressive three-pointers. Layups were not happening, just a slow approach to the basket with no jump, and then he'd reach up and put the ball in. Ginny wondered how often Dash practiced. She tried not to let this break her heart. She backed away from the door and retreated to her practice court.

Ginny picked up the phone on the second ring.

"You'll be in town next weekend, right?" Tilly said.

"Yeah. Why?"

"We're going to Philly. Something's happening with Barry, but Renée didn't want to talk about it over the phone."

Ginny had never been to Philadelphia. She stood gaping in its 30th Street Station, a nine-storied open room with floor-to-ceiling windows and square inset lights in the ceiling grid. It was impressive.

"Don't gawk like a tourist," Tilly said. "Let's get a cab."

Renée and Barry lived in Old City in a former artist's dwelling that they had renovated to have proper rooms. Ginny and Tilly put their bags down in the foyer and stared at the beautiful furnishings and the perfectly even walls and floors.

"Are you two alright? You act like you've never seen an apartment before."

Renée seemed calm, too calm for a person with marital troubles.

"We haven't. Not like this."

"This is gorgeous, Renée."

"Thank you. Come sit in the living room. Leave your stuff in the foyer for now."

The living room had a huge stone fireplace, which was currently in use, a comfy couch, and matching chairs. The paintings on the walls were real, not prints, and there were museum-quality sculptures on the end tables. This was luxury compared to how Tilly and Ginny lived in New York. A foyer? A fireplace? Sculptures?

"I made sandwiches and iced tea. I'll be right back. Make yourselves comfortable."

Ginny and Tilly sat on the edge of the couch, careful not to knock anything over or set anything on fire. When Renée returned, she looked at her friends and laughed.

"Why are you two sitting like that? Relax. Take your shoes off. Wanna smoke a joint?"

The fire made the room warm and cozy. Why not smoke a joint? Even Ginny agreed.

"Careful, Ginny," Tilly said. "You haven't smoked in years."

"And?"

"You no longer have a tolerance."

"I couldn't find the giddy pot," Renée said as she lit the joint. "But I like this mellow high. It's good for talking."

"Do you want to tell us what's going on?" Tilly said.

Renée handed Tilly the joint. "When I first talked to Barry, he was defensive and angry. Accused me of trying to make trouble. Accused me of being paranoid. It got really ugly, but things got a little better after that."

"I suspect that's not the end of this story," Tilly said.

"Last week, he admitted it. He's been sleeping with the clinic's receptionist."

This was said so matter-of-factly Ginny and Tilly couldn't react right away.

"He said he's in love with stupid Casey now and wants a divorce." Renée said this with venom but then burst into tears.

"I can't imagine him finding someone better or more beautiful than you, Ren," Tilly said.

This made her cry harder, but she managed a "Thank you."

"He'll probably dump Casey in six weeks and come running back to you," Ginny said.

"I don't want him back. Stupid Barry."

"Very Stupid Barry," Tilly said.

"He's obviously not getting something he needs from me."

"This isn't about you, Renée. This is about him," Ginny said. The urge to tell her about the wedding and what a pig he had been even then was tempting, but she held her tongue.

"I don't know what I'm gonna do. I guess I need to get a lawyer."

A gloomy silence fell over the three friends. All eating and smoking stopped.

"Do you both own the apartment?" Tilly said.

"Yes. He said I could have it, but who knows what'll really happen?"

"Where is he now?" Ginny said.

"Packed a couple bags and moved out. I guess he's with Casey. Damn, I'll have to see both of them at the clinic on Monday."

"Call in sick."

"I may have to. Anyway, let's not talk about him anymore."

"How about we blow off some steam?" Tilly said. "Do you have a stereo in this place?"

"Yes. Barry's."

Renée went to a cabinet, opened the door, and revealed a high-end stereo system.

"We could give block parties with this thing," she said.

She put on an oldies station. Soon, the friends were dancing around Renée's living romm in their pot haze. For a moment, everyone felt better.

The next time Ginny was at the practice courts, she could again hear dribbling behind one of the doors. Dash was practicing again. Ginny watched for a few seconds and then loudly cleared her throat.

"Ginny!"

Dash walked to her. His limp made it hard for him to move too quickly, so Ginny met him halfway.

"It's good to see you," he said.

Dash bounced the ball a couple of times and then nervously tossed it from hand to hand. Ginny had a thought.

"How about a short scrimmage?" Ginny said.

"You want to play a lame, lumpy old man?"

Ginny laughed. "As long as the lame, lumpy old man doesn't beat me."

To take some pity on him, Ginny avoided darting in and out too much until she realized Dash was killing her with his three-pointers. Then, it was all-out war. Ginny took advantage of her layups, so it was Ginny's layup, two points, Dash's long shot, three points. It turned out the three-pointers had the upper hand, and Dash won 21–18.

"That was great. Thanks, Ginny."

"I'll want a rematch."

"I look forward to it."

As Ginny walked out of the building, she felt a sudden wave of sadness. Dash would certainly not want her pity, but she couldn't turn off feeling bad for him. She shook off most of it by the time she arrived home, but the feeling lingered all night.

Chapter 20
Going Pro

In April 1996, the NBA founded the WNBA, or one should say, they finally founded the WNBA. This league had a chance, and more importantly, they were hiring. This begged the question: Did Ginny want to become a professional coach? Or was she happy being an assistant coach at Flushing U?

The answer was yes, she wanted to become a professional coach, and yes, she wanted to stay at Flushing U with Frank. Who could have predicted that there would ever be a professional women's basketball league, one that might have staying power?

Ginny applied for several WNBA coaching jobs. At 37, she was too old to play for them. Frank was applying, too. Maybe they would get hired by the same team. If she could land anything with the pros, that would satisfy a lot of those feelings of opportunities lost.

Tilly meanwhile bought three tickets to see Patti Smith. Ginny had been playing Patti's latest album, *Gung Ho*, nonstop for the last few weeks. It was time to hear the band live.

Tilly and Renée insisted on standing up front by the stage. While seeing Patti up close was a great experience, people were packed on top of each other. Ginny's diabetic paranoia was emerging, and she couldn't relax. If she was going to have low blood sugar issues, this would be a bad place for that to happen.

"Back in a minute."

Not wanting to be jostled while she was testing, Ginny made her way through the audience, out to the main corridor, and found a corner. She took out her meter, now about the size of a wallet, and tested: 172.

"Are you okay?"

A stranger had approached her.

"What?"

"I saw you check your blood sugar. Are you okay?"

Ginny stared at this intruder.

"My cousin is a diabetic," he continued. "I know all about it."

Ginny thought, *This is none of your business*, but instead, she said, "I'm fine," so that he would go away faster.

Since, apparently, she was being watched, she wandered around the main room of the venue until she found the ladies' room. She ducked into a stall, took a unit of insulin, and then went back to find her friends. It wasn't easy; the crowd did not like her pushing to the front, nor did she like doing it. Ginny made it back in time to hear Patti sing one of her favorites, "Wing."

Ginny received offers from all three of her favored teams: New York, Cleveland, and Los Angeles. Frank received assistant offers from Cleveland and Charlotte and a head-coaching position from Utah.

"Well, we could flip a coin."

"That's unhelpful, Frank. Do you have a three-sided coin?"

He laughed. "Okay, what about this? What does your gut tell you? I know what mine tells me: that I should finally get my head-coach position, even though it's in Utah, of all places. Might as well be Mars. But my heart tells me that if you decide to go to Cleveland, then that's where I will go."

"My heart says go to Cleveland if you go to Cleveland. My gut tells me to stay in New York. But my gut is always telling me to stay put."

"I don't think staying in New York is a bad plan for you. New York gets under your skin. If you like it here, there's no reason to leave. I would never leave if it wasn't for work. But both our hearts are saying Cleveland. How do we really feel about Cleveland?"

They looked at their laps.

"I thought so," Frank said. "So that means Utah for me. What about you? L.A. or New York?"

Ginny thought for a moment. "I have friends here. And family in Rhode Island. And—"

"Then I don't think this is a hard decision. The three-sided coin has spoken. You're going to be an assistant coach for the New York Liberty. You're going pro."

They looked at each other.

"We're breaking up," Ginny said.

"I'm going to stupid Utah."

They took a moment to feel the full impact of their decisions.

"Well, we don't have to go anywhere right away," Frank said. "Let's go out and celebrate. This is not a completely sad moment."

He kissed her, and after a moment, she said, "Or we could stay in." They continued kissing, and he said, "The Thai place delivers."

They stayed in.

Ginny and Frank passed Dash on their way to the Athletic Center. He waved but didn't approach them. He had congratulated Ginny a couple of days earlier, but not Frank. Ginny hadn't asked him, but she wondered if Dash had applied for a job at the WNBA as well. She guessed not; he could have approached the NBA years ago. And why would he settle for coaching women? Maybe he wasn't like that, or maybe he wasn't like that anymore, but just in case it was a sore spot, she kept this question to herself.

Ginny had almost suggested to Frank a few weeks earlier that Cleveland would have been close enough to New York that they could maintain a relationship. Something stopped her from saying anything. If Frank felt the relationship was more important than basketball, he could have stayed in New York with her. And if they both felt that way, the two of them would be going to Cleveland.

This would be Frank and Ginny's last one-on-one scrimmage, after which it would be their last lunch, their last dinner, and their last lovemaking. Frank was leaving for Utah in the morning.

Several people entered the court to watch their final game. Though Frank had a distinct height advantage, Ginny was more nimble than Frank, who was all arms and legs. The score stayed close, and when Ginny tied it 20–20, they both stopped and said, "Let's end it here."

The onlookers groaned, but Ginny and Frank were happy.

Ginny had been keeping busy these last few weeks prepping for her new job. She met with the other coaches and the players (including nine-foot-tall Rebecca Lobo, star of UConn fame!). Her days were packed. Ultimately, it didn't matter. Frank's imminent departure loomed large.

When Ginny returned from accompanying Frank to the airport, she headed to the university's Athletic Center. She was going to meet Dash to work out a little and get her mind off the overpowering feeling that she and Frank had made the wrong decision. What was that song? "You Can't Put Your Arms Around a Memory"? Johnny Thunders. She remembered when Ken first played that for her. Stupid Ken.

Dash wasn't in the gym when she got there. Had she picked the wrong day? She turned to leave when she heard her name.

"Ginny!"

She turned around. Dash was approaching her, using a cane.

"Where are you going?" he said.

She waited for him to catch up with her.

"I didn't think you were here today," she said.

"Had to ice my ankle. Overdid it yesterday."

"Okay, so no scrimmage today. Wanna get some coffee?"

The vintage coffee shop she had gone to with Frank that first time was gone. Now, it was an Indian restaurant. There was a tiny five-dollar-coffee place on the next block. She didn't want to force Dash to walk too far, so they went there.

Dash said, "So, Frank's the new head coach for the Utah Starzz. Good for him."

"Is it my imagination, or do I detect a sense of irritation in that statement?"

"You do, yes."

"I didn't realize you didn't like Frank. Is there a history there I should know about?"

Dash tried to take a sip from his cappuccino, but it was too hot, and he put it down. "I don't really know him. It's just that he's got everything I want."

"But you got *his* head-coaching gig at Flushing. He should feel that way about you, but he doesn't."

Dash stirred his cappuccino with more concentration than it needed.

"Don't make me spell it out for you," he said.

It took her a long time, then she said, "Ohhhhhh. Is this about me?"

He nodded. "It's all about you."

"But ... But ..."

"I always regretted not calling you after that night we had together. I hesitated because I figured you thought I was an asshole."

"I did."

"... and then too much time passed ..."

"Yes. And I met Ken ..."

"Right. Why did you sleep with me, anyway? Was it just to lose your virginity?"

Charming. The glimmer of the old Dash came shining through. Since he was being blunt, Ginny would be, too. When she could pick her jaw back up off the floor, she said, "Yes."

"I thought so. It wasn't like you were all over me like the others." He paused. "I liked that."

They sat in silence, finally able to sip their hot coffees. Neither of them knew what to say.

"You know, Lila came on to me at one of our frat parties," Dash said. "She sought me out. We did it in my bedroom with the party going on in the main room. I think it was for the same reason, because she didn't want anything to do with me afterwards."

Ginny smiled broadly. "Wow. And neither one of us ever told the other. Too embarrassing."

"Because it was me?"

"That, and just the whole situation."

"What happens now? Does this mean you won't come shoot hoops with me anymore?"

"No, I will."

"I don't suppose ... with Frank in Utah ..."

Ginny shook her head.

"Sorry," Dash said. "Too soon. I get it."

To avoid the impending awkward silence, Dash said, "Hey, would you introduce me to Rebecca Lobo?"

Ginny laughed, then, seeing the look on his face, said, "Oh. You're serious. Sure."

She hoped Rebecca wouldn't be mad at her for this introduction. Rebecca was almost a foot taller than Ginny. She could squash her like a bug. This was Dash, after all, though a shadow of his former cocky self.

Ginny now wished she hadn't lost contact with Lila. Things just happened over the years. A person gets busy, people move, and the next thing she knows, she's lost contact. But she would have liked to discuss Dash with her. Maybe in their next lives.

Ginny wanted a place where she could practice on her own on her days off. She found an athletic club in Woodside, Queens, that had courts to rent, right on the subway's 7 line, maybe 15 minutes from her apartment. She thought this could get her mind off Frank on days when it got too much. Playing with Dash was great, but she liked being able to do her own thing sometimes.

She came home one night, exhausted from coaching, and, after a snack and a much-desired shower, fell into bed. She fell asleep right away but, after a couple of hours, was awakened by a low blood sugar crisis. She was shaking so hard she almost fell out of bed. She reached for her Ike and Mike's and took a handful. Then she pried the cap off her juice, gulped some down, and waited for this drama to subside. Her thoughts were muddled. All she could do was lay there staring at the wall. The bottle she was holding tipped and spilled the remaining juice onto her clean nightshirt and sheets. She couldn't react.

When her brain finally engaged, she felt the liquid on her skin.

"Damn it."

She righted the bottle and put it on her nightstand, then sat up and tried to dry up the juice with some tissues. Everything was sticky.

"*Damn* it!"

She got up off the bed, peeled off her nightshirt, and tossed it across the room into the laundry basket.

"Three points! The crowd goes wild. Yay!"

Rather than taking another shower, she washed off her chest and arms, got a clean nightshirt, and then pulled the sheets off the bed to change them. This process was annoying at best, but even more so at three in the morning.

She climbed back into bed, now wide awake.

"I want to call Frank," she said aloud. "What time is it in Utah, anyway?"

It was one o'clock in the morning in Utah; it was too late to call.

Stupid Frank, she thought.

Ginny was feeling sorry for herself. Everyone seemed to move on without her. Even stupid Freddie, in a way. Ginny stayed the same, and Freddie changed. Ken moved to fricking Minnesota, and Frank just moved to Utah. Was her resistance to change just an excuse to be alone? Was she too stubborn to change? Should she have followed Ken or Frank, even though they had gone to places she didn't want to go?

There had to be a better solution than *that*. And no, unlike the advice given by Stephen Stills, she was not going to "Love the One You're With." Poor Dash would have to get over her.

The first WNBA game was played on June 21, 1997. It was the New York Liberty versus the Los Angeles Sparks. Ginny expected more media attention, more pageantry, more razzle-dazzle, more ... something. Maybe this wasn't a big deal compared to men's sports, but this was a very big deal for women. How many leagues had tried and failed, and for how many years?

There were a little over 14,000 in attendance at the Great Western Forum in Los Angeles. Ginny wasn't sure they'd have done much better in New York, although that same number of people would have been louder, especially since New York won, 67–57.

This could be the start of something, if not big, at least enduring.

The Liberty were scheduled to play the Utah Starzz on July 5th in Utah. Ginny and Frank had been communicating via telephone since he left, but this would be the first time they had seen each other in months.

Ginny was nervous and excited as she approached the restaurant. She looked around. Frank was casually reading a newspaper at a window table.

"Hi."

Frank folded the newspaper and stood up.

"Hi." They fumbled a kiss before sitting down.

"I wasn't really reading this newspaper. I was trying to appear nonchalant."

Ginny smiled. "I'm nervous, too. It's great to see you."

"You, too. I see the Liberty are doing well."

"They are! Think we'll kick your butts this afternoon?"

"Yes. Our team is not at their best at the moment, to be diplomatic."

"Hmm. I won't tell my women that. You never know when a team will rally."

"True. Although I've never seen this team rally."

"Are you liking Utah?"

"Not really." He laughed. "I've been too busy to have seen much of it, but so far, no."

There was a pause, and then they both started talking at once.

"Go ahead," Frank said.

"No, you go ahead."

"I've made a big mistake," he said. "I thought it would be good to be a head coach, and it is, but not this team and not this place. And most importantly, not without you."

"I was thinking about that the minute you left. I thought, 'What were we thinking?'"

Frank reached for her hand.

"We'll see each other more often now that the season has started," Ginny said.

"Yup. In 12 days, I'll be in New York. Not that I'm counting."

"Right. Me neither."

"Should we try this, the long-distance thing?"

"I think we should."

They continued to hold hands until their food came. Then, they didn't want to let go.

Chapter 21
Party Like It's 1999

While New York businesses were all abuzz over Y2K and what it would mean to everyone's computers when calendars turned over to the year 2000, Ginny was enjoying being part of a coaching staff on a winning team. The Liberty made it to the Finals in 1997, was third in the Eastern Conference in 1998, and 1999, so far, was looking good. NBC televised games, and Madison Square Garden was selling out. Women's basketball was here to stay, and there were no unitards or smaller courts.

Frank wouldn't be in town until Sunday, so Ginny stopped by the university to have a scrimmage with Dash. He was in good form today, and soon he was winning 19–12. He got the rebound and headed to the backcourt.

"Where are you going?"

At six foot seven, he was taller than Frank, and Ginny never bothered trying to block him. The best she could do was steal the ball or maybe annoy him, like a gnat. Now, he continued past the center circle almost to the opposite free-throw line and turned around. He bounced the ball a few times in place and, with a clumsy jump, took a shot.

It sailed across the court, spinning as it traveled, and went in with a swish, nothing but net.

"Wow! Show off!"

Dash beamed.

"That wasn't a basket; that was a touchdown," Ginny said. "You should get six points for that."

He laughed. "Just don't ask me to do it a second time."

That made it 22–12. Ginny tossed the ball back to Dash, who was slowly approaching her.

"Frank still out of town?"

"He'll be back Sunday."

"Wanna go get lunch?" Dash winked at her.

"Dash ..."

"You can't blame a guy for trying."

She laughed. "Yes, I can."

The phone was ringing as she entered the apartment.

"I have news," Frank said without saying hello.

"Oh?"

"NYU is looking for a head coach for their men's team."

"Uh ... they're not exactly Division One."

"No, they're Division Three. But maybe I can do something about that. Some say coaches can make a difference."

"First, change their name. They're the Violets. Not very intimidating."

"No, it's not. They should be the Dope Fiends, or the Water Bugs, or the Sewer Rats, or something. But the school has great new facilities. I put in an application. I figured I better do it now before my reputation is destroyed by my current job."

"This would be so great!"

"I mean, it's not Utah, but I think I can make the grand sacrifice."

"I think you'd better!"

This was great news, but Ginny soon struggled with a bout of depression that made her doubt her and Frank's future. Would he even get that job at NYU? Would he get it, then resent her for making him come back to New York? Would they be able to just pick up from where they left off, or had they changed too much to keep the relationship going? These were all foolish, unanswerable questions, but they stayed in her head for a while, torturing her, until the melancholy finally lifted.

It took a couple of days, but once she was feeling better, she called Woodside and reserved a half-court for the afternoon. She needed to bounce and run. She dribbled all around the half-court in one direction, then turned around and went the other way. Then she stopped to dribble between her legs, switching hands and turning as she did.

"Ginny the Globetrotter!" she said aloud. "Meadowlark has nothing on me!"

She pivoted and shot. She missed.

"Okay. Meadowlark would have gotten that one."

She had rented it for an hour, but she had her fill of endorphins after 45 minutes. Her blood glucose was 62, so she drank some juice and spent the rest of the hour cooling down.

Tilly's invitation read:

"We will be celebrating the last day of the last month of the last year of the last decade of the 20th Century, and you're invited. Please dress for the occasion."

Ginny and Frank liked this idea. How often did they get to dress in something other than sweats and sneakers?

"What do you think?"

Ginny had waited until the day of the party to model her new outfit for Frank: a clingy, black mini dress with glitter pantyhose. Frank stuck out his tongue and panted.

"Okay, slugger, calm down. We have the whole evening to get through first."

"You're going to freeze in that dress."

"I have a long coat. Besides, it's warm for New Year's, like 35 degrees."

Tilly lived close enough to the subway that it made sense to take the train, even though Ginny was wearing silver spike heels that she was having trouble steering. Outside the stop on the Manhattan side was a vendor selling New Year's Eve souvenirs. Ginny and Frank each bought a hat and glow sticks. Other revelers on the street were laughing and blowing noisemakers. The longer Ginny was in her shoes, the more uncomfortable they became, and as the wind picked up, she and Frank quickened their pace to Tilly's.

"Ginny! Frank! Come in! You look great!"

Till was already sipping champagne. She was all in black except for a bright pink boa that clashed with her hair.

"Coats are in my bedroom, and there's champagne in the kitchen. Help yourself."

Frank took Ginny's coat and headed to the bedroom. Ginny could feel a blister forming on the bottom of her foot. She slipped out of her shoes.

"Yeah. I took mine off before anyone arrived," Tilly said. "They were nice, but damn ... I guess you didn't invite Dash here tonight."

"No. While I feel sorry for the guy, he and Frank are not a good mix."

"You think he's home alone?"

"He said it's what he wanted, though he definitely would have come out if I had asked him."

"Poor Dash."

"Good decisions were never his forte. Is Renée here?"

"She and Carlos will be here a little later. They had another party uptown."

"Have we met Carlos?"

"No. They've only been dating a couple months."

Someone was handing Ginny a glass; Frank had returned with champagne. As she reached for it, he pulled it back.

"Wait. You can't have this, can you?"

Ginny smirked. "Bite me."

"Later."

As they retired to the living room, a monolith of a man stood up to greet them.

"Ginny Eastman! Wow. I remember when you played for UCLA. How are you?"

"Hi. And you are?"

"Max Seidemann. UCLA, class of '79. I played for the Bruins with Dash Hollander. I wonder what ever happened to ol' Dash? Haven't seen him since he had that injury."

"He's head coach at Flushing," Frank said.

"Really? He's in the city? I should look him up."

"I see Dash pretty regularly," Ginny said.

"You do?" Frank said.

"I have his office number." She scribbled it on the back of one of her business cards. "Here...."

"Great. Thanks," Max said. "It's good to see you, Ginny."

As midnight grew nearer, Tilly flicked on the TV so everyone could watch the ball drop in Times Square. As the countdown started, Tilly said, "I wonder if all our computers are going to freak out."

"All our information will disappear."

"There will be no subways or busses."

"The banks will collapse."

"Two, one ... Happy New Year!"

People on the TV were going crazy, but there was a moment of silence at the party.

"Think we're okay?" Tilly said.

When they all decided they were, everyone started kissing each other and cheering.

"Happy New Year, Frank."

"Happy New Year, Ginny."

Once the century turned, a new diet fad arose, namely "low carb." Now there were hundreds of products that replaced sugar with aspartame, or the new sweetener, sucralose, or the dreaded mannitol or sorbitol, sweeteners okay for diabetics but still a carbohydrate that had to be counted. Plus, those sugar alcohols were baby laxatives, so for practical reasons, a person shouldn't consume too much of them. During the low-fat craze, it was almost impossible to find low-sugar products. Now, it was almost like the days of cyclamates.

Although Ginny didn't want to admit it, her energy was starting to falter. She would be out of breath just walking home from the subway. Practices were more of a chore, and it took longer for her to warm up. She had to force herself to do pushups, and often she skipped them. It could have been her age; she was turning 41 this year. Maybe she was simply in a rut. Still, this was distressing.

Her New York doctor had retired but gave Ginny three names of diabetes specialists in the area. Having nothing to go on, she arbitrarily picked one. The office told her to get bloodwork a couple of weeks before her appointment. Could they figure out what was going on with her energy? This was worse than her bouts of depression; she could work through those. The lack of energy was constant.

Dr. Xander read her name from her chart.

"Ginny ... How long have you been diabetic?"

"Uh ..." She calculated. "Thirty-four years."

"Lente and Ultra Lente are unusual for Type 2 diabetics ..."

"I said *thirty-* four years. 1967."

"You're how old?"

Read my chart. "Almost 41."

"How's your vision?"

"It's fine." Ginny did not like this guy.

"Tingling in your feet? Numbness?"

"No. But I think I'm depressed." She just blurted it out.

He looked surprised and said, "Why are you depressed?"

Ginny didn't know the answer to that question. It didn't occur to her she needed to answer that question.

"Uh ... I don't know ... But my energy is failing."

The doctor opened her folder and checked her bloodwork.

"Well, here's a reason for your sluggishness," he said. "Your thyroid numbers are low. I'll prescribe Synthroid. You'll feel like yourself again."

"That's it? That's all I need?"

"That's all. Why, is there something else?"

She wanted to say, "I've been feeling detached and morose off and on since grade school. That can't be my thyroid." But instead, she said, "Just seems too simple."

The first day on Synthroid, Ginny felt her energy return. That familiar, disengaged feeling she always had was still there, but her energy was much better. However, soon it seemed the Synthroid was working a little too well. In the middle of the night, she sat up in bed, suddenly wide awake.

Frank rolled over to face her. "You okay?"

"Sorry. These meds are making my heart race."

"Are you sure it's the meds?"

"It's the only thing that's changed. I didn't read that insert that came with the prescription, so I'm not really sure."

"You better call in case it's something else."

She rarely called doctors since she saw them so often, but this was unnerving.

"It'll subside. Give it a week or two," Dr. Xander said.

"I won't run out of heartbeats?" Ginny wasn't serious, but her doctor didn't laugh.

"You can't run out of heartbeats." He said this with some annoyance. She really didn't like this guy.

Ginny's heart did calm down, and she didn't run out of heartbeats. This doctor rubbed her the wrong way. She would be looking for a different one. There were two more on the list.

The post office was delivering the mail later and later in the day. Today, it didn't arrive until around four o'clock, after Ginny got home. She went through the stack of bills and political notices and advertising mailers and ... what was this? An invitation? She tried calling Renée, but when the machine picked up, she called Tilly.

"Renée's getting married again?"

"Yes. Carlos asked her about a month ago."

"And no one told me?"

"Sorry. It looks like you're out of the loop."

"Well, put me back *in* the loop."

"This is a small wedding. Little fanfare."

"Still ..."

Ginny had to get a dress (and hey ... why wasn't she a bridesmaid?) and buy a present. Or maybe she and Frank would just write checks.

"Ever notice how time moves faster the older you get?" Ginny said. She was trying to make a decent dinner for her and Frank, although neither of them had high hopes.

"Waxing philosophically, are we?" Frank said.

"I was just thinking, now that Renée is getting married again. When I was in high school, a month seemed like a long time. Now, although it's been years, it feels like Renée just got married to Barry."

"And if I refuse to participate in this 'we're getting older' discussion?"

"Fine. But I expect a banner when I'm about to turn 48 and I've been a diabetic for 40 years."

"You got it."

Ginny put her lasagna in the oven and set a timer.

"That smells good. Did you make that sauce?"

"No. Paul Newman did."

"He's a good cook."

"Hey. You've created some culinary disasters yourself, Bucko."

"True, true. That's why the pizza guy is on speed dial."

Renée's wedding was low-key and tiny, maybe about a dozen guests. There were no bridesmaids. Ginny and Tilly were the official witnesses, and no, neither Ginny nor Frank were in charge of the food. But most importantly, Carlos only had eyes for Renée, which was how these things were supposed to be.

Chapter 22

What Other Clever Things Can You Do?

Diabetes Forecast was back to putting damaged, wholesome-looking people on its cover. For the April 2001 issue, there was a woman on the cover who was missing part of her foot. Ginny shuddered and thought darkly, *Diabetics don't die; they are taken out in pieces.* As much as she had some renewed faith in this publication since Bret had been on the cover 14 years earlier, she was still hesitant to read it all the way through.

She flipped through the pages, then stopped. There was a full-page ad for something called a GlucoWatch. This was too good to be true ... a watch that read blood sugar? Not having to stop what she was doing, not having to explain herself to people, just look at the watch, like Dick Tracy? It was the 21st century. There were no flying cars, no robot armies, and no cure for cancer, but maybe these GlucoWatch people were onto something.

Ginny was now going to a Dr. Yang. She saw him every three months or so, and she had no complaints in the past couple of years.

"How are you feeling? Your numbers are good. Your A1C is 5.6. That's excellent."

Ginny made a *mezz-a-mezz* gesture with her hand.

"I'm okay. I have these bouts of intense listlessness, but I've been feeling like this off and on since grade school."

"Do you feel sad? Disconnected? Emotional? Think maybe you're depressed?"

Yes! Yes! She was depressed! Yes!

"Well, yeah."

"Twenty-six percent of diabetics suffer from depression."

"The gift that keeps on giving."

"I'm going to prescribe an antidepressant called Effexor. You might feel it right away, but it could take as long as two weeks. Either way, you should start feeling better."

"Will this change my personality? I don't like change."

"If you consider depression part of your personality, yes. If not, then no."

This made Ginny laugh.

"Dr. Yang, do you know anything about the GlucoWatch?"

"Do you think you might like one?"

"I want to look into it. If it works, then when I'm at practice or a game or a concert or something, I don't have to stop what I'm doing to check my blood."

"The cons may outweigh the pros at the moment. First of all, it requires frequent finger pricks to keep it calibrated. Then, there's an electrical current that goes through the body, which most people find uncomfortable, even painful. Plus, often there's a rash where the sensor touches the skin. There are also accuracy and consistency issues."

"Oh, no, no, no, no. I'll just have to wait to become Dick Tracy."

Dr. Yang laughed. "Dick Tracy? No, we're not there yet."

Ginny picked up the bottle of Effexor from the pharmacy. Was this going to make her manic? Would she split into two personalities? Laugh inappropriately? Talk backwards?

She got over herself and took one of the pills.

The next day, she started to feel the cloud of sadness lifting. In two days, she was sleeping deeper than she had in decades. Once she was awake, she felt like herself again, her whole self, before her chronic depression started. She hadn't felt a transformation this big since her first shot of insulin.

The events of September 11, 2001, changed New York City. In fact, the whole country changed. For a couple of months, there was a feeling of comradery, togetherness, unity. Then, there was talk of the United States maybe invading Iraq, and the country was again divided. The economy was tanking as well, and New York City was bleeding jobs. Ginny wasn't very knowledgeable when it came to public affairs, but she could feel the tension in the people around her. If one were to ask her what teams were likely to win the NCAA Finals and why, she was your girl; she and Frank were both singularly focused on basketball. Any other information seeped in unintentionally. She wasn't even sure who Frank voted for or if he voted at all.

In other news, George Harrison was dying of cancer. Heroes were supposed to outlive their usefulness; someone needed to explain this to them. Ginny started listening to all her George albums in order, a couple each night. Frank was being a good sport about it; he sat through *All Things Must Pass*, even the *Apple Jam* LP. When Ginny got to *Somewhere in England*, the song "The Writing's on the Wall" made her burst into tears. No, this wasn't affecting her at all.

He didn't make it to the end of the year.

When the war in Iraq started in 2003, Ginny thought about Asher often. Would he have been opposed to it? Wouldn't he have been opposed to any war after seeing what he had seen? Ginny had to admit that she tended to agree with

Asher, but she never expressed this opinion to anyone except Tilly and Renée. There was a general feeling at the time that one shouldn't be anti-war, that this undermined the troops. Silence, as the Tremoloes once sang, was golden.

"I know you don't like change, but we're going to have to change your insulin."

"What? Why?"

"They're discontinuing Lente and Ultra Lente."

She liked Dr. Yang, but what was he doing to her?

"I'm going to prescribe Lantus, which is a long-acting, base insulin. It will cover about 24 hours. Then there's Humalog, which is a faster-acting insulin, which you'll take at meals."

"Fast? How fast?"

"It starts working in about 15 minutes and lasts around four hours. You'll have time to eat if that's what you're worried about."

"That's what I'm worried about."

Insulin each meal? That was so old school. That was so inconvenient. That was so ...

"We'll adjust it depending on how much you choose to eat."

Choose to eat?

"Wait. Does this mean Lantus doesn't have peaks? I won't go into insulin shock if I eat late?"

"That's right. Of course, nothing is perfect. We'll see."

What would this stuff do to her? Would the Humalog kick in too fast and leave her convulsing on the floor? No, Dr. Yang wouldn't tell her to do something that ridiculous. She would keep a large bottle of juice by her side, just in case.

She took her first shot of Lantus, and there were no fireworks, no jumping up and down, no reaction of any kind. This insulin wasn't trying to kill her. Now, she just had to deal with the Humalog.

She took her dose of Humalog and then ate her usual breakfast. If this worked, it could mean greater flexibility. Also, no mandatory snacks.

She forgot about it until around ten o'clock when she checked her blood. 135. So far, so good.

By noon thirty, her number was back down to 90. This was working. Amazing.

Two things were off, however. Three or four hours after eating, her blood sugar would often drop, sometimes as low as 35. And sometimes in the morning, it would rise to 180 or higher. Okay, the system was not perfect, but it had great promise.

The coming week was rocky. When her number went low, she'd take some juice or candy, but then it would bounce up to 200 and she'd panic and take more insulin, which brought it too low, and so on. Her numbers were bouncing around like a basketball. She called Dr. Yang.

"You haven't hit the sweet spot yet."

Ginny groaned. Dr. Yang laughed.

"Sorry. That was bad. We'll adjust what you're taking. But listen, if your glucose goes up after a low, let it go. Wait it out. Only if it stays up or starts going too much over 180, take insulin, but don't overdo it. You're making yourself crazy."

"Yes. I am."

"This will be better in the long run. I promise."

"Not like I have a choice."

"Well, you could get a pump, which I don't recommend for you."

"I agree. Wait. A pump?"

"You're an athlete, and there's the issue of tubes, which I think would make you crazy."

"Tubes? Oh, no, no, no."

"Stop reacting to every little thing and call me in a week. If there needs to be another adjustment, we'll figure it out."

There were still mysterious highs and lows, but overall this did seem to work better. Sometimes the Humalog continued to lower her blood glucose hours after she had taken it, often quite a bit. This was opposite from what she was used to, lows before eating. She'd have those bouncy days often, her blood sugar going high and low all day. One thing that seemed to help was keeping her morning glucose close to average. She started setting an alarm for five a.m. so she could take a unit or two of Humalog to bring down her morning highs. Not the best solution, but a solution.

With Frank heading to NYU today, Ginny rented a half-court at the Woodside gym to run her bounce and run drills. She did the whole sequence twice; then, she practiced some of the shooting drills she ran with her players. She circled back to do some layups, first on the right side, then the left. As she came around to do the right side again, she started trembling. Her momentum kept her moving forward, and she continued into the layup, but her knees buckled on the landing. Her ankle twisted under her, and she fell on it, full weight. There was a loud crunch.

"Owwwww."

Ginny's whole body was shaking. Her bottle of juice was several feet away, and her right foot was dangling pathetically from her leg. She used her left leg for traction and shimmied on her butt over to the sidelines. With some difficulty (stupid bottle cap), she got the juice open and guzzled it as fast as she could without making herself nauseous. It was several minutes before she felt normal again.

She took a moment to think back on her Humalog intake, but there was a more pressing issue: How was she going to get out of there? Her ankle was swelling and turning purple.

"Eventually, someone will find me," she said aloud. Maybe it was time to consider getting one of those cellular phones.

They were smaller now and more affordable. She had to have a plan for right now, however.

She ate a couple of Ike and Mike's to ensure this crisis was over before she started on the next one. She put her bag on her shoulder, dragged herself over to the bench that was against the wall, and climbed onto it. The door seemed lightyears away. She couldn't hop there, could she? She slid down to the end of the bench and stood on her left leg. Leaning against the wall, she pivoted on that leg to the door. She put her full body weight on the push handle and almost fell over when the door miraculously swung open, but she stopped herself in time.

There was a payphone just outside the court.

It was only four hops to the phone. Using the wall for balance, she grabbed the receiver and called 911.

Frank greeted her in the ER with, "You broke your ankle?"

"That's what they're saying. Messed up some ligaments, too. Looks like I won't be able to walk properly for months, much less play. I really screwed up."

"How did you do this?"

"I was doing a layup and missed my landing. Fell straight down onto my ankle."

Ginny didn't want to admit her low-blood-sugar issue. She was worried someone in the hospital would find out and keep her there indefinitely.

"The only times I've been injured have been off the court," Frank said. "Fell off a curb. Tripped on one of those metal basement doors sticking out of the sidewalk. Slipped in the shower and got a concussion."

"Good God, Frank."

"I know. But I've been lucky: never while playing. Can I sign your cast?"

"You can, but they'll take it off tomorrow when I go to surgery."

"Surgery?"

"Yeah. Looks like I need a few pins and stuff."

"Ouch."

Ginny was nervous. She would be under anesthesia for a couple hours. She didn't like not being in control for that long. However, if she wanted to run again, this was how that was going to happen.

When she woke from surgery, she was alone in a room attached to an IV. Her first thought was to test her blood sugar, but her meter was with her bag and clothes, wherever they were. A friendly male nurse walked into the room. Ginny thought maybe he was the only male nurse on the floor; all the other nurses she had seen were women.

"You're awake. Your surgery went well. Your doctor will fill you in in a little while. Can I get you anything? You must be hungry."

Come to think of it ... "Yes. I'm famished. And could I get a cup of coffee?"

"Absolutely. They gave you your insulin this morning?"

"The Lantus, yes. But I'll need some Humalog if I'm going to eat."

"I'll get that for you and some food."

"Could you test my blood sugar? It's often a little high in the morning."

"No problem."

What was she worried about? This place had it down.

It took most of the day, but she was eventually transferred to a semi-private room where she was reunited with her belongings. Frank arrived the next day with some *Sports Illustrated*

magazines and Diet Cokes. While he was leafing through one of the magazines, Ginny took out her meter and tested her blood. 272. Damn. She rang the bell for a nurse.

"Can I help you?"

"My blood sugar is high."

"You're not scheduled for insulin."

"I need some Humalog. Now. I'm not sitting here with it high like this."

"I'll have to call the doctor."

"Call him."

"We'll have to do a finger stick."

"Do it."

Frank observed this dialogue and frowned.

"Why is it high?"

Ginny noted that his question wasn't, "Why aren't they listening to you?"

"They cut my dose of Lantus this morning. They're worried it'll go too low. It went down to 29 while I was in surgery, so now they're being overly cautious."

"How could they let that happen?"

"Good question. If I was in here specifically for diabetes, they'd be checking my numbers every minute. They wouldn't leave me alone. I suppose this is better, in a way."

"Why don't you take your own insulin and not wait for them?"

"It makes sense to use theirs. That way, they'll have a record that I took some."

The nurse came back, checked Ginny's blood sugar with the hospital's meter, and, having ascertained that it was indeed well over 200, went to order the insulin.

"All this for three or four units. Next time, maybe I will just use my own."

Ginny escaped the hospital after a week with all her parts intact. She was a little unsteady on the crutches, but she found she could still coach. Otherwise, she would have missed months of work.

It could be worse, she told herself. *I still have my foot and all my toes.*

This injury was causing her a lot of anxiety. Frank had to practically carry her up and down the stairs to their building. She couldn't ride the subway yet, and she was spending a fortune on cabs. Would she ever walk without a limp, or would she be like Dash, hobbling around for the rest of her days? Most importantly, would she ever be able to bounce and run again?

Speaking of Dash, she had promised to meet him at Flushing's Athletic Center today. She called him at his office.

"You broke your ankle? I'm so sorry."

"Yeah. I'm still struggling with the crutches, but I've been able to coach."

"You know ... I took my career for granted. Before I got injured, I never had to fight for anything. I just gave up. Now I see how you women play your hearts out, only to be still in the shadows of the men."

"Dash ... are you being understanding?"

He laughed. "Yeah. I guess that's not like the Dash you knew."

"Not really, no."

"Listen. Do all the PT. All of it. It might take a year or more, but keep at it. You'll play again. You will."

"Thanks, Dash."

For a moment, it reminded her of something Asher might have said.

Because Ginny wasn't getting around very well, Frank invited Tilly and Renée over for dinner.

"I should have guessed that the only way I'd get you two to Queens was to break my stupid ankle."

"We came when you first got this place," Tilly said.

Ginny laughed. "That was almost 20 years ago."

The pizza they ordered was just okay, a little under-cooked and the sauce was too sweet. It wasn't so bad that they wouldn't eat it. Ginny had had her foot up on the coffee table but put it down to make room for the food. It started to throb. Ginny reached for her crutches and moved to the sofa chair so she could put her foot up on the ottoman.

"Anyone want to smoke a joint? It'll relieve some of your pain, Ginny."

"In that case, yes. But no dancing."

It did take over a year, but Ginny was able to bounce and run again, though somewhat slower than before. She started using the team's treadmill to practice running. She even prac-ticed running backward. Things got better, but there was always that fear they might never be the same.

One afternoon, Frank returned home looking pleased with himself.

"Guess who's the new head coach for the Utah Jazz?" he said.

He knew something Ginny didn't. That was unusual.

"It's not you, is it? Have you lost your mind and accepted another job in Utah?"

"Dash," he said.

"No kidding! He's finally working for the NBA. Guess he got tired of Queens."

"Guess he got tired of you leading him on."

Ginny threw a pillow at him.

"I did *not* lead him on. I merely encouraged a bimonthly scrimmage."

"That's what you call it." Frank smiled. "I could see how a fellow might be smitten with you, Ginny Eastman."

"I guess I should go see him before he leaves."

Frank sighed. "I compliment you, and you talk about Dash."

"That was the main news item, wasn't it?"

"Yes. But now I'm changing the subject. What do you think, Ginny? Should we finally get married?"

Ginny raised her eyebrows. "Whoa. That was out of left field."

"You don't have a basketball metaphor for that?"

"Let me think. No, sorry."

"Is that a 'no' to the metaphor or to my proposal?"

"The metaphor."

"We've been together for decades now. It's unlikely we would jinx anything with a simple ceremony. We could go to City Hall."

"We're happy. Why would we change that?"

"You're right. It's a symbolic gesture."

"Okay."

"Okay? City Hall, okay?"

"Yes. Okay."

"I don't feel much enthusiasm here."

"I said 'yes.' Don't make me change my mind. Look, I'll jump up and down for you."

Ginny hopped up and down like a pogo stick.

Frank laughed. "Never mind. I'll take my 'yes' before this turns any less romantic."

Ginny went to Flushing U the next day and went straight to the practice courts. She could hear someone bouncing and maybe running. She entered, waited a moment, and called out, "Utah? You're going to Utah?"

Her voice echoed in the empty gym. Dash turned and

smiled at her. "Ginny."

"I guess congratulations are in order. What's chasing you out of Queens?"

"You assume I wasn't drawn to Utah."

Dash bounced and limped around in a circle, then casually tossed the ball into the basket.

"I need a change. I'm bored."

"And you think Utah is going to fix that?"

"Head coach for an NBA team? Yes. I need to step up my game before I get any older. It's past time to stop feeling sorry for myself."

Ginny calculated. He had to be 49 by now, maybe 50.

"And Utah was your epiphany?"

"Yes. Shoot some baskets with me?"

It was bittersweet, this last scrimmage with Dash. It marked the end of their weird friendship. Ginny was feeling time passing faster all the time. She wanted to dig her heels in and tell it to stop.

Before she knew it, Ginny's 48th birthday was approaching. She and Frank made plans to go out to dinner that night, and then they might go to a movie if they were both awake enough. Ginny didn't want anything fancy this year.

She put her key in the door and thought she heard people talking. Damn, had Frank planned a surprise party? Her birthday wasn't for a couple weeks. Maybe she had nothing to worry about. She opened the door.

Tilly, Renée, and Frank were standing with dopey grins on their faces under a gold banner that read, "40 Years with Diabetes."

She always joked that she wanted a banner. These idiots took her seriously. At best, this was a dubious achievement. She hoped no one took her picture with it to send to *Diabetes*

Forecast. She looked at their smiling faces and just couldn't tell them they had misread her. Maybe they were kidding, but she just wanted the banner to go away.

"Wow. Uh, thanks, guys."

From Ginny's lukewarm reaction, Tilly suspected something wasn't right. She spoke quickly. "We brought excellent, giggly pot and Edy's sugar-free chocolate ice cream."

The giggly pot appealed to her. It almost made her forget about the huge tacky banner hanging in the sitting room.

"Great. Let's get high. And thank you, ice cream is perfect."

They all settled down to smoke, and Frank said to her, "Do you like your banner?"

Don't push it, Frank. "Hey, I earned it. Where did you get it?"

"There's a place in Rego Park that makes all kinds of signs and banners and stuff. They make commemorative balloons, too, but I thought that would be too much."

"Definitely too much. And please don't get me a banner if I reach the 50th."

He kissed her. "You'll reach the 50th. I bet you'll reach the 60th and the 70th as well, and beyond. You're supposed to live forever, remember?"

Chapter 23

Do You Really Want to Live Forever?

The year 2017 came down harshly on Ginny. Her feet were starting to tingle, not in an obtrusive way, but it was noticeable, annoying, even. There was even some numbness in her pinky toes. The year before, she had gone to an optometrist to get reading glasses, and during the exam, he said, "Are you a diabetic?" She was shocked and panicked. What had he seen in her eyes? She immediately found a retina specialist, who said the retinopathy was "manageable," but she would have to come back every six months to monitor its progress. This development greatly upset her. She didn't even tell Frank; diabetic complications were just not who she was. How could this be happening? The impending 50-year diabetes anniversary was coming with some unwelcome bonuses.

Dr. Yang didn't seem that worried about her symptoms.

"We'll deal with these things as they happen. Don't worry."

Easy for you to say.

"I'm going to write you a prescription for something that should cheer you up," he said.

The doctor took out a plastic device. It looked like a complicated syringe.

"What's that?"

"It's an applicator for a continuous blood-glucose monitor, a CGM. Reads your blood sugar. You can check it on the reader or on your phone."

"On my phone?" There was an implied collection of question marks and exclamation points after that sentence.

"You have a smartphone, don't you?"

She and Frank were the last people on the planet not to have one.

"Er ... I'll get one."

"Okay. In the meantime, you can use the reader. Try it out and tell me what you think. I think you'll be pleased."

Ginny picked up her prescription the next day. Her insurance didn't cover all of it, but if it worked, it would be worth the money. There were three boxes, one each for a reader, the sensors, and a transmitter. She read the instructions, which she found a little confusing, but she managed to get the sensor attached to her abdomen and started it up. It would be two hours, and then she could calibrate it using her meter. She was beginning to think this whole thing was too complicated.

Then, it started working. She could check her blood glucose on the reader. There were even arrows that indicated in what direction the numbers were going and how fast.

"Oh my God," she said aloud. The next step would be to get a smartphone so she could carry only one device. This could change everything. What would it have been like if she had this forty years ago?

Ginny's CGM did make her life easier, although at first, she was obsessed with checking her glucose levels. Her numbers started bouncing around like they did when she first started taking Lantus and Humalog. Eventually, she calmed down, and there were days when, as Dr. Yang had said, she hit the "sweet spot." There were still, however, those bouncy days.

Another issue she had, and it was not inconsequential, was the beeping noise that sounded for low blood sugar. It couldn't be turned off, not even if the reader or phone's sound was off. Plus, it kept going even after treatment. It was embarrassing to be in the middle of something, say, a movie, and have the reader loudly beeping every five minutes. The only way to keep that from happening was to turn the reader off entirely, which defeated its purpose.

Ginny expected more and more things to go wrong with her body as she inched closer to 60. She figured no matter what finally took her out, people would say she died of "complications from diabetes." Choked on a chicken bone? Shot by a sniper? Hit by a bus? Complications from diabetes.

She and Frank were watching reruns on Antenna TV when there was a commercial for CGMs. This station was flooded with them:

"Diabetics! You know the pain of having to prick your finger ..."

Ginny muted the TV.

"Argh! Shut up!" she said.

Frank laughed. "Problem?"

"Finger pricks are not a big deal. They act like it's such a frigging hardship. Makes me crazy. CGMs are great. They don't need to sensationalize them."

"They should get Tilly to do a commercial. She'd come up with something interesting."

"The commercials with Nick Jonas are okay. They're straightforward. I don't mind those."

Ginny was one of those diabetics who had already seen the light. CGMs were indeed an amazing innovation. Loud but amazing.

Ginny spent the morning of her 58th birthday at the Woodside courts. When she had first gotten her CGM, she tried to keep her phone tucked into her waistband so she wouldn't have to leave the court to test her glucose. It kept falling. She broke the glass on her phone a number of times trying that. Now, she kept the phone on the sidelines and walked over if she wanted to check. It would beep loudly if she moved too far away from it or if her blood sugar dropped too low. This was not a bad thing when she was alone and working out, but Ginny would have preferred to have the information before it got too low. Or too high. On days when her blood sugar was bouncing around, she'd want to check it every few minutes until it settled down.

The Woodside courts had served Ginny well over the years. Today, she was enjoying bounce and run drills. She was pretty fast for someone pushing 60. Actually, she was pretty fast for a 30-year old and even some 18-year-olds. She was still the queen of the bounce and run.

Frank had stayed home to start cooking. He was making something "special," he said. Ginny wasn't sure what that meant, but she was intrigued.

"No, no, you can't go into the kitchen."

"Oh, c'mon. I want to get a soda."

"Stay there. I'll get it for you."

He backed into the kitchen. Ginny stayed put. Why ruin his surprise?

"Okay. Here you go."

"I can't even peek?"

"No. Go sit down. Why don't you open your present? It's on the coffee table."

She was more interested in finding out what food he was concocting than her present, but she begrudgingly went over to the couch. She unwrapped it, and she was confused.

"An Apple Watch? Why did you get me an Apple Watch?"

"I did some research. Which means I Googled it. Your

CGM can be read on a smart watch. You have an iPhone, so it needs to be an Apple."

Her eyes went wide. She ripped open the box. Following the set-up instructions, she got the watch paired with her phone. Then she hit the button on the watch, chose the app, and presto! Blood glucose: 111.

"Damn, where have you been all my life?"

She threw her arms around Frank. Dick Tracy was alive and well and living in the 21st century.

Tilly and her boyfriend, Pete, bought a place on East 85th Street by the newly opened 2nd Avenue Subway. The apartment had two bedrooms and a terrace, although it was on a lower floor than Tilly would have liked. She felt terraces worked better when they were higher than the third floor. Tilly invited her friends over for a housewarming, and Pete chivalrously stayed in his study, leaving the women alone to visit without intrusion.

These days, Tilly had bright, cherry-red hair. She had started to dye it about a decade earlier when it began growing in white. Conversely, Renée bleached her hair pure white, which she considered better than the gray it was turning. She kept it cut short, and it looked stunning. Ginny's hair was basically the same, just dyed a richer color to cover grays and her mousy brown hair, something she wished she had tried years ago.

"I don't know. Sometimes, I think I'm still 18," Tilly said. "My body thinks I'm close to 60, but my mind still wants to get high and dance."

"Dance while we still can," Ginny said.

Renée laughed. "God, Ginny, that's bleak."

"I know. Don't mind me. Frank and I have been discussing retirement. I'm feeling old."

"You get a pension, right?"

"Frank, yes. He's got a few more years. Me, no. I have a 401K, and I'm lucky to have it. Our league isn't as rich as the NBA. You should see how small some of the players' salaries are. That's why a lot of them spend time playing in Europe."

Tilly passed the joint to Ginny.

"Here. Have a mood enhancer. This stuff will make you love yourself."

Ginny took a long hit and handed it to Renée.

"Carlos doesn't like it when I smoke in front of him," Renée said.

"But behind his back is okay?" Tilly said.

"For some reason, yes."

"It's not like we're wild. Some giggling, some eating, some dancing," Ginny said.

"He doesn't like that it's illegal."

"We don't either," Tilly said.

"It's legal in Vermont," Ginny said.

"Tell him it's medicinal," Tilly said. "Tell him it cures what ails us." She stood up and called out, "Alexa, play the Violent Femmes."

As the song "Kiss Off" played, she started to dance. Renée and Ginny joined her. They danced less vigorously and more carefully than they did in the past, but they were still dancing.

Resources

American Diabetes Association
2451 Crystal Drive, Suite 900
Arlington, VA 22202
website: diabetes.org
email: askasa@diabetes.org
phone: 1-800-DIABETES (1-800-342-2383)

JDRF (Juvenile Diabetes Research Foundation)
200 Vesey Street, 28th Floor
New York, NY 10281
website: jdrf.org
email: info@jdrf.org
phone: 1-800-533-CURE (2873)

Abbott Diabetes Care
1360 South Loop Road
Alameda, CA 94502
website: freestyle.abbott
phone: 1-855-632-8658

Dexcom
website: dexcom.com
phone: 1-888-738-3646 M-F 6a.m.–5p.m. PST

About Atmosphere Press

Founded in 2015, Atmosphere Press was built on the principles of Honesty, Transparency, Professionalism, Kindness, and Making Your Book Awesome. As an ethical and author-friendly hybrid press, we stay true to that founding mission today.

If you're a reader, enter our giveaway for a free book here:

SCAN TO ENTER
BOOK GIVEAWAY

If you're a writer, submit your manuscript for consideration here:

SCAN TO SUBMIT
MANUSCRIPT

And always feel free to visit Atmosphere Press and our authors online at atmospherepress.com. See you there soon!

About the Author

Connecticut born, **ROBIN D'AMATO** moved to New York City to attend New York University, fell in love with the City, and never left. She has worked in the publishing industry as a Macintosh pre-press specialist since 1984. She also spent several decades pursuing dance and choreography. Her first novel, *Somebody's Watching You*, won a 2021 second-quarter Firebird Book Award for fiction, and her second novel, *Don't Poke the Bear*, was a 2023 Page Turner Awards finalist. She currently lives in Manhattan's East Village with her 3,000-LP music room and her two cats.

Website: www.robindamato.com